To Mary So for being great Neighbors!

STARBUCK

Nantucket Redemption

A Novel

By

Garth Jeffries

ISBN-13: 9780999906705

Library of Congress Control Number: 2020908034

Dedicated to the amazing women in my life.

To my mom, for making it all possible.

To K for her thirty-five plus years of love, support and encouragement.

And to M for being the best daughter - and editor - for which a dad could ever ask.

And to FFT, the most remarkable man I have ever known.

Many men can make a fortune
but very few can build a family.

J. S. Bryan

PROLOGUE

P eter Bois opened his eyes. He was lying on a hard, wooden floor and gasping for breath, pain radiating from the back of his head. He was also violently nauseous and could taste bile. What the hell just happened?

Slowly he rolled over and opened his eyes to a piercing blue sky, dappled with soft, white clouds occasionally covering the sun. The air was warm but damp, and he could smell the salt from the ocean. His body lay crammed up against a wall, his head and neck twisted at an uncomfortable angle against what looked like a short wooden bulkhead. A few minutes ago, he had been standing at Great Point at the tip of Nantucket Island, his toes in the water. How the hell had he gotten here? The shock and pain left him feeling confused and completely unsure of where he was. Flits of recent memory passed through his mind. He remembered the sun and the blue sky, the picnic with Charlotte and the kids, and the sound of the waves crashing onto the beach. He could still hear the waves, but they were strangely muted as if distant.

As he gathered his senses, he could feel that the floor was moving under him, swaying back and forth and making him feel physically uncomfortable. Suddenly, interrupting the motions was the sound of a thump followed shortly by a vibration he could feel deep into his body. It had an awkward mechanical feeling and reminded him of a time when he had gone charter fishing with some friends from the club. They had booked a fifty-three-foot sports fisherman out of Nantucket harbor and went deep offshore looking for tuna and marlin. They had been much more successful drinking beer and telling stories than catching large game fish but, in the end, had managed a few blues and a couple of stripers that salvaged the trip and made for some delicious meals with the family. The weather had blown up in the afternoon, and despite its size, the boat struggled a bit on the return. Most of the group had gotten seasick as it crashed through an angry ocean filled with large swells and whitecaps.

The motion under him felt similar, but clearly, he was not on a sportfishing boat. Peter's confusion with his situation grew more intense, and for the first time in a long time, he felt the uncomfortable stab of fear.

Gradually he worked up the strength to raise his head and look out over the wall. Waves stretched out as far as he could see. The water was a dull gray-green with gentle swells, the shadows of the clouds reflected on the surface. He could see gulls flocking in the distance and just barely make out their calls. He twisted his head around, looked up, and was shocked to see a large wooden mast with acres of white canvas all connected by a spider-web of ropes. Squinting, he could just make out two men at the very top of the mast standing inside what looked like metal hula hoops and looking out across the sea.

As his mind was wrestling with this new reality, he felt a fresh breeze on his cheek, followed by an unholy stench. The warm, moist air had been replaced by a putrid, foul-smelling smoke that brought back his nausea. He rolled over and wretched out that morning's breakfast, a breakfast that now seemed so long ago.

The sound of men started to filter in through the calls of gulls, and he could hear them shouting loudly from one to another. It was English but with an unusual dialect and many words unfamiliar to him. He also heard what he thought were other languages; Portuguese for sure and maybe Spanish. There was an urgency to their voices but with the disciplined air of men working together. They did not share the panic he was feeling.

The kick to his gut was shocking and intensely painful.

"The hell are you doing laying there green hand? Are you going to take a nap, or are you going to get back to work?"

Peter looked up as a tall, bearded man towered over him. His bulky figure blocked the sun, and his brown eyes glowered down on him. He was wearing a dark woolen coat, white shirt and had black knee-high leather boots. Oddly, Peter's first thought when seeing those boots was of Charlotte and how she looked when he had taken her out to dinner for their fifteenth anniversary. It had been a chilly evening for early October, and she had purchased the black leather boots, especially for the occasion.

The captain's boot drew back and struck him again - this time in the hip. Peter cried out in pain.

"For God's sake, man, it was only a slight thump from a pulley. You act as if you'd been harpooned like a whale. Get up and get back to work or I'll have you flogged! You know I'm not one to spare the cat-o'-nine-tails."

Peter struggled to his feet and looked about him. *What the fuck?*

CHAPTER ONE

T he white Gulfstream G5 jet crossed the south shore and touched down at Nantucket Memorial Airport just after 4:00 p.m. The pilot deployed the spoilers and reversed the engine thrust, quickly slowing the plane and allowing it to make the left onto the HS 2 taxiway. After making the turn, she proceeded over to the apron space reserved for general aviation and deftly rotated the plane following the ground crews' visual instructions. They chocked the tires as the turbines wound down.

Being a Friday afternoon in the heart of the summer season, it was easy to understand how this rather small airport could be the second busiest in Massachusetts, trailing only Logan in Boston. The sleek G5 was cheek to jowl with dozens of other business jets, turboprops and private planes. It looked like half the wealth of the free world had descended on this irregular-shaped speck of sand thirty miles off the mainland.

The stairs descended, and Peter Bois appeared in the opening, his six-foot frame filling the doorway. He had put some weight on over the past few years, and as he said to himself nearly every morning, he needed to start exercising and drop a few pounds. He paused briefly, his light brown hair blowing in the wind, taking in the beautiful blue sky and inhaling a deep breath of the fresh, salt-tinged ocean air. Bois looked and played the role of a Nantucket summer resident perfectly. Just forty-four, he had made a fortune with his plastics company and was now one of the wealthiest men on the island, a pretty significant accomplishment when you consider the competition. And he looked the part as well with his youthful appearance and boyish good looks, features that attracted stares from most of the women who saw him. Those stares occasionally returned by his penetrating blue eyes.

This was usually his favorite moment of the weekend - a week's work behind him and a full two days of relaxation ahead. But not today. The day's events weighed heavily on him, and there was an uncomfortable feeling in his gut that he was struggling to understand. Usually, he'd have been able to unwind fully during the short flight but found himself tense, almost anxious about the upcoming weekend, and how things were going to be with Charlotte. He fought the urge to turn around and get back on the plane. Instead, he stepped quickly down the stairs and walked through the general aviation terminal and out into the arrival area.

Charlotte was waiting at the curb in their black Range Rover. Peter hopped in the passenger side and gave her a quick peck on the cheek. She looked fabulous as always, and despite the tension in their relationship, she still never failed to take his breath away. Her dark brown hair was cut short, and her dazzling blue eyes were just visible through new sunglasses.

She pulled out of the parking space and drove towards the airport exit. She looked over at Peter and smiled. "We certainly missed you this week, and it's so good to finally have you here. How was your flight?"

"It was fine. And quick. Wheels-up to touchdown was just over thirty minutes. It was a short flight but long enough for the new flight attendant to screw-up my cocktail. Not only is she unattractive but incompetent behind the bar as well," Peter said and paused for a minute. "I think I'll have her fired."

"Fired for being unattractive?" Charlotte asked with a tinge of anger. Although she had no evidence Peter had ever cheated on her, she did see his eyes wander when there was an attractive woman nearby. And as a woman, she boiled at the thought that this young lady could be fired based on looks alone.

Peter ignored her comment. "I mean, how difficult is it to make a Manhattan? Take some good whiskey, add the bitters and sweet vermouth, and stir." He glanced out the window as the scrub oak, and pitch pine barrens rolled past. They came to the end of Nobadeer Farm Road and took a right on Milestone Road. For nearly three hundred years, this seven-mile stretch connected the bustling town of Nantucket with the quiet village of Siasconset or Sconset for those in the know. Summer was in high gear, and traffic down this narrow two-lane confirmed it. Hordes of mopeds, most with two people aboard, buzzed along at thirty miles per hour managing to do little more than back up faster traffic. Cars waited patiently for a clearing in the oncoming lane to pass them. Unfortunately, traffic the other way was just as busy dealing with their own menace of the powered bicycles, so opportunities were few and far between to dispatch the pests. Peter clenched his jaw and grudgingly accepted that it would be thirty or less all the way to Sconset.

"I wish they would ban those damn things," he said.

"What things?" asked Charlotte, glancing over at him.

"Those fuckin' mopeds. Dealing with them is a pain in the ass. All they do is slow things down for everyone," replied Peter.

Charlotte rolled her eyes, it was not the first time she had heard this argument from her intolerant husband. "But honey, for a lot of people, it's the only affordable way to get around the island. Rental cars are brutally expensive, and the taxis and Ubers in summer are so busy that it can often mean hours before one becomes available."

"Then maybe those tourist assholes shouldn't come here at all if they can't afford it. Go somewhere cheaper, like the Cape. Or maybe just stay home and leave the island to those who have the money to enjoy it properly," said Peter.

Not wanting to hear another of her husband's rants on the current state of tourists on the island, Charlotte quickly changed the topic. "So how did she screw it up?" she asked.

"Who screwed up what?" asked Peter tersely, rolling his eyes.

"Your flight attendant. If I may quote you, you said," Charlotte dropped her voice down a bit and said in a mildly mocking manner, "Our new flight attendant really screwed-up my cocktail. Not only is she ugly and not sexy at all but incompetent as well. I'm going to have her fired."

Peter turned from the window, his eyes sparking anger at being mocked by his wife. "I didn't say I was going to fire her, and I didn't say she was ugly. Only unattractive and apparently incompetent behind the bar. I asked for a Manhattan, and the bitch made me an Old Fashioned. And she used the wrong whiskey. You know I prefer Makers', but she just pulled the well crap we got for the golf outing with the guys last month," Peter snapped.

"So she used the wrong whiskey and added sugar when she shouldn't have. Do you think perhaps she could have been a little nervous? After all, it was her first week on the job and the first trip with you. Don't you think it would be the right thing to do to give her another chance?" asked Charlotte.

"I suppose you're right. Let's see how she does on the return trip Monday morning. We'll see if she can get coffee and cream right," Peter said caustically.

He turned and looked out the window watching as the scrub oak and pine gave way to open moors with its low growing vegetation of bushes and grasses. Across the moor, he could just make out the cranberry bogs and in the distance Sankaty Head Lighthouse. He lowered the window and breathed in the scents of the moor - an aroma that always takes him back to being a child when he'd ride his Raleigh ten-speed along the Milestone bike path that paralleled the road. Back to a time when things were simpler, happier, and more carefree. Back to when he wasn't worried about quarterly results, the stock price, or what new contracts his company was landing this year that would continue to drive revenue growth in the high single digits.

Although he had been coming here since he was an infant, his first memory of the island wasn't until he was nearly five. He had been playing in the little park next to the Sconset Market, imagining the tree was his ship, and he was the captain, sailing the high seas in search of whales. Descending the tree to head home, Peter had stepped on an old rusty nail. His screams were followed by a trip to the ER at Nantucket Cottage Hospital. They dressed his wound, gave him a shot - which he remembered being as almost bad as stepping on the nail - and sent him home with his foot bandaged and instructions to forego his captain career for a few weeks.

"Peter?" Charlotte asked.

"Oh, sorry. I was thinking about when I stepped on the nail when I was a kid. Remember that story?" said Peter.

"Of course, especially since you remind us of that at least once a season...if not two," Charlotte said, teasingly.

Peter replied with a chill, "I'm sorry if you have to hear it every year. It's just that it stands out so vividly in my mind and certainly a defining moment of my childhood." He paused briefly. "Seeing that nail poking out of my skin scared the crap out of me. Not to mention it hurt like a sonofabitch and made me scream like a baby. It was the first time I ever remember being scared, afraid of what might happen to me."

Charlotte looked at her husband of nearly twenty years. The take-control CEO, master of the universe, and the father of her two children looked like a hurt little boy about to cry. She sensed there was more to this than just recalling a bad experience from his childhood. "Is something wrong?" she asked.

Peter looked back out across the moors. "The offices were picketed again today," he said.

Charlotte took her eyes off the road and glanced at Peter. "What do you mean picketed...again?" she asked. "When have your offices ever been picketed?"

Peter shifted uncomfortably in his seat. "I haven't told you, but for the past few months, an environmental group, Clean Seas Forever, has been picketing our offices. They have spent the last few Friday mornings in our lobby, disrupting our business and claiming that the plastics we produce are killing the oceans and the wildlife in it."

Charlotte wasn't sure which made her angrier, that this organization was targeting her husband's company or that he hadn't bothered to tell her it had been happening in the first place. She looked at Peter, "Who are these Clean Oceans people?"

"Clean Seas Forever," he corrected her. "They are a very well funded group and claim to have research linking our products to the deaths of hundreds of thousands of whales, dolphins, and other marine life. They believe that these animals ingest our products, thinking it's food, and it fucks up their insides, and they die. Personally, it's all a bunch of hysterical bullshit and just gives these people a cause, another reason to protest."

"Is there any truth to their claims?" she asked. "About killing marine life?"

"Absolutely not! Yes, our products can last for many years in water, but in no way will they be mistaken for food. They are clearly exaggerating the situation and using it to siphon donations from sympathetic housewives who don't know any better. And they need the money - and the cause - because I don't think any of these fruitcakes could get a job in the real world."

Charlotte looked at him, "Well, that might be, but these 'fruitcakes' could potentially harm your business. What if they started picketing some of your biggest customers?" she asked. "Do you think they might succumb to that kind of pressure? I'd think that could potentially be bad PR for them."

"I don't think you understand my business," said Peter condescendingly. "My customers and their customers need our products. We produce value-added plastics that people use thousands of times a day. It makes their lives easier and more enjoyable. They need us. They depend on us," he finished.

"But what if more of them start answering 'paper'?" said Charlotte.

"What the fuck are you babbling about?" asked Peter, looking at his wife like he would dogshit on his shoe.

She stared back at him, her blue eyes blazing with anger, "I'm the one who shops for this family, Peter. And when I go to the store, they ask me every single time I check out - paper or plastic?"

"Don't bait me."

"Bait you?"

"Yes. You know that we don't produce those types of plastics. Those are commodity items made overseas in crappy factors using low-quality plastics and cheap labor. Our products are made of the highest quality resins and used by several premium brands in the food and beverage industry. Yes, they might end up in the ocean, but it's guilt by association with this bunch of wackos."

"I understand that. After all, I've been there with you since you bought that company," Charlotte scathingly reminded her husband.

"But it's that guilt by association that worries me. If more and more people respond with paper as their answer, then their perceptions and preferences are changing."

"Meaning?" asked Peter, already tired of the argument.

"Meaning that they might start cutting plastics out of their lives where they can. Maybe these people will realize that they can probably still live a happy life without your products?" she finished.

Peter looked at her, unsure of how to respond.

"I think what I'm trying to say is that you should consider transitioning out of plastics."

"What the fuck?" said Peter, nearly apoplectic. "Plastic products make up almost our entire sales portfolio. They generate hundreds of millions per year in revenue. And if we don't make them, then one of our many competitors no doubt will," he snarled. "Is it my fault that people don't recycle or dispose of their trash properly? And how the fuck can I keep a whale from eating a piece of plastic floating on the surface of the ocean?" Peter was bristling now, the recollection of the morning's activities helping to fuel his displeasure.

"I'm just trying to help," Charlotte said shakily. "Anyway, I thought your guys in R&D had developed a new type of plastic using natural materials that would degrade quickly in water."

Peter snorted, "Those 'guys' are very highly paid chemical engineers, and yes, they have developed some resins made from natural materials. In our preliminary studies, they appear to disintegrate fairly quickly when exposed to water, especially saltwater. But we abandoned that work last year."

Taken aback, Charlotte said, "Abandoned? It sounds like it might be a perfect solution to this problem!"

"We had to abandon it because they were proving to be too damn expensive to make. Even looking past the very high capital needed to rework the production equipment, converting our entire product line would cost us over fifteen percentage points of margin. Do you know what that means in terms of dollars?" Peter stared at her intently.

"I don't," said Charlotte, "Especially since you won't share the financials with me."

Peter ignored the dig. "Over one hundred million. Per year! Do you know what that would do to our stock price?" Peter waved his arms to make the point. "Our stock price would tank and with that a lot of my net worth." He slumped back into his seat. "I think you like the way we live. Plastics have taken care of us financially, and I seriously doubt you would want to give it all up to clean the oceans," he said mockingly.

"But what about the wildlife some of your plastics are hurting? Like the whales?" Charlotte asked.

"Fuck the whales. I have margins to maintain and profits to deliver," Peter replied with an icy tone.

They drove the remaining few miles to their house in silence.

CHAPTER TWO

C harlotte pulled into their driveway, shell-covered and lined on each side with neatly manicured hedges. The hedges were a landscaping staple in Sconset, and nearly every house was fenced by these privet bushes, perfectly groomed, arrow-straight and flat-topped. More creative types pruned them into shapes like a whale, a basket, or a simple arch over an arbor, but regardless of the form, the privets defined the little village.

Growing down the center of their driveway was a thin strip of grass whose survival depended on being out of reach of the tires, and Peter hated it. It had always made him feel a little sloppy, that he wasn't keeping the grounds manicured to the level he preferred and expected. But Charlotte loved it for its charm and the way it helped to soften the approach to the house. She had convinced Peter to keep it that way.

The driveway was reasonably long and allowed them a great deal of privacy, even in this small village. Many summer residents who lived in Siasconset were familiar with the entrance, often using it as a backdrop for family pictures. They were completely unaware of the beautiful home that resided at its end.

The house was named Fernweh, German for 'longing for unseen places,' and Peter had known it all his life. More of a small compound than a house, it had been built in the 1820s by Charles Litchfield, a very successful whaling captain who preferred the quieter life on the eastern shore of the island versus the hustle and bustle of town. Initially sitting on over ten acres of land, over time, much of that land had been sold off as it passed through the generations of the Litchfield family. It was a rather large house and expensive to maintain, so when the Nantucket economy struggled as the whaling industry declined, descendants were forced to sell the land to keep the house afloat financially. In the end, it became too much for them, and Peter's grandfather purchased the home and the remaining three acres in the 1950s after it had sat abandoned for nearly two decades.

Bringing the house back to its original glory had been an expensive proposition, but one Peter's grandfather had relished. Having made his money in manufacturing during World War II, he took to the task of restoring Fernweh with teams of carpenters, painters and other tradesmen. They were on-site for nearly three years attending to every detail of the house. The work also addressed the carriage barn, converting it into a large garage with a comfortable guest suite on the second floor, and building a small but charming guest cottage. The only structure that was not included in the restoration was the outhouse as modern plumbing and sewage had been installed. Unlike most of the houses in the village, Fernweh was sided in white painted clapboards versus the traditional shake shingle, a common trend in the 19th century as a way of demonstrating one's financial success and position.

Peter inherited Fernweh at the age of twenty when his parents had been killed in a plane crash. They had been traveling home from a ski trip in Vermont when their small plane encountered a snow squall crossing the Massachusetts border, disorienting the pilot who failed to maintain altitude as he approached the Berkshires. The aircraft had impacted one of the higher peaks killing all aboard nearly instantly. An only child, Peter had heard about the accident from a family friend as he was preparing to head home for spring break. He had been very close to his parents, and the news was devastating, particularly after the loss of his best friend a couple of summers before. He toyed with the idea of withdrawing from school to manage their affairs, but in the end, though, he decided to honor his parent's memory and get his degree in business administration.

Over twenty years later, and now the third generation of his family to oversee Fernweh, Peter took the responsibility very seriously. This house was both his first love and his third child, and he used much of his considerable fortune in maintaining it to a very high standard. The environment on Nantucket was harsh, and in Sconset, it was particularly challenging. The air was frequently damp due to summer humidity and the frequent fog banks that rolled in off the Atlantic. Nor'easters and the occasional hurricane added their own damages to the mix with high winds and torrential rains. Constant upkeep was critical to ensure that nature didn't get a finger hold on the house and damage her through rot, decay, or sheer force. It was an endless battle that Peter was determined to win for when the time came to pass it along to his children, Spencer and Sophie.

Charlotte wheeled the Range Rover up to the front of the house, and Peter jumped out. He grabbed his backpack from the back seat and headed straight to his study. Charlotte sighed and watched Peter retreat into the house from the driver's seat. After a few minutes, she slowly got out of the car and made her way up the brick path that led from the driveway to the entry.

The front door opened into a well-lit center hall with large rooms spread across either side of the house. A generous staircase led to four bedrooms upstairs. To the right was the living room and formal dining room. To the left were the family room and kitchen. Large double-hung windows covered the exterior walls bathing the house in beautiful natural light and offering gorgeous views to the lush lawn and the moors beyond. The decorations were simple and had been collected over time. There were original pieces from Peter's grandfather as well as antiques that Charlotte had found locally from trusted sources. The soft, light blue walls and glossy white wood trim created a bright and airy space that usually brought Charlotte joy. But not tonight. The short drive from the airport had left her with a heavy feeling.

Their summer nanny, Jess, had just finished feeding Sophie and Spencer their dinner and was rinsing the dishes in the sink and putting them in the dishwasher. The children had disappeared to the family room, eager to utilize their one hour of screen time.

"Did they give you much trouble?" asked Charlotte.

"No, they were great, as usual," replied the nanny. "Sophie still doesn't like fresh fish very much. I prepared some bluefish for her tonight, but she only picked around the edges. Spencer, of course, would have licked his plate if I had let him," said Jess, smiling.

Charlotte stood next to the nanny with her arms crossed. "Well, bluefish can be pretty fishy. I know I didn't like it much when I was younger. Maybe next time we should try swordfish or grouper."

"Hmmm. She might like that," replied Jess. She placed the last of the dishes in the dishwasher. "Can I get you anything, Mrs. Bois?"

"Thanks, but I'm okay. I had a late lunch at the club, and I think I might just have some cheese or fruit in a little bit."

"Okay. Do you need me for anything more tonight? I was going to head into town and meet up with some friends if that's okay."

"Of course that's okay. I can get them to bed. Please, go out, have some fun and see your friends. Just do me a favor and don't drink too much," she said with a smile.

"I won't, Mrs. Bois," said Jess sweetly, and she walked out of the kitchen, anxious to start her evening.

Charlotte watched her leave and then headed past the sink and through the kitchen to Peter's study. He was at the laptop as usual and utterly oblivious to the beautiful sunset out his window. The moors were bathed in a golden hue, and the sky had streaks of purple, pink, and red. It was stunning.

"Did you want some dinner, Peter?" she asked.

Peter replied without looking up from his screen. "No, I'm good for now. I had a snack on the plane with my crappy drink." He continued tapping on the keyboard.

"Can we talk?" asked Charlotte.

"Not now. I've got to get this pricing information out to the Asian team," Peter replied. "They are presenting this weekend to one of the biggest food producers in Singapore, and I really want to get that business." He briefly looked up at Charlotte. "Give me thirty minutes, and then maybe we can meet for a drink on the patio?"

"Sure, hon," said Charlotte reluctantly. She sighed and walked back to the family room to join the kids for some *Penguins of Madagascar*. The family room had a large overstuffed, and very comfortable leather couch that could probably seat eight in a pinch. They sat spread out on the couch with their eyes intently focused on the large flat-screen television hung over the whitewashed brick fireplace. It was Charlotte's favorite room in the house, especially in the fall, when she and Peter could curl up and watch some college football with a fire roaring in the hearth. Spencer and Sophie laughed out loud several times at the antics of the four penguins and were both very disappointed when the credits started to roll.

"Okay, you two, time for bed," said Charlotte. "Go upstairs, get your PJ's on, and brush your teeth. I'll be up in ten minutes for reading time." Sophie and Spencer reluctantly went up the stairs. Charlotte stood and took a minute to reorganize the numerous pillows and neatly fold the wool blanket that Sophie had wrapped around her as she watched television. She walked over to the window and looked out over the lawn. The sky was nearly black but held just the faintest light of purple close to the horizon. Off to the west, she could clearly see Venus and several stars and closer to home, a handful of rabbits eating the grass over by the carriage house.

True to her promise, Charlotte was upstairs with two minutes to spare. She, Spencer, and Sophie spread out on her large bed in the master suite. Spencer clutched one of his favorite stuffed animals, a little dog named Floppy, and snuggled in on Charlotte's left while Sophie curled up on her right. Reading at bedtime had been part of their nighttime ritual since they were barely out of the womb and her favorite time of the day. Tonight they were continuing with a treasured classic from her childhood, *The Wind in the Willows*. She read for nearly thirty minutes before she reluctantly put the book down. She could have gone on for hours, the escape into the lives of Mole, Toad, and the others a welcome distraction. Charlotte paused at the end of a chapter and noticed that Spencer had fallen asleep. Glancing at her daughter, she saw that Sophie was struggling to keep her eyes open. "Okay guys, bedtime."

Sophie reluctantly scooted off the big bed and made her way through the door and down the hall to her room. Charlotte nudged Spencer awake, helped him off the bed, and then led him down to his room. He climbed in his bed, hugged Floppy to his chest, and closed his eyes. Charlotte brought the blanket up and tucked him in. "Good night, love," she said. "Sweet dreams."

She stood and made her way quietly out the door and down the hall. Sophie had already crawled under the sheets and was fluffing her pillow when Charlotte came in and sat on the edge of her bed. Sophie looked up at Charlotte, her greenish eyes fighting against sleep. "Why doesn't dad ever want to join us when we watch TV or read?"

Charlotte felt a lump in the back of her throat. "Oh, honey. He's just so busy with work right now. I know he wants to, but there is a lot he needs to do for the company."

Sophie's face clenched. "I hate that company," she said with a grumble and rolled over. Charlotte paused and stared at the beautiful child below her. Peter was missing some of the best years of her life and worse, Sophie was noticing. She brushed Sophie's blond hair away from her cheek and leaned down to kiss her. "Just remember daddy loves you, honey," she whispered soothingly. "And so do I."

Charlotte stood and quietly exited the bedroom. She glided softly down the stairs, careful to miss the two creaky treads, and walked to the kitchen. She opened the refrigerator and pulled out a bottle of sauvignon blanc. She poured herself a glass, walked through the french doors to the patio, and settled in on the chaise. Laying back and looking up at the sky, she could clearly make out the Big Dipper to the north and Orion's Belt to the south. As her eyes adjusted, more stars and constellations came into view, disrupted briefly every fifteen seconds or so from the sweep of light from the Sankaty Head lighthouse. Muffled by the distance, Charlotte could just make out the faint roar of the waves breaking on Sconset beach.

Pulling out her phone, she checked the display and saw that it had been well over an hour since Peter's promise to join her for a drink. She raised up a bit and looked over her shoulder back toward his study. She could just make out a tuft of Peter's hair through the panes where he was still at his desk, hunched over the laptop. Her eyes returned to the sky, and she took another sip of her wine. The night air was getting chilly, and Charlotte could feel the fog rolling in. She reflected on Sophie's comment about the company and had to agree she was starting to hate it too. Yes, it provided for them financially, but it was also taking more and more of his time and focus away from the family. She could happily share him with his other loves of Nantucket and Fernweh. But sharing him with this company? In many ways, it was worse than him having a mistress. And she knew, deep in her heart, that she was going to need to make him see what his company, his precious Shimmo Plastics, was doing to their family.

She took a last sip of wine and accepting that Peter was not going to deliver on his assurance to join her, decided to call it a night. She got up from the chaise and walked into the kitchen, closing and locking the French doors behind her. Placing her wine glass in the sink, she looked across the kitchen into Peter's study. He was still at it, his face buried in the laptop's screen. She saw he must have grabbed a bite at some point as a dirty dish and a half-full glass of beer sat on the corner of his desk. Rather than cede to her nature to want to clean up his meal, she headed back through the family room to the stairs, turning lights off as she went. Casting one last look through the house toward his study, she ascended the stairs and headed for the master bedroom.

CHAPTER THREE

Peter turned off the light in his office and went into the kitchen. With Charlotte and the kids asleep, the house was quiet, the only noises being the typical creaks and groans of an old home and a slight hum from the refrigerator. Peter grabbed a beer and headed out onto the patio. He knew that he had let Charlotte down again, having promised to meet her for a drink on the patio hours ago. He just couldn't seem to make her understand the importance of his business and how critical it was to their lifestyle and his feeling of self-worth. As he had done hundreds of times before, he told himself that they would need to accept it as part of who he was and if they couldn't do that, well, there were other options available.

He finished his drink quickly and went in for another. Returning to the patio, he planted himself on one of the chaises and looked out across his lawn. The fog had settled in and shrouded the house and the grounds in a gray embrace, bolstering Nantucket's nickname the *Gray Lady*. Many people didn't like the fog; some even found it sinister, if not outright scary. But Peter loved it. The isolation both in sound and sight comforted him and made him feel like he was home. Not the little "h" home that represents where you rest your head every night and where you get your mail but the big "H" Home that defines who you are and from where you come. And although he considered Nantucket and Fernweh Home, Peter knew sadly that he was not considered a native by the islanders. He hadn't spent winters here or gone to the local school. He hadn't played Whaler football or participated in any of the myriad of other activities that the native kids did. He and his family were just another one of the thousands of summertime residents who filled the streets and restaurants and raised the prices of everything for everyone.

Peter took a sip of his beer and wondered about how things might have been different. He had tried to talk Charlotte into living on the island year-round, right after they had married. He knew he could find a job that would pay the bills, if not take full advantage of his education, and find a small rental cottage in town. But Charlotte wanted no part in that adventure. She enjoyed coming in the summer and fall for a few weeks but could not envision herself here year-round, particularly in the winter. Citing high rates of alcoholism and drug abuse as confirmation of her thinking, she had put her foot down. In the end, they had landed in Greenwich, where he commuted into the City working in private equity on Wall Street. The hours had been brutal, but the money was excellent, and they managed to escape to Nantucket for weekends and the occasional longer stay of a week or two.

The opportunity to buy Shimmo Plastics had changed all of that.

It had all started with an accidental meeting of an old friend from Deerfield. He had been having drinks after work at the White

Horse. As usual, the big swinging dicks from the financial district were filling the place, and Peter was sitting at the bar with a few colleagues. After settling his bill, he was getting up to leave when he was bumped from behind hard enough to lose his balance. He turned quickly, ready to rail on this act of rudeness, and stared straight into the wavy brown hair and hazel eyes of Charles "Chuck" Thompson. Anger quickly faded into delight, and the two friends embraced.

Chuck was in the City for meetings on Wall Street. He was the chief financial officer of a plastics company in Connecticut, and they were looking to raise capital for a significant expansion. Despite strong financials and a solid business plan, he had been rebuffed from all of the firms he had approached, citing the company's small size and projected single-digit returns. After calling Charlotte to let her know he was staying in the City, Peter and Chuck grabbed a booth and settled into the green leather benches. They ate and drank and talked, catching up on each other's lives and filling in the gaps since they had last seen each other at graduation.

They also talked about Chuck's business and the frustrations he had experienced trying to secure investors for the firm. After hearing more about the company and the business plan, Peter started to ferment an idea. He had managed to save quite a bit from his few years of work, and he had access to his parent's money, which had sat in trust since their accident. Maybe this was the opportunity to go out on his own and control his future.

It was well into the early morning hours before they finally parted company. Peter gave Chuck a final hug and put him in a taxi then turned, walking up Bridge Street in search of a hotel.

After that initial meeting, it didn't take long before Peter found himself a majority investor in Bridgeport Plastics Company, and he quickly went about making changes. He shed unprofitable product lines, streamlined the workforce, and renamed and rebranded the company Shimmo Plastics. Within a year of his arrival, they had increased profits substantially and had secured several significant new customers in the food and beverage industry. But his hours and workload had gone from brutal to insane. Eighty hour weeks were not uncommon, and he spent most Saturdays and Sundays at the office. Two years in, he fired his old friend. Chuck was not strong enough from a financial skills perspective and had not been willing to put in the same hours as Peter. Despite offering to provide a strong reference, they had not talked since.

The money started to flow to Peter but with it came some costs. Sophie had been born while he was at a major industry conference in Asia. Spencer was born while he was pitching for new business in Europe at one of the world's largest water bottlers. The first words he heard from either were over a cell phone. And it was lucky if he and Charlotte were able to have dinner once or twice a week. Now here he was, over ten years after taking over the company, wealthy and successful but struggling on the home front. He admitted to himself that even though the hours were better, it was not unusual for him to work sixty hours a week. And even when he was home, he often spent hours in his office. But it was the price he had to pay for the lifestyle they enjoyed.

And it was a great lifestyle. In addition to Fernweh, they had a large home in Weston, Connecticut sitting on over four acres, the best schools for the kids, private jet access, and complete financial security. They wanted for nothing.

Peter stared through the fog, "Why can't Charlotte understand that this is what it takes?" he whispered to himself. Sighing, he finished his beer, left the empty bottle on the small table next to the chaise, and made his way over the lawn to the guest cottage. He climbed the stairs to the second-floor suite and turned in; the maids had already prepared the room for guests. The long week and the beer allowed sleep to come quickly.

* * *

Peter dreamed again of the summer he lost his best friend. In his dream, he was carrying one end of a bundle of drywall sheets up temporary stairs in a newly framed house on the south side of the island. His best friend on the island, Jack Tate, had the other end. Together they were working as laborers for a contractor who was building several new homes in an area known as Tom Nevers. It was on the south shore of the island and just a few miles along the beach from Sconset. Their jobs were pretty simple - be the muscle to move whatever materials were needed on the site: studs, drywall, bricks, cedar shingles (lots of cedar shingles), mulch, dirt, whatever. It wasn't much fun, but it paid reasonably well and allowed Peter to enjoy the entire summer on the island before he started college in the fall.

It also gave him the chance to spend more time with Jack, his best friend on the island. Unlike Peter, who only spent summers here, Jack was a native Nantucketer. His family was able to trace their lineage on the island back to one of the original nine founders. This group of men purchased the land from the natives in the mid-1600s and set about making a community focused on raising sheep, spinning wool, farming, and fishing the abundant waters that surrounded the island. Many, many generations later, Jack and his family were still on the island but were now active in local government as well as supporting the flourishing tourist business. It was Jack's uncle, one of the largest contractors on the island, who had hired them as laborers for the summer.

"Man, that was fun last night wasn't it?" said Jack. His flaxen hair was wet with sweat, and his green eyes shimmered in the heat. "I'm not sure I've ever seen The Box so busy and with so many good looking women."

"That probably explains why it is the best bar on the island!" said Peter. "It looked like you were getting along okay with that one blond. You bailed on me - I'm assuming everything worked out?"

"Pretty much," said Jack, smiling. "We took her Wagoneer and parked down by the Coast Guard beach. She just happened to have a couple of blankets, so we went down by the water and did some whale watching if you know what I mean."

Peter smiled back, "I thought so, you lucky devil. She was gorgeous. Are you going to see her this weekend?"

"She left this morning on the 6:30 ferry," replied Jack. "She's a nanny for a family from Philadelphia. They had a rental in town and were only here for a couple of weeks." Peter and Jack carefully lowered the drywall in an upstairs bedroom and leaned it against the newly framed wall. They turned back down the stairs to get the next load. All told they would be moving several tons of drywall, which would undoubtedly help further shape their physiques. A summer of hard work and weekends on the beach had turned them into modern-day Adonises, which worked well for them as far as the ladies were concerned.

"Well, that sucks," said Peter. "Any chance she could come back on her own?"

"I asked," Jack replied. "But she's committed to this family through Labor Day and then is heading back to school the following week." Jack looked over at Peter and grinned slyly, "So, I'll need to find another girlfriend." They pulled five sheets off the back of the delivery truck and started back into the house. "What about you?" asked Jack.

"Oh, I had fun, but nothing happened. Met a few pretty girls, but either they already had boyfriends or just weren't interested. I struck out." He looked across the drywall at Jack. "What about that cute older sister of yours? Jen. Do you think she'd ever consider going out with me?"

Jack laughed. "You don't give up, do you?"

"Not when there's a beautiful woman involved."

"Well, trust me, that dog won't hunt. She's getting serious with that guy from New Jersey, and I'm pretty sure they're going to get engaged when they graduate next year."

"Bummer," said Peter. He was walking backward through the front door and started up the temporary stairs. "How much more of this shit do we have left?"

"By my count, we have six more trips, and we will be done positioning the upstairs drywall for the rockers. The downstairs will be a bitch but not as bad as we won't have to deal with those friggin' stairs. I'm guessing we should finish-up by three."

"Man, I can't wait. I was not born to do this type of work," said Peter. "What's say we hit the beach for a quick swim when we're done. Get cooled off and figure out what we're doing tonight."

"Sounds good, man."

After several more grueling hours, Peter and Jack pulled the last of the drywall sheets off the truck and maneuvered them into the framed out kitchen area. They checked in with their site manager, who released them for the day.

"God, that water is going to feel good," said Peter. They walked over and jumped in Peter's old, red Jeep CJ-5. It had been in the family for years and reflected that history with over a dozen of the annual beach permit stickers neatly lined up on the rear bumper. Peter's dad had taught him to drive with this truck on the beach when he was just ten. Lacking both doors and a top, it was the perfect summer vehicle for the island. Peter started it up, crunched the shifter into first, popped the clutch, and headed for the South Shore. Jack slipped an AC/DC disc into the stereo, and they cranked up some *Big Gun*, excited for the possibilities that the rest of their day offered.

They followed some of the back trails from Tom Nevers over to Low Beach Road, the Jeep bouncing on the ruts of the narrow path. The road smoothed out when it turned to tarmac and, after a few hundred feet, pulled into the beach entrance just past the Loran station. Peter and Jack jumped out of the Jeep and ran toward the beach, struggling in the hot, heavy sand. There was no one on the beach and not having bathing suits, they stripped down to their boxers and jumped into the lukewarm water. The waves were nearly perfect for body surfing, and both Peter and Jack managed some impressive rides. "This feels so good after hauling all that goddamn drywall," said Peter. "And these waves are awesome. Let's see if we can grab some of them a little farther out."

"I'm okay," replied Jack. "I just want to relax and enjoy the water. Besides, I'm beat. But let's see what you can do you, bastard," he said teasingly.

"You wimp," Peter said good-naturedly. "I'll show you how to do some kick-ass bodysurfing!"

Peter turned and started swimming farther out from the shore just beyond where the current swells were breaking. He was trying to line himself up for one of the bigger waves when he felt the first grip of the rip current. It was almost as if someone had grabbed his ankles and started pulling him out to sea. Peter tried to swim back toward shore but felt himself moving farther out. He tried to swim harder, but he quickly tired, already exhausted from their long day of work. Peter began to panic, flailing his arms about, and struggling to keep his head above water. The wave he was lining up to bodysurf instead broke on top of him, the whitewater filling his mouth and pushing him under the surface.

Jack had been floating close-in to the shore, enjoying the water and thinking about the evening ahead. He turned to see if Peter was showing off yet when he saw his flailing arms just a foot or two out of the water. "Oh, shit!" he said out loud and started swimming out to Peter. He ducked under the breaking wave and kicked harder. Peter was still fifty feet away and struggling when Jack shouted to him, "Don't fight it! Swim parallel to the shore."

Peter shouted back, his mouth full of water and difficult to understand. "I can't, Jack. I'm too tired!"

"Don't panic, Peter," Jack yelled. "I'll be right there." Jack had spent a couple of summers lifeguarding and was a good swimmer as well. He closed the distance to Peter quickly, and as he neared him, he could feel the grip of the current and sensed himself being pulled out to sea along with his friend.

Peter was struggling to keep his head above the water. Jack finally reached him and came up from behind. Peter was clearly in a panic now, and Jack was extra careful not to let him take them both down. "Hang in there, Peter. I got you," Jack said as he slipped one arm around his chest. Careful to keep Peter's head above water, he used a sidestroke to pull the two of them out of the strong current. After several minutes of swimming and his muscles burning, Jack finally felt the rip release its grip on the two of them. He changed direction and started heading into shore, trying to leverage the breaking waves as much as possible to ease the burden of carrying his friend.

"We're going to be okay," said Jack. They were just twenty feet from shore now, and he was exhausted. "Do you think you can make it the rest of the way?"

Peter nodded his head and mumbled, "Yes, I think so."

Jack released his hold of his friend and made sure he was okay and swimming in the right direction. Jack held back a few feet just in case and was starting to follow when he again felt the strong grip of the rip current.

Peter swam slowly into shore. His muscles ached, his eyes burned and his throat was sore from all of the saltwater he had ingested. Mostly though, it was embarrassing. He had been trying to show off to Jack and had nearly gotten them both killed. Approaching the shore, he finally felt the soft sand beneath him and was able to stand up and walk onto the beach. He heaved himself up out of the reach of the surf and sat down heavily in the dry sand. He looked out on the water expecting to see Jack. He thought he had been right behind him but now didn't see him.

"Jack? Jack!"

He jumped up and ran up and down the beach, looking for his friend. For the second time in just a few minutes, he was panicking and felt the warm rush of adrenaline through his body.

"Jack!"

Peter frantically called out his friend's name, pacing back and forth along the shoreline. But Jack was gone. Peter slumped to his knees and sobbed into his hands. "Oh, Jack. I'm so sorry. So very sorry."

Jack's eighteen-year-old body washed up three days later on the west end of the island, near Madaket beach.

CHAPTER FOUR

I n August, dawn comes early to Sconset with the first lightening of the eastern sky just after four in the morning. Peter was sound asleep as the sun approached the horizon, and when it did break the surface of the ocean just before six, the rays flooded into his bedroom on the upper floor of the carriage house. He woke, his eyes squinting against the sunlight streaming in through the windows, turned on his bed, and propped himself up to look out the window. The fog had retreated back out to sea and been replaced with a bright blue Nantucket sky. *There is nothing quite like a Nantucket blue sky*, he thought. A vibrant, deep blue that extended from horizon to horizon, unsullied by clouds or haziness.

Dreaming of Jack always left him with a heavy feeling, a void in his heart, and feelings of guilt from being the cause of his death. *If only I hadn't tried to show off, Jack would probably be alive.* He looked out at the sky and wondered what Jack would be like now. Would he have kids? Would we still be best friends? Would I be a different man?

He swung his feet over the edge of the bed and started to dress. He wasn't sure how Charlotte was going to react to him spending the night in the guest room. No doubt, she was going to be upset, but he knew he could make it up to her. He slipped on his boat shoes and headed to the house. The maids could make the bed.

Peter walked across the lawn towards the house, stopped briefly on the patio to grab his empty beer from the night before - really earlier this morning - and then opened the French doors into the kitchen. Charlotte was sitting at the island in her robe, sipping a cup of coffee and reading the paper.

"Morning, hon," he said as he walked into the kitchen. He grabbed a mug from the cabinet and poured himself a cup of coffee. "How did you sleep?"

She looked up from her paper, her eyes were red. "I slept fine. That is until about two o'clock when I woke up and realized you still hadn't come to bed." She crossed her arms. "So I came downstairs looking for you, and all I found was an empty beer bottle on the patio. Where were you?"

Peter looked down at his coffee, "I ended up sleeping in the guest suite. It was late, and I didn't want to disturb you or the kids."

"Really? So now you're sleeping in the guest suite?" Charlotte asked, her eyes reflecting the pain in her heart. "What is wrong with you? Why don't you want to be with us as a family?"

"What? Of course, I want to be with you and the kids. What a dumbass thing to say. I just honestly was afraid I'd wake you."

"Did you ever think that maybe I want you to wake me? You're gone so much, I'd love time with you even if it's in the middle of the night. I feel so disconnected from you."

He walked over to her and tried to give her a hug, but she pulled quickly away. "I'm so worried about us," she said sadly. "We're not going to make it if things continue."

"I promise things are fine," said Peter angrily. "I know I put long hours in, but that's what it takes for us to be successful."

Charlotte looked at Peter, her eyes tinged with anger. "Things are most certainly not fine. Success, to me, is more than money and things. In fact, I don't consider us successful. Rich, yes. But not successful. For that, we need to be together as a family."

Peter looked down at the floor, quiet.

"Do you know what Sophie said to me last night?" Charlotte asked.

He looked at her.

"She said, and I quote, I hate that company."

"What?" said Peter, anger, and irritation in his voice. "Doesn't she know how much that company provides for this family?"

"She's nine years old, Peter. She only understands that she rarely sees her dad, and when she does, he doesn't seem to be all here," replied Charlotte. "And to be honest, I'm starting to have similar feelings," she said as she stood and walked over to the French doors. Looking out over the patio, she continued, "I used to see that company as our future, and as you know, I supported you every step of the way, the long hours, whatever it took to make it successful. But now that it's successful, I don't understand why you can't dial it back. Can't you hire someone to run it for you? Or better yet, why don't you sell it and retire?"

Peter stared back at her, disbelief in his eyes, "Retire? I'm forty-four fucking years old. What the hell am I going to do with the rest of my life?"

Charlotte walked over to him and grabbed his hands. Looking into his eyes, she said, "You could spend the rest of your life with us. In fact, we could have more children if we wanted. We could travel, we could give back, there are so many possibilities. But the important thing is we could do it together."

Peter's face flushed, and he pulled his hands from hers. "I can't retire. This company needs me. My employees need me." She started to speak, but he raised a hand to stop her. "But, I hear you, and I promise that I will look for ways to cut back my time."

"You've said that before and look where we are. I couldn't even enjoy a glass of wine with you last night."

"I know. But this time it will be different. I'll start thinking about how I can make some changes and will put a plan together."

"Are you sure?" asked Charlotte, her voice soft and questioning.

"Yes, I'm sure," said Peter, and reached out to hug her. This time she acquiesced and let herself be pulled into a hug. Rubbing her back, he said, "I love you guys so much. You are my life, and I'm sorry to have caused you pain."

He pulled back slightly and kissed her on the lips, his hand moving up to gently stroke the back of her neck. Just as he thought it might lead to more, he heard a creak from the stairs. Seconds later, Sophie ran into the kitchen dressed in her pink polka dot pajamas. "Hi Daddy!" she yelled and ran to him. Peter kneeled down and embraced her. "Morning, babycakes. Did you sleep okay?"

"I slept okay. But I had an awful dream," she replied, her face twisting at the memory.

"I'm sorry, sweetie. Do you remember what it was about?" asked Peter.

"I dreamed that you disappeared," said Sophie.

"What do you mean, disappeared, hon?"

"I dreamed that mom and Spencer and I were here and we wanted to go to the beach, but we didn't know where you were. We looked and looked and looked but we couldn't find you anywhere. It was like you vanished," she said, her small voice trembling.

"Oh, honey, I'm so sorry," said Peter as he reached out to gently stroke her forehead. "But please don't worry, I'm not going anywhere, I promise."

"Cross your heart promise?" asked Sophie quietly.

"Yes, cross my heart promise. Absolutely," said Peter, He leaned over to give Sophie a hug and kissed her forehead.

"What's say we wake Spencer up and head to Downyflake for breakfast?"

"Yay!" shouted Sophie.

Peter rose up and looked at Charlotte, "What do you think, hon?"

"I think that would be great," said Charlotte, smiling and relaxed from their talk. Peter stared at her, the golden light of the morning sun reflecting off her skin, her blue eyes sparkling with love as she looked at her daughter, and thought he was the luckiest man on earth, that is if he didn't screw it all up.

CHAPTER FIVE

S ophie volunteered to wake up Spencer and ran full steam up the stairs and into his room. Charlotte and Peter could hear her feet pounding on the floor down the hallway to Spencer's room. At first, it sounded like Spencer wasn't too happy to be woken up, but that seemed to change when he heard the reason. They heard a faint shout of "yay" and then more footsteps on the stairs. Sophie burst into the kitchen dragging Spencer by one hand, his other wiping the sleep from his eye with the knuckle of his index finger.

"Let's go, daddy!" said Sophie.

Peter looked at her with a smile spreading across his face, "Um, Sophie. Don't you think you're forgetting something?"

Sophie looked back at her dad with intense concentration. Finally, she replied, "I don't think so."

Peter walked over to her and knelt down. "I don't think we should go to Downyflake in our pajamas." He gave her nose a playful swipe with his finger.

Sophie looked down and surveyed herself and then glanced over at Spencer. She smiled and then started giggling. "Oopsie," she said, looking up at Peter. At that moment Peter saw the face of Charlotte, the face he fell in love with, the face that remained burned in his brain for weeks after he had first met her. "Why don't you take Spencer upstairs and get dressed. Mommy and I need to get ready too."

"Okay, daddy," she said and looked over at Spencer, "Come on, let's go get dressed!" Then the two of them exited the kitchen much the way they entered but in reverse, Sophie tearing out of the room holding Spencer's hand and pulling him up the stairs. Charlotte and Peter could once again hear the pounding of feet on the floor above augmented this time with the sound of drawers being open and shut and closet doors slamming. They looked at each other and laughed. Peter stepped forward and embraced Charlotte, kissing her first on the forehead, then tenderly on the nose and then finally firmly on the lips. "I love you," he said, pulling back from the kiss.

"I love you, too, honey, with all my heart," replied Charlotte. They embraced a few moments longer before Peter broke away. "Why don't you run upstairs and get dressed. I'll get the car and pull it up to the front."

She gave him one last quick kiss and then turned and headed upstairs.

The kitchen fell silent. Peter took a moment to look around him, his eyes settling on objects around the room, all of which held some meaning for him. Over the living room mantle was the large oil painting depicting an early America's Cup race that his father had purchased for his mother just after their marriage. On the floor was a large and gorgeous oriental rug his parents had found at

Brimfield when he was just a boy. Across the room was the 18th-century Irish cupboard that he and Charlotte had purchased on their honeymoon, their wedding china displayed on the open shelves above, his grandparents' china stored in the cabinet below. For the first time in weeks, he felt a sense of calm and ease. Fernweh was like a wool sweater on a cold day. It embraced him, protected him, and made him feel warm.

He walked over and turned off the coffee pot, grabbed the keyfob from the junk drawer, and headed out to the carriage house to retrieve the Range Rover. It was still early, but already he could feel the dampness in the air and his blue Nantucket sky had started to turn hazy from the humidity. He opened the garage door via the code panel on the trim, started the car and backed slowly out. He usually backed the car into the garage, but Charlotte preferred to park nose in. He wasn't sure why that bugged him so but it just didn't seem orderly. He closed the doors with the button on the rearview mirror and wheeled the Rover up to the front of the house.

Waiting for Charlotte and the kids to join him, he opened the sunroof and lowered all of the windows. He then turned the radio on and hit the memory button for the classical station from Cape Cod. Ludovico Einaudi's *In un'altravita* came over the speakers. He settled back in the driver's seat and closed his eyes, the beautiful and haunting melody filling his ears. He could smell the blooms of the roses on the side of the house and the salt in the air. He felt satisfied.

The shell driveway crunched with the sound of Spencer and Sophie's approach as they ran from the house. Charlotte closed and locked the front door then jumped in the passenger side. She looked over at him, "This music is beautiful," she said. "Who is it?"

"It's Ludovico Einaudi. He's an Italian pianist and composer. I don't know the name of the song, but I have always liked his compositions."

"Well, it's lovely," replied Charlotte. She turned to the back seat, "Are you two buckled in?"

"Yep," said Sophie. Spencer was silent but gave her a thumbs up, his face buried in a book.

Charlotte smiled at them and turned to Peter, "Let's do it," she said as if they were getting ready to rob a bank or storm a beach. Peter smiled back at her and started the car. They pulled out of the driveway and headed toward Milestone Road. "What do you think if we take the long way and go via Polpis Road?" asked Peter.

"Sounds great. And it's such a beautiful day," she replied.

"Yes it is," said Peter. Rather than taking a left on Milestone, he instead crooked a right and took a shortcut over to Sankaty Road. Turning left, they headed out of the village.

After a few minutes, they could see the lighthouse off to their right across the golf course, its white brick and bright red band standing proudly on the bluff. Continuing, they passed the blue waters of Quidnet, the small brackish lake where Peter had sailed a small Sunfish sailing dinghy as a boy, actually winning a race much to the surprise of the people around him, including himself. It was then on through the moors, the road curving left and right, with the fresh air blowing through the open windows. Peter looked over at Charlotte, her hair rustling in the wind, looking very Audrey Hepburn-ish in her Aviators.

Charlotte caught him looking and smiled. "Do you think there is going to be much of a line?"

Peter made a face of concentration and then said, "Hmm, let's see. It's 8:30 on a Saturday morning in August. If we're lucky, we should be able to sit down by early afternoon," he said teasingly.

"Peter!" said Charlotte and playfully cuffed his shoulder.

"Seriously, I think we will be fine," said Peter. "You know their service is great. It'll probably be twenty to thirty minutes. Besides, we can wait outside, and on a day like today, it will be a pleasure."

They made their way into town, rounded the rotary, peeled off on Sparks Lane, and pulled into the small parking lot of Downyflake. As predicted, it was busy, and there was a small crowd of people standing outside of the door. Charlotte jumped out to put their name down on the waitlist while Peter hung back like a vulture waiting for another car to leave and free up a parking space.

He was admiring a nicely restored early Ford Bronco when a couple jumped into their SUV and backed out. It was a bit of negotiation for the two cars to pass, but in the end, Peter got the Rover parked, and he climbed out with the kids. They caught Charlotte as she came out of the door.

"Ten to twenty minutes," she said.

"Oh, that's great," said Peter. Looking down at Sophie and Spencer, he said, "What kind of donuts are you going to get today?"

The Downyflake was an institution on the island, having opened its doors in the 1930s. Peter fondly remembered his grandfather bringing him to town as a young boy to get donuts at the original restaurant site downtown. At the time, and still today, there were just a few varieties of donuts available, all cake-based. There was a sugar-covered option, not that white powdered sugar, but real granulated sugar sprinkled over the fried circular dough. Then chocolate-covered with real chocolate poured over the cake. Maple glazed and coconut rounded out the flavored options, and for those who preferred their fried dough the natural way, there was always the plain cake donut.

Spencer smiled and nearly shouted, "Sugar!"

Sophie looked up at him, beaming, "I want chocolate!" Peter tousled her hair and turned to Charlotte, "What about you, honey?"

"You know me. I simply can't resist the sugar-coated." She threaded an arm through his as they stood.

Sophie looked up at Peter, "What about you, daddy?"

"Me? I don't know, it's a really tough choice. But I'm thinking…"

Just then, his iPhone buzzed. Charlotte gave him a stern look, but he pulled his phone out anyway.

"Sorry, guys. Let me take this, and I'll be right back." Peter accepted the call and walked into the parking lot.

Charlotte watched him intently and noticed that his smile soon disappeared replaced with first a frown, and then anger. After a few minutes, he dropped the phone and ended the call. He turned and walked back to Charlotte and the kids.

"What was that about?" asked Charlotte, tensely, for fear of the answer.

As she asked, the hostess came out of the door. "Bois, party of four?"

Peter ignored the hostess and looked at Charlotte. "That was Janet, our office manager. Apparently, the auditors have found some issues with the company's financial statements we released last week. And it sounds serious. I need to get back."

"What? Need to get back? Now?" Charlotte was clearly upset. Sophie and Spencer looked at each other with confusion in their eyes and uncertain how to handle this sudden shift of emotions with their parents.

"Yes, now. I'm sorry, but I have to go. But I'll make it up to you, I promise."

Charlotte was silent. And angry. "What about our discussion this morning? That things were going to be different?"

"And they will be hon, I promise. I'll start to put a plan together. But I have to take care of this. I don't have another option."

"Fine," said Charlotte, coldly. "You just do what you have to do for that company."

Peter looked at her, "And I'm sorry about breakfast. We can come back next weekend."

Charlotte stared back, her blue eyes blazing, "On no. We're staying. You can take the car. We'll Uber home." She turned to find the hostess. "Hi, we're Bois. But it's just three."

The hostess nodded and headed back into the restaurant.

Kneeling down, Peter gave Sophie and Spencer a quick hug. "I'm sorry, guys, but I have to go. Have a donut for me and I'll see you in a few days." He reached out to embrace Charlotte but was rebuffed. "Have a safe trip," she said unemotionally. She grabbed Sophie and Spencer by the hand and led them into the restaurant. No one looked back.

Peter watched the door close and then walked dejectedly back to the car. Climbing into the driver's seat, he was tempted to call Janet back and tell her he wasn't coming, that they could deal with whatever the problem was next week. But his sense of duty and drive kicked in, and he pushed those thoughts out of his mind. Calling the jet service, he confirmed an 11:00 a.m. departure which would have him back at the office by early afternoon. He started the car, turned off the radio, and drove back to the house with the windows up and the sunroof closed. The only sounds coming from the rumble of the tires, the wind over the side-view mirrors, and the hum of the air conditioning.

He got to the house and quickly backed the car into the garage. Running up to the master bedroom, he changed into more appropriate work attire and ordered a taxi. He grabbed his laptop and stuffed some papers into his backpack, and headed out the front door. The taxi arrived as promised and deposited Peter at the airport with time to spare.

It took a few minutes to find his place among the dozens of jets on the ramp. He spotted the white G5 about halfway down, parked on the eastern edge of the apron, with the clamshell door open and the stairs down. He made his way over and, nodding to the pilot, quickly climbed the stairs and settled into one of the large chairs at the front of the aircraft.

He heard the thump of the door closing and the whine as the engines were started. The pilot taxied to the runway and paused, waiting for clearance. Peter looked out the window and thought again about staying and rushing back to the Downyflake to be with his family. He was about to get up and say something to the pilot when he felt the brakes release and engines spool up. The jet accelerated down the runway and was quickly airborne. As they climbed, Peter could make out the lighthouse in the distance where just a couple of hours before he had driven by with Charlotte, the promise of a fun day together stretched out in front of them. That feeling of lightness and satisfaction had disappeared, replaced with a sense of regret and dread. Peter pulled his eyes from the window and reached into his backpack for his laptop.

The plane banked left and continued climbing on its way to Connecticut.

CHAPTER SIX

It was the summer of 1995 and Charlotte was nervous. She had known Peter Bois less than a year, and here she was traveling to visit him and his parents on Nantucket Island. As a girl who grew up outside of St. Louis, she was entirely unfamiliar with the geography and culture of the East Coast. When Peter had told her about their summer home, she had to pull out a United States map to even understand where it was located. And that map hadn't been particularly helpful. It just showed a speck of land south of Cape Code and east of Long Island out a bit in the Atlantic. Her mother though had been the smart one. She and Charlotte had gone to a local bookstore and purchased a travel guide named *Cape Cod & The Islands*. Fearing embarrassment with Peter's family, she had read it cover to cover to fully orient herself with the area, its history, and the strange names of the towns, like Hyannis, Madaket, Wauwinet, Yarmouth, and so many more. Being the detail-oriented person she was, she even made a cheat sheet on an index card as if she was going to an art history exam.

She and Peter had met the very first day of orientation at the University of Richmond in Virginia's capital city. He and his roommate were throwing a party in his dorm room and invited their orientation groups to join. Charlotte had reluctantly agreed to the invitation more out of boredom than any curiosity or desire to meet more people. And her first impression of Peter was certainly not very flattering. She had arrived at his dorm and found him quite busy with a short, busty blond. He stopped kissing her long enough to say hello and invite Charlotte to join them on a trip downtown. Having been warned that very day about going out with hormone ridden college males, she politely declined. She had a few sips of a very cheap beer and then headed back to her room, hoping that she'd not run into him again.

And that desire had been granted, at least for a few days. Charlotte had signed up for French 101, which met Tuesdays and Thursdays for two hours, starting at 11:00 a.m. The first class was the Tuesday after Labor Day, and she arrived and promptly took a seat in the front row. With her textbook laid out in front of her, she opened a new college-ruled notebook and neatly labeled the date, ready to capture the notes from the lecture. The professor was in the middle of introducing the semester's syllabus when Peter stumbled into the classroom and plopped down next to Charlotte. He was wearing bright yellow Bermuda shorts, a navy polo, dirty bucks with no socks and a pair of Ray Bans. His hair was still wet from the shower, and he clearly had not been up long despite the class's late morning start time.

He apologized to the professor for his tardiness - had actually used the word tardy - and leaned over to Charlotte and mentioned that he'd not been able to get to the bookstore and purchase his textbook, would she mind if he shared hers. She smiled faintly and reluctantly angled her book to him. Little did she know that this minor event would totally change the course of her life and her future.

At first, they had just been friends, sharing notes from class, and occasionally studying together. They would talk about girlfriends and boyfriends, good dates and bad, and events around their Greek life. Over the semester, their friendship grew, so when Peter asked her to join him for their social after the last home football game of the year, it was easy to say yes. Following the game, they had gone to his fraternity house for a party and danced the night away. Despite that terrible first impression in his dorm room, she found Peter to be charming, kind, considerate, and with a sense of humor that often had Charlotte in stitches. She found herself falling in love, and it wasn't too much longer when he shared similar feelings for her.

Things had gotten more serious during the spring semester, and their relationship became a staple on campus. When May rolled around and with it the end of their freshman year of classes, they had talked about if and when they would see each other during the summer. Charlotte would be working for her father in his law office in St. Louis and had some flexibility for travel. Peter would be working construction on Nantucket and only had weekends free. They had agreed that Charlotte would come for a week's stay in July - right in the middle of the summer - so they would only be apart for a month or so on either end. Not knowing Peter or his family, her parents had reluctantly agreed to the trip, but only after her mom had a long conversation with Peter's.

Now here she was, on a small commuter flight, preparing to land at Nantucket, and feeling very nervous, partly because she had never been on such a small plane but more so at what lay ahead of her with Peter and his family. She knew his family was wealthy and was afraid they would look down their noses at a simple midwestern girl.

The twin-engine Cessna 402 eight-seater landed at Nantucket and taxied to the commuter terminal, where the pilot swiveled the plane and shut down the engines. The propellers rapidly slowed to a stop sending a shudder through the airframe. One of the ground crew opened the door while another went to the nose to empty luggage. With the low ceiling of the plane, Charlotte stooped and awkwardly walked to the exit stairs and then took the two steps down to the tarmac. She looked over at the terminal, saw Peter, and waved. He smiled and waved back. A buzz of excitement went through her, and she hurried into the terminal where Peter met her with a ferocious hug and a long, lingering kiss.

"Welcome to Nantucket!" he whispered into her ear. "I'm so happy you're here!"

"Me too! I have missed you so much," she replied. He took her hand and they walked over to the baggage area. Belaying the wealth that came through the airport every day, the baggage claim was nothing more than an angled wooden deck where the bags were thrown after being retrieved from the plane. The luggage cart pulled up, and Charlotte pointed out hers as they slid down towards them. Peter slung the duffel over his shoulder, grabbed the suitcase in one hand, and with the other grabbed Charlotte's hand and led her out of the terminal. The family's red CJ-5 was parked just outside. Peter threw the luggage in the back and helped Charlotte into the passenger seat. She had never ridden in a Jeep, let alone one without a roof or doors, and found it exhilarating.

Peter crunched the Jeep into first and popped the clutch. Charlotte cried out in delight and grabbed the windshield header to stabilize herself - the last thing she wanted to do was fall out of the car. He accelerated slowly out of the parking lot and then shifted up to second when they got on the street. He looked over at Charlotte, "How was your flight?"

"Oh, it was fine," replied Charlotte. "But I have to admit I was more than a bit nervous on that little plane. It bounced around quite a bit, and it seemed like we were flying awfully low."

"Yeah, it's certainly a different way to fly than on the big jets the airlines have."

"For sure. And why is the airport called ACK? That just seems really weird."

Peter chuckled. "Well, the urban legend says it used to be known as Ackerly Airport until it was renamed Nantucket Memorial. But the truth is that the Navy had exclusive rights to three-letter airport designations starting with N. So since NAN was out as an option, they picked the next logical three letters, which ended up being A, C and K or ACK."

"Hmm." Charlotte thought for a minute and said with a smile, "Well, I guess it could have been worse. It could have been ANT or UCK."

Peter laughed and looked over at her, his brown hair tugged by the wind, "Very true!" Charlotte reached over and grabbed his hand. "God, I've missed you. The last six weeks seem more like six years."

"Me too. It feels like it has been forever since I've seen you, and I'm so glad you're here." He paused for a minute to check traffic as he turned right onto Milestone road. "Are you ready to meet my parents?"

"As ready as I'll ever be. I have to admit that I'm really nervous about it. What if they don't like me?"

"They're going to love you, hon, trust me. My parents might seem a little intimidating at first but they are pretty down to earth. you're going to knock their socks off."

And she did.

Charlotte found Peter's parents warm and welcoming and thoroughly enjoyed spending time with both of them during the week. And with Peter being an only child, she could also see the very soft spot they had for him. She, of course, had to know what they thought of her and finally screwed up the courage to ask Peter during one of their many walks through Sconset. They were on Ocean Avenue, holding hands and he turned to her. "My parents love you. They think you're sweet, kind and above all a lovely young lady. In fact, the other night, when you were getting ready to go out, my father came over to me and said, 'oh my god, her eyes. I could stare into them for the rest of my life'. So, yes, I think they approve," said Peter with a wink. Charlotte smiled broadly and fought the urge to start skipping as they walked.

She also learned much more about Peter and realized that he was a different person here. At school, he was distracted with classes, making grades, and fraternity life. Here, on Nantucket, he was relaxed, easy-going, and very open to sharing more of his past, including his ongoing sadness with the loss of his close friend the summer before. He had told her about it when they were still just friends, but it was the first time that he truly opened up to her about the impact it had on his life and his deep feelings of sadness and regret. He also shared more about his four years away in boarding school and what it was like to be living away from home at the age of thirteen.

"It certainly made me more independent and resilient, but it was also emotionally tough to be in that environment at such a young age. It definitely made me hesitant to get too close to people and to rely more on myself, and what I know I can control," he had said as they sat on the beach, looking out over the waves breaking on the shore, the gulls flying low and the terns skittering up and down the sand. She didn't know how it was possible but realized she was falling ever deeper in love with Peter.

Peter had made it a point to show Charlotte as much of Nantucket as possible and was happy to be a tourist for the week. They went to the Whaling Museum, where Charlotte learned that this small island had once been a significant economic force in the world. They explored the shops along the cobblestone Main Street, had lunch and milkshakes at the pharmacy, and went for a sunset sail in the harbor. They rode their bikes to town on the bike path and up to Sankaty Head lighthouse. But Charlotte's favorite of all had been the picnic at Great Point, the sandy arm that makes up most of the island's eastern edge and only really accessible by four-wheel drive. The entire experience of driving on the beach and sitting by the water was exhilarating and so thoroughly opposite her life in the landlocked midwest. She wished she could bottle that day up and carry it with her for the rest of her life.

Despite being from the midwest, Charlotte had fallen in love with Nantucket. She was charmed by the old-world atmosphere, the gray shingled homes, the glorious open spaces, and the lovely beaches. And Siasconset had wholly captured her heart. Originally an old fishing village, over the centuries, it had been transformed into an escape. First, from those from town wanting to distance themselves from the noise and smells of the whaling industry, then actors seeking refuge from the heat and humidity of Broadway in New York and now, well-heeled residents, tourists, and vacationers looking for shelter from modern life. While there were a few elegant old homes, like Fernweh, most were small, simple cottages, many built in the mid to late 1800s. It quickly became Charlotte's favorite place on earth.

When Peter was at work, she explored Sconset walking every street and getting to know this very unique village from the Bluff Walk to the old well. She was charmed with the manicured privets, the profusion of blooming hydrangeas ranging in color from light pink to deep purple, and the ever-present climbing roses, their numerous blossoms in red, pink, and white adorning the trellis-covered walls and roofs of the quaint cottages. She watched through the hedges as they played tennis at the Casino - dressed in all white of course - and was fascinated by the sundial next to the old bike bridge. When Peter returned from work, they would go down to the beach to sit and talk and then head to town for dinner.

It was a wonderful week, and it went by way too quickly. Before she even realized what had happened, she found herself back at the airport and getting ready to board the small commuter plane to start her trip back to the midwest. "I'll see you in a few weeks," said Peter, holding her hand and fighting back tears. She squeezed his hand, sad to be leaving him and Nantucket. "I'll still miss you," she said, sniffling through her tears. He pulled her toward him and hugged her tightly. "I love you," he whispered into her ear. "And I want to spend the rest of my life with you." Charlotte pulled back and smiled. She kissed him on the lips and hugged him harder. "Me too, Peter. Me too."

Her flight was called. They shared one final kiss and slowly pulled away from each other. Charlotte reluctantly turned to follow the handful of other passengers out onto the tarmac. She ascended the steps into the plane and shuffled to her seat directly next to the pilot. The door thumped closed, and the ground crew gave the pilot the thumbs up to start the engines. She watched as the propellers on the right engine started to turn, caught, and then roared with a belch of blue smoke from the exhaust. With the left engine started with the same belch of smoke, the pilot eased the throttles forward and taxied out on the runway.

From her front seat, she had a fantastic view out of the windshield and again thought about the sheer beauty of this little island. The pilot turned onto the runway and immediately started accelerating, the roar of the engines rumbling through the airframe. She looked past the pilot toward the terminal and could just make out Peter waving and blowing her kisses. She felt a lump in her throat as the plane lifted off the runway, heading north to Boston. Through the windshield and her tears, she watched sadly as Sankaty Head lighthouse, and then Great Point receded past her.

CHAPTER SEVEN

Peter's jet landed on runway 29 at Westchester County Airport just before 11:00 a.m., the flight having taken just over a half-hour. The pilot taxied the plane to the general aviation terminal on the north side of the airport. Peter descended the stairs as they were opening and quickly walked across the ramp and through the hanger to a waiting car from his usual service. Being midday on a Saturday, traffic was relatively light, and the driver pulled into the Shimmo offices just thirty minutes from touchdown. Peter thanked the driver and headed in the front door where his chief financial officer, Don Aires, was waiting for him.

"Hi, Peter. Good flight?" asked the CFO, more than a bit nervous at having interrupted his boss's weekend.

"Never mind that, Don. What the fuck is going on?" said Peter angrily. He hadn't been in the office in nearly three weeks between business travel and a few precious days on Nantucket and was feeling very disconnected from the operations team that managed the day-to-day affairs of his business.

"I'm so sorry to have disturbed your weekend, Peter. And trust me, I wouldn't have called if I didn't think it was critical to have you here. Let's head upstairs to the Executive Conference Room. The team is there and ready to brief you on the issue."

Peter took the stairs two at a time, his CFO struggling to keep up.

Immediately he could sense the feeling of unease and nervousness radiating from his senior team the moment he walked in the door. They were all there, the head of information technology, the regional accounting directors as well as the vice president of operations, the VP of human resources, and his chief marketing officer. Pretty much the entire C-Suite and their direct reports were on hand totaling over twenty people.

He settled into the large leather chair at the head of the glass table. "So, does anyone here want to tell me what the fuck is going on?"

Steve Rhodes, the director of information technology, was the first to speak. "As you know, we closed the books for the second quarter last month and released the results a week ago Friday. Everyone agreed the numbers looked good, but…"

"But what?" demanded Peter clenching his fists.

"Purely coincidentally, the auditors were here over the last week completing a standard review of the financials and…," his voice trailing out.

"And?"

"They discovered some issues in our recorded revenues."

"Issues? What sort of issues?" Peter challenged.

"It appears based on the preliminary assessment that we have overstated revenues for the quarter by over ten million dollars and year to date by nearly twenty million."

Peter's eyes went wide in shock. "Why are you telling me this and not him?" said Peter, pointing his finger at the CFO.

"Because, unfortunately, we believe the error is due to a glitch in our accounting software," replied the IT director nervously.

Peter leaned forward and slammed the top of the conference table with the palm of his right hand. "A glitch in our accounting software? Would this be the custom software you recommended we develop and install? The software that has cost me over two million dollars in capital expense?" he asked, his face red with anger. "You recommended this approach, you asshole, and now you're telling me our financials are all fucked up?"

Steve's face turned red at being the focus of Peter's ire. "Yes, sir." He fumbled with his hands. "Clearly we didn't fully test and validate the closing process. We've already started to identify the issues and fix the process."

Peter sat back and stared intensely at his IT director. "You mean that the system screwed up because you didn't test it sufficiently, and now that you've fucked me with bad financials, you're going to look to see what caused the problem and fix it?" Peter was shaking with rage.

The IT director stood silently, too afraid to respond.

"I'll tell you what we're going to do," said Peter. "First off, you're fired. Get the fuck out of my sight right now, and get the hell out of this building." Peter turned to his VP of HR. "Please escort him the fuck out of here and make sure you secure his laptop, card access, and corporate credit cards. And terminate his email and system access, goddammit!"

Dejectedly, the IT director left the room, escorted by HR.

Peter sat in his chair, clenching his fists and trying to cool down so he could address these problems clearly and rationally.

Taking a deep breath, he turned to Don, "Step one is that we need to correct and republish the financials. What is involved with that?"

"Well, we know that the divisional accounts are correct. The issues happened when we used the software to consolidate those numbers into the corporate books. So, we can complete that process manually. It's going to be time and labor-intensive, but then we know it will be right."

"Ok. What do you need from me to make that happen?" Peter asked.

"Just your approval on the approach. We'll need to hire some accounting temps, but our incremental spend will be pretty low, and I can cover that within my operating budget."

"Great. Let's get that started. How long do you think until we're ready to restate the numbers?"

"If we get started Monday, and we can find the temps we need, I'm thinking at most a few days. That includes a little wiggle room in case we need additional time to address things."

"Ok. Please keep me apprised on your progress."

Peter turned to his VP of Operations, Sally Wurth. "Ok, step two. I know Steve only had a dotted line to you, but I hold you partially responsible for this fuckup. You need to put a plan together on how this is going to be fixed. I'd like your recommendation on my desk first thing Monday morning."

"Yes, sir," said Sally. She pulled out her Android and immediately started texting the team that they were needed at the offices for the rest of the weekend.

Peter turned back to Don, "Anything else we need to discuss?"

Don pulled his glasses off and rubbed the bridge of his nose. Clearly, he hadn't had much sleep over the past few days, and the stress of the situation had taken its toll. "Unfortunately, yes. Since we released inaccurate results, we're technically in violation of our bank covenants. We need you to talk with the bank and advise them of the issues and that we will have corrected numbers to them shortly."

"Sure, I can manage that. I play golf with our loan officer, and we've got a great relationship. In fact..." Peter picked up his iPhone, "let me see if he's available to play tomorrow." Peter typed out a text and sent it.

The CFO continued, "I've already informed the SEC of the situation, so no real concerns there. But I'd recommend that we put out a press release so that our shareholders know what's going on and get the facts directly from us. Although we didn't do anything intentional or illegal, I don't want anyone to think this is another Enron type of situation."

"Totally agree," said Peter. He looked down the table, searching for Paul Lord, his chief marketing officer. "Paul, how quickly can you get a release drafted and on my desk?"

The CMO looked at his watch; it was a little past one. "I'll need to connect with the agency but should have something for you to react to by 5:00."

Peter nodded, "Make sure you emphasize that this was a result of a systems failure and not an intentional act to overstate revenue. I'd also suggest you make it clear that the people responsible have been terminated, and the plans are in place to restate the numbers quickly."

Paul was taking notes on a legal pad in front of him. He looked back when Peter finished and said, "Absolutely. We can spin this in a positive light, and I've no issues whatsoever with throwing Steve under the bus for this entire fiasco."

"Perfect," said Peter. He turned his attention back to the assembled team and pointed his finger one by one at the faces around the table. "I expect that addressing this issue will be your number one priority and the most important thing in your life for the next two weeks. I don't care if you have a vacation planned, if your kid is getting married or if you have to go to your parent's funeral, I expect you to be here, whatever it takes, to get our books right." Peter stood up and walked out of the conference room and headed to his office.

The rest of his day was spent reviewing the original financials to fully understand the implications of the revenue issues and develop talking points that he could use with the loan officer as well as with any stakeholders that sought him out for comment. And the more he looked at it, the more upset he got. At one point, he slammed his notes on his desk when he realized that this issue was going to be a problem for him for months, if not years. Even if it was an honest mistake, many would think it was indeed an intentional act and that they, Shimmo Plastics, had gotten caught cooking the books, just like so many other companies in the news lately.

"Fuck, fuck, fuck!" Peter shouted at the ceiling.

He swiveled his office chair to look out the large, floor-to-ceiling windows of his office. The light outside had taken on the golden hue of an approaching sunset. Glancing at his watch, he realized he hadn't connected with Charlotte since saying goodbye this morning. That omission certainly wasn't going to help him improve things with her, but he hoped she'd understand. He quickly fired off a text to her to let her know he was alive and would call later with the ugly details of his day.

Peter grabbed his backpack, stuffed his notes in the back pocket, and walked out of his office, turning off the lights as he went. He did a quick circle of the offices to see who was still there and noted with some satisfaction that the IT director's office was dark and the door locked. "Fucking asshole," he muttered to himself.

His car service took him back to their Connecticut estate, Sheldon House, a classic 18th century New England colonial sitting on over four acres of prime Weston, Connecticut land. They had purchased it after the IPO of Shimmo, when they had become truly rich, and spent several hundred thousand in renovations. They had maintained the historical charm of the old house but had made needed updates in the kitchen, bathrooms, and most of the living spaces.

Part of the renovation project had also included an outdoor living space with a large bluestone patio, outdoor kitchen, and a saltwater pool. The car dropped Peter off at the foot of his driveway, and he strolled directly to the terrace and grabbed a beer from the outdoor refrigerator. He pulled out his iPhone and made a call to his favorite local eatery and arranged to have dinner delivered. He hung up with the restaurant and then dialed Charlotte. It went straight to voicemail. He left a message with some details of the day and asked for her to call him back when she could. He disconnected the call and then headed up to the house. After disarming the security system, he dropped his backpack in the kitchen and went upstairs to change. Although he spent a lot of time here alone, the house still felt eerily quiet and empty. He missed Charlotte and the kids.

Dinner arrived as promised, which he enjoyed while watching the end of a Yankees game. They were visiting the Red Sox, and unfortunately, his beloved Yankees were trailing their Fenway rivals. A tendril of memory invaded his thoughts and took him back to his friend Jack, a diehard Red Sox fan. The two of them had many spirited discussions about who had the better team. Many a beer was bet although neither really minded losing as the winnings were always shared with each other. Peter felt a sudden deep sadness at the thought of Jack and again wondered how his life would be different if he still had his dear friend in it.

He turned off the television, and beer in hand went back out on the patio to clear his head. So many conflicting and confusing emotions were going through him. The fuckup at the company, his strained relationship with Charlotte, his feeling of being disconnected from Sophie and Spencer, and a sense of loss and guilt about Jack. He gazed up at the sky and could not help thinking that his life was at a turning point. He just wasn't sure if it was going to turn for the good or the bad.

CHAPTER EIGHT

P eter spent Sunday morning at the offices and didn't really have an agenda other than to track who was working and the progress being made. Thinking he had been a bit rough on the team Saturday, he arranged for a breakfast of fresh bagels, doughnuts, and coffee to be delivered first thing. He also made a point to speak with each person of his team during the morning to offer support and his appreciation for their efforts and made a mental note to take everyone out for a happy hour and dinner after the new results were released. He wanted them to think he was at least partly human.

His afternoon was spent at the golf course playing with his loan officer. Peter had also invited a couple of club friends to join them, and they had a pleasant day on the links. It was between holes ten and eleven, and after a couple of beers that Peter broke the news about their inaccurate financials. He also managed to get in the fact that some people were totally incompetent, but you didn't always find out until they completely and totally screwed the pooch. That got a hearty chuckle from the loan officer, and by the time they teed off on thirteen, it was all water under the bridge. They had a few more drinks at the nineteenth hole but no more discussions about Shimmo or the financials. It had been a successful outing.

Peter picked up some take-out on the way home and tried to call Charlotte. Again it went straight to her voicemail, which got him wondering if she had blocked his number or more likely that her phone had died and she had forgotten to charge it. He felt a bit anxious when he didn't get an answer on the house line but was reassured when Charlotte texted him with apologies that they had been at the beach and as he expected her phone had died. Seizing the opportunity, he called up her number on his iPhone and was finally able to connect. It turned into a halfway pleasant thirty minutes hearing about their events of the past day and a half, their time at the beach, and a stray cat who was apparently trying to take up residence in the carriage house. Spencer and Sophie had their turns as well, and hearing their voices made Peter smile and wish that he were with them.

They said their goodbyes with a promise that they would talk again on Monday. Peter disconnected and sat quietly for a few minutes and wondered if perhaps the turning was for the better.

* * *

He was at the office early Monday morning and started the day with a quick staff meeting to be updated on the progress, and if Don had secured the necessary temps he needed to get things rolling. He ended the session and headed for his office, where he was intercepted by his admin, Aleta Paddington. "Mr. Bois?"

"Yes, what is it?" Peter responded a little shortly. His admin was a lovely lady, but sometimes her timing was not always the best.

"There is a gentleman here to see you. A Mr. Jasper Norrington," she said hesitantly.

"Who? I don't recall having any appointments today," replied Peter.

"No, sir, he does not have an appointment. But he says it's quite urgent and could have a major impact on the company," said Aleta.

"Hmm. That must be something regarding the financials. Is he with the press?"

"I don't know, sir. He just said it was urgent and that you would want to talk with him."

"Okay. Send him in."

Peter was at his desk reviewing email when Jasper Norrington walked into his office. He was slender and tall, a shade over six feet with dark hair, brown eyes and a thin but handsome face. Peter stood and offered his hand, "Good morning. I don't think we've met, but I'm Peter Bois."

"Yes, Peter. I know who you are. I'm Jasper Norrington, the acting CEO for *Clean Seas Forever*, and I wanted to talk with you about your company and the damage you're doing to the world's oceans."

"What!" said Peter loudly. "How the fuck did you get in here? Get the hell out of my office right now!" He called out to Aleta, whose desk sat just outside his door. "Aleta! Get security! Have them come to my office immediately."

Jasper looked at Peter with pleading eyes. "Mr. Bois. Please wait. I'm not here to attack you or your company. In fact, I was hoping we could have a collaborative discussion on how we could start working together."

Peter stood up. "A collaborative discussion? Working together? What the fuck have you been smoking? You assholes have picketed my offices. Why the hell should I listen to a damn thing you say? Aleta!"

"Sir, please. I apologize for barging in without an appointment, but now that I'm here, just give me five minutes. I promise that you'll find it beneficial, and in fact, you might even find it profitable."

Peter was angry and feeling unsettled from this sneak attack. "Profitable? I'd love to hear how you're going to make that happen."

The security guard appeared at the door. "Everything okay, Mr. Bois?"

Jasper looked at Peter with pleading eyes. "Please. Five minutes. That's all I need. And if I don't manage to sell you on this, then I will leave quietly and with a promise to never picket your offices again."

Peter thought about it briefly and relented. "Okay. Five minutes. But then you're out of here." Turning to the guard, he said, "We are fine. But don't go too far." He settled back into his chair.

"Thank you." Jasper reached into his briefcase and pulled out an empty water bottle that was heavily damaged and discolored. "This is one of your products, is it not?"

Peter picked up the empty bottle and surveyed it. Finding the company mark on the bottom, he looked up at Jasper. "Yes, it is. It's hard to read the date code, but I suspect it was made in the last year or so." He put the bottle back down on the desk. "So?"

"So, this bottle was removed from the stomach of a dead humpback whale. It had beached itself on Cape Cod, and a thorough necropsy was completed by the marine biology team at UMass. In addition to this bottle, they found a number of other plastics in its GI tract as well as severe lacerations around the fluke from discarded netting."

Peter stared at him, dispassionately. "I'll say it again. So?"

"Our organization is dedicated to helping to eliminate plastics from the world's oceans and work with industry leaders such as yourself to put in place measures that would help prevent future plastics pollution," said Jasper. "With that goal in mind, we have two requests for you."

"You have two requests for me? I have one for you - get the fuck out of my office!"

"Mr. Bois, please. I think you'll find these requests rather straightforward."

Peter turned away and stared out the window briefly before responding. "Okay. I'm listening. Doubtful, but listening."

"Number one is that we would like Shimmo Plastics to join our industry roundtable. This group is comprised of other plastic producers like Shimmo and meets quarterly to identify problems, develop processes and solutions, and workshop new products that longer-term could help eliminate plastics altogether. At least those that have the potential of entering the world's oceans."

Peter turned back and said tauntingly, "Funny you say that, my wife suggested the same thing just the other day. And I'll say to you what I said to her. Transitioning out of plastics would cost us hundreds of millions per year in revenue!" Peter smacked his desk with his palm. "I thought you said our discussion was going to be profitable."

"Mr. Bois, we've done our research, and we know that consumer sentiment is building against the widespread use of plastics. We also know that Shimmo provides bottles and containers to a number of the world's premium food and beverage brands."

"True," he confirmed. "And we make them to the exact customer specification."

"I understand that," said Jasper. "We also know that these brands have images they need to maintain. They spend hundreds of millions, if not billions each year, nurturing those brands. Do you think they want their logo on a piece of plastic that kills a whale or a dolphin?"

Peter sat back in his chair, absorbing the claims Jasper was making. He hadn't really thought of it from the brand's perspective. But it's not exactly like they had come running to him either. It was probably just a bunch of liberal, sentimental bullshit. "So, what was the second thing?"

"We want you to license your new resin technology, the one made from natural materials that break down quickly in saltwater," said Jasper.

"How the fuck do you know about that?" said Peter angrily.

"Your chief scientist gave a presentation on it last year at the Asian plastics conference," Jasper smiled wryly. "And one of my associates found it when she was doing some online research." Jasper paused to pull out a single sheet of paper and placed it on Peter's desk. "This is our preliminary estimate as to potential licensing deals and subsequent royalties you would earn."

Peter picked up the sheet and reviewed the numbers. Most of his primary competitors were listed as were several others that produced for adjacent industries. The volume estimates were significant, as were the potential licensing fees. He looked up at Jasper. "Why would I agree to this? Why would I share our proprietary technology when we could have the global exclusive for years?"

Jasper stood quietly and carefully selected his words. "Because you have the opportunity to not only do a very good thing for the world but also earn a tremendous amount of money for your company."

"Bullshit," said Peter. "This is just tree-hugging bullshit, and I don't believe a single company on your sheet would agree to this."

"But Mr. Bois…"

"Enough! I told you I'd give you five minutes, and you've taken closer to twenty," said Peter angrily. "Now, please get the hell out of my office and let me get back to work."

Jasper turned and walked toward the door. He slowed and looked back at Peter. "What do you know of whaling, particularly in the 18th and 19th centuries?"

Peter decided to play along. "A little, I guess. I've been to the Nantucket Whaling Museum. I've read *Moby Dick* and *Heart of the Sea*. Is that what you mean?"

"Mr. Bois, in the 18th and 19th centuries, hundreds of thousands of whales were killed to supply oil for industry and for light. But what a lot of people don't know is that they were also killed for baleen, which some called whalebone."

Peter stared at him without responding.

"Baleen is often referred to as the plastic of the 19th century as it was flexible, light and strong and used in everything from women's corsets to buggy whips, canes, and even brushes."

"And your point?"

"My point, sir, is that hundreds of thousands of whales had to die back then to supply people with products they desire. And they continue to die today because of companies and people like you. Honestly, Mr. Bois, you are no different than a 19th-century whaler, raping the oceans in search of profit." Jasper turned and walked out of the office.

"Fuck you!" Peter shouted at Jasper's back. He sat fuming in his chair for a few minutes then opened his laptop to check email.

CHAPTER NINE

C harlotte wheeled the Range Rover into the circular drive of her best friend's house off Polpis Road. While Charlotte preferred the village life in Sconset, her friend, Amy Stephens, and her husband favored a more rural and isolated location for their home on the island. Charlotte liked to tease Amy that it was more of a compound than it was a house. Besides the main home, there was a large barn with an in-law suite, a smaller two-bedroom cottage on the north side of their land, and a substantial pool house that could sleep four if pressed. All of this sitting on over three acres of land with spectacular views over Polpis Harbor. Charlotte, by her nature, was not a jealous person. After all, she had a pretty good life herself. But she had to admit feeling a bit envious of her friend's situation. Not so much the buildings but definitely the land and the view. She felt like she could sit and stare at the water for hours on end.

"Hey, friend!" Amy cried out from the spacious front porch. "Be right there, just need to get the baby and grab the boat bag." Amy turned and ran back into the house.

Charlotte smiled and waved up to her friend. Then she turned and looked at Spencer and Sophie. "Now, I need both of you to be on your best behavior today. Okay?"

"Ma-om," said Sophie in a sing-song voice. "I'm always good" and crossed her arms. Charlotte smiled at her, "I know you are hon." She turned to look behind the driver's seat.

As usual, Spencer's head was buried in a book. He had been in love with them ever since he picked up his first picture book in his crib. Since he had learned to read, it was not unusual for him to go through several a day. Feeding this voracious appetite had become a bit of a challenge for Charlotte. They would hit the Nantucket public library, The Atheneum, a couple of times a week often leaving with a canvas boat bag stuffed full with books. Fortunately, Charlotte had a partner in crime at the Atheneum with one of the older librarians. She had taken a shine to Spencer and his love of reading and would usually have a list of titles she thought Spencer would enjoy. She had also convinced Charlotte that Spencer was ready for more adventurous and challenging material. On their last visit, she had introduced Spencer to *A Watership Down*. Although the political and social commentary went well beyond his understanding, he relished the story of a bunch of rabbits looking for a new home and the adventures they encountered along the way. Secretly, Charlotte had hoped that Spencer and Peter could read it together at bedtime as a way to strengthen their relationship. But Peter was off-island so much, and even when he was here, he never seemed to be in the moment. When she had last brought it up with him, the discussion had turned into a nasty fight and since she had let it lay.

"Spencer?"

Spencer looked up from his book, his blues eyes sparkling and his tawny hair showing streaks of blond from his time in the sun and in the water. "Yeah, mom."

"I need you to be on your best behavior today, okay? This is the first time we've been to the beach with Mrs. Stephens and her new baby."

"Okay," said Spencer, and he turned back to his book.

Charlotte smiled at him and, for the tenth time today, thanked her blessings to have two wonderful and well-behaved children. She had heard horror stories from her friends about their kids and knew just how fortunate she was with both Spencer and Sophie. She looked up to see Amy walking down the brick walkway toward the driveway, the baby on her hip, and a bag slung over her shoulder.

"Sorry that took so long," she said.

"No worries at all," said Charlotte. "I remember those days all too well of trying to get going and having to pull all the baby stuff together."

Amy opened the rear door balancing Constance on her hip. "Well, it didn't help that I had to change her diaper at the last minute. She had some fruit for breakfast, and it just went right through her," said Amy, wrinkling her nose. "And thanks for bringing the car seat," she said and gently lowered the baby in. After buckling the seatbelts, she closed the door and hopped into the front passenger seat. She looked at Charlotte as she was putting on her own belt. "So, where are we headed?"

"I was thinking of Pebble Beach. Spencer loves to play on the dunes there, and it's usually not too crowded," said Charlotte.

"Sounds good." Amy climbed into the front passenger seat and slammed the door. "Let's do it!" she yelled playfully.

Charlotte smiled sadly, remembering those same words she had said to Peter last Saturday. She started the car and headed back to Polpis road. Although the beach was only a few miles as the crow flies, there wasn't a direct route, so Charlotte followed Polpis back through Sconset and then took Milestone out to Tom Nevers Road. She then followed Tom Nevers all the way to the end, past the old Naval station, an active base during World War II, and the site of the 1960s presidential nuclear bunker. It was now mostly a local recreational space that also had one of the best yet least known beaches on the island. Road maintenance had ended with the base closure, so the last mile or so was a patchwork of macadam and dirt pockmarked with deep depressions and large bumps. The Range Rover swayed over them, more than up to the task, and within a few minutes, Charlotte had found a good parking spot, and they unloaded the car.

It was a perfect day for the beach. The sky was a deep blue with just a few wisps of high clouds. The temperature was in the seventies and with low humidity the air was quite comfortable. They followed a path down from the parking area through the dunes and found a flat spot free of seaweed and other beach detritus. Amy spread out a large blanket and unfolded their chairs while Charlotte screwed an umbrella anchor into the sand. She inserted the umbrella into the base and then opened it, providing instant shade. A fresh shore breeze was just enough to keep them cool and frustrate the sand flies.

"Spencer, Sophie," Charlotte called out. "Let me spray you." Spencer and Sophie dutifully lined up for their mist of sunscreen. "Now, stay out of the water unless I'm with you. And please, don't stray too far. Stay where I can see you."

As soon as Charlotte had finished, they tore off across the sand. Spencer was quickly busy playing with his toy trucks on the dune while Sophie was actively engaged in making a sandcastle from shells and dead sea life. The baby was sound asleep in her little pumpkin seat in the shade under the umbrella.

"This is just about perfect," said Amy as she settled into one of the beach chairs. She pulled the cooler over and opened it handing Charlotte a seltzer and grabbed one for herself.

"Yes, it is," replied Charlotte, with just a hint of sadness in her voice.

"What is it?" asked Amy. She had known Charlotte for years and could tell that something was bothering her.

"Oh, it's nothing, Ames."

"I don't believe you. I can tell that something is on your mind. Talk to me."

Charlotte looked out toward the water. A small flock of sandpipers was skittering across the beach just out of reach of the oncoming waves and stabbing their peaks into the sand looking for food. Gentle swells driven by the breeze, approached and broke a few feet from shore. The waves rushed up the beach, scattering the sandpipers and dimpling the sand. The sandpipers chased the retreating water back toward the edge and renewed their efforts to find a tasty buried morsel only to scatter again with the next breaker. As she watched, Charlotte imagined that the waves and sandpipers had been doing this dance for millennia. And in some way, that knowledge gave her comfort and a sense of permanence.

Charlotte turned her eyes from the sea and looked at Amy. "It's Peter."

"Peter? What's going on?"

Charlotte paused for a minute. "You know, Ames, when Peter and I were first married, it was like a dream come true. We were so in love and so close. We could talk about anything, and it seemed like we laughed all the time. And he couldn't keep his hands off me."

Amy looked at her friend compassionately. "And now?"

"And now?" Charlotte scoffed. "It's just not the same anymore. He's not the man I married. He's not the husband or the father I thought he'd be. Hell, he hasn't touched me in months."

"Oh, Char, I'm so sorry. What's changed?"

"What has changed is that fucking company of his," said Charlotte, angrily. Amy's face registered shock and surprise at the use of profanity. Charlotte was by no means a saint, but she rarely used that kind of language. "Ever since he bought that company, it has become the most important thing in his life. We just don't measure up," she said, gesturing towards Spencer and Sophie. "And he doesn't have time for us. He usually gets here late Friday, and he leaves first thing Monday morning. And even when he's here, he's not. He is on his laptop dealing with email or on the phone with customers," said Charlotte, her face showing exasperation.

"Have you talked with him about it?" asked Amy, taking a sip of her seltzer.

"Yes, I've tried, most recently last Saturday morning. He arrived late Friday afternoon as usual and then proceeded to lock himself in his office and work past midnight. He ended up sleeping in the guest cottage."

"What, you kicked him out?"

"Actually, no, that was his choice. He claimed he didn't want to disturb me, but I think deep down, it was easier for him to sleep in the guest room than to come inside and face me. I guess he thought I was going to be angry with him."

"Well, I wouldn't blame you if you were," said Amy.

"At this point, I'm happy to get any time from him. Just some moments to reconnect and feel like a family again."

"But are you happy with just that?"

Charlotte looked down the beach at Sophie. Her sandcastle was growing with walls and turrets. It looked like she had some crab shells as guards on the towers with larger quahog shells dividing the rooms. She smiled at her daughter's imagination and turned to Amy. "If I'm honest with myself, then I have to admit that I'm not."

Amy leaned forward out of her chair. "Then what are you going to do?"

"Peter promised me he was going to put a plan together that would allow him to spend more time with us. So I have to give him a chance and hear what his plan is."

"And what if it's just another broken promise?" asked Amy.

Charlotte was quiet and reflecting on the discussion she'd had with Peter on Saturday. "If he breaks this promise, then I think the only logical next step is a separation and maybe even a divorce."

"Charlotte, no!" exclaimed Amy.

She looked at her friend. "Amy, it's the only option I have. I can't spend my life waiting for Peter to show up, and it's certainly not fair to Sophie and Spencer. They only see Peter a day or two a week if that. And it's no different when we're home in Connecticut. He lives at that damn office."

Amy wasn't sure how to respond. Charlotte continued, "You know Amy, there is so much more I want to do with my life. And on this island. We're so lucky and fortunate. I want to be more involved on the island and give back."

"But if you get divorced?" asked Amy, her voice trailing off.

"Well, it will mean changes for sure, especially here on the island. I might not have the history on Nantucket that you and Peter do, but I love it nonetheless. So a divorce would mean finding another house here."

"Maybe we could be neighbors!" said Amy, only half-jokingly.

"As much as I'd love to be your neighbor, Ames, I really don't want to leave Peter or Fernweh. It would tear up the kids, and I don't want to cause that pain."

"I know, I was just kidding, sort of," she paused. "Can you just give him an ultimatum?"

Charlotte looked over at Spencer on the dune, lost in play. "Peter doesn't respond well to ultimatums. He'd just get pissed and shut down. That wouldn't work."

"So what are you thinking?" asked Amy.

"Well, he's flying in today for the weekend, and I managed to get reservations tonight at 56 Union. I'm hoping he'll be ready to talk about his plans. And if not, then I think I need to come clean with him and tell him what I'm thinking."

"How do you think he's going to take it?"

Charlotte turned her gaze back at the sandpipers running back and forth across the sand in their continuing dance with the waves. "I think he's going to be angry, but I hope I can make him see what he's doing and that he needs balance. And that we can do so much good for this island."

"Well, remember, I'm here anytime if you need to talk," said Amy. "If there is anything I can do, please don't hesitate to reach out."

"Thanks, Ames. I will. And anyway, let's stop being so serious and enjoy this day and the weather. Besides, Constance will probably wake up soon, and I'm sure Spencer and Sophie are getting hungry. Ready for some lunch?"

"Sounds good, Char."

The two friends shared lunch while they watched the children play, the baby sleep, and the sandpipers dance.

CHAPTER TEN

P eter landed at the airport late Friday afternoon, his flight had been delayed an hour due to thunderstorms over Long Island Sound. But the new flight attendant had made him a couple of very good Manhattans, which he enjoyed while he reviewed the corrected financials. The latest quarterly numbers for Shimmo Plastics were still looking good despite the revenue issues the auditors had found.

Charlotte was unable to pick him up - something about going to the beach - so he had to wait nearly forty minutes for an Uber to take him to Sconset. The young driver had a Jamaican lilt to his voice and had talked most of the way, usually about the traffic, the mopeds, and the day-tripping tourists that always made weekends so crazy busy in the summer. They pulled into the driveway a little after six o'clock, and Peter exited the car without saying a word to the driver and headed into the house.

Walking into the kitchen, he found Charlotte by the pantry, putting some food and containers away. "Hi, hon," he said and kissed her lightly on the cheek. She grudgingly accepted and resumed cleaning up the remnants from their day at the beach.

Peter felt the chill but was hoping that dinner tonight might help smooth things with her.

"How was your flight?" she asked tersely.

"It was fine until I landed. It took me forever to get an Uber and then traffic was a complete bitch all the way from the airport," he complained. "Where are the kids?"

"Jess took them over to the Casino for movie night."

"Hmm," said Peter. "What are they seeing?"

"I think it is the latest Toy Story," she said and turned to Peter. "I hope you're still up for dinner. I have been looking forward to it all week," said Charlotte, her voice not betraying the tension she felt.

"Of course," said Peter, although it had been a long week, and there was nothing he would rather do than get comfortable and have a lazy evening at home. He wasn't up for dealing with the traffic, the parking, and the crowds of Nantucket in August, but it wasn't an option; he could not let Charlotte down again.

"What time is our reservation?" he asked.

"7:30. And it was really difficult to get. I had to pull a few favors with them."

"Well, given how much I have spent at that restaurant over the years, I'd hope that they would make room for us, even if it's the busiest time of the year," said Peter annoyed. He walked over to his study, dropped his backpack next to his desk, and came back to the kitchen where he tried to embrace Charlotte. She pulled away.

"What is that about?" said Peter, irritated.

"I'm sorry. It's just that you left us unexpectedly at Downyflake last Saturday, and you knew I was upset. But I barely got more than a few texts and a single call from you all week. You can't expect to walk in here and act like everything is great," replied Charlotte testily.

"You're right. I'm sorry. You know I had that financial issue to deal with and it really stressed me out. I'm sorry that I took that out on you."

"It's not just me, Peter, it's the entire family," she said. "It's really been a rough week, and I'm worried about us."

"I promised you it would be okay, hon," he said softly as he again tried to embrace her. This time she relented and wrapped her arms loosely around him. Peter looked into her eyes and kissed her gently on the mouth. "You look beautiful as usual." She was wearing white pants with a blue checked blouse and accented simply with a strand of pearls and matching earrings. Her graceful arms were burnished by the sun.

"Thanks, hon. You look quite handsome yourself." Peter had changed out of his suit on the flight and had arrived at the house in pressed tan dress slacks, a simple striped button-down, and a navy blazer. He had a personal rule of never wearing a tie on the island and had only had to violate that a few times during his nearly five decades here.

Looking at his watch, Peter said, "We have plenty of time for a drink. What can I get you?"

"I guess just a glass of wine."

"Red or white?"

"Sauvignon blanc, please. I picked up a few bottles of Kim when I went to the store yesterday," said Charlotte.

Peter poured the wine for Charlotte and grabbed a cold beer from the refrigerator. "Let's go sit on the patio and enjoy this beautiful evening."

Charlotte followed Peter out the French doors onto the patio, and they each took a seat at their teak dining table. They sipped their drinks in silence, the conversation struggling to take hold.

Finally, Peter asked, "How was your day?"

"It was good. I took the kids to the beach with Amy and the baby."

"It looked like a great day for it."

"It was. And I can't believe how quickly the baby is growing!"

"I'm sure," said Peter, the topic quickly fizzling out. Charlotte wasn't ready to talk about things yet and she sure as hell wasn't going to ask about that damn company. "How was your flight? Did that stewardess screw up your Manhattan again?"

"Actually, she quit on Monday. Something about another opportunity she had with a charter company."

"Hmm, that's interesting. Especially after the Manhattan-gate fiasco," said Charlotte, teasingly.

Peter was defensive. "I did not say a word to her. In fact, I tried to make an effort to put her at ease as you recommended. Clearly, I failed." He took a sip of his beer, signaling a close to that line of discussion.

After ten minutes of uncomfortable silence, Peter finished his beer and looked at Charlotte. "Ready?"

"Sure," said Charlotte, happy for a change of circumstance.

Peter eased the Range Rover out of the carriage house and headed down the driveway and proceeded toward Milestone Road.

When Charlotte had visited Nantucket after their freshman year, she had remarked on the number of deer she had seen on the side of Milestone Road when they would travel into town for dinner. Together she and Peter had counted six deer on the seven-mile trip and the return journey later that evening. During the week, they continued counting deer every evening they headed to town, and by the end of her visit, they had created a guessing game to see who would get the nights' deer count correct. Over twenty years later, they were still playing the game, although the numbers had gradually increased as the deer population swelled.

"What's the over/under tonight?" asked Charlotte, knowing that this might not only help occupy their fifteen-minute drive into town but also might reconnect her with the Peter she fell in love with so many years ago.

"I'm thinking eight," said Peter.

"Hmm." Charlotte paused a minute. "I'll take the over. I think we're going to see a lot tonight."

Peter smiled slightly. "You're on. And are we playing for the usual prize?"

Charlotte blushed faintly. "Maybe, but let's see how dinner goes first."

After seeing four deer, all single does, they arrived at the restaurant a few minutes before their time, and as usual, parking was a challenge. The space in the restaurant's lot was full, as was the street out front. Peter thought briefly of parking in the open handicap space but, in the end, was able to squeeze into a small spot on York Street. Charlotte and Peter crossed over Union Street and into the restaurant.

The hostess looked up as they came through the door. "Good to see you two here again!" she said and hugged Charlotte and then Peter. She stepped back behind her lectern and checked her notes. She looked up and said, "It will just be a minute. We're clearing your table now."

"Okay," said Peter acidly. He didn't like to wait.

"Hon," said Charlotte, squeezing his arm. "Please." And then to the hostess, "Thank you."

A minute turned into nearly ten before they were seated at their table. The hostess presented the menus and asked, "Can I get you started with some drinks?"

"Please," said Peter irritated. He turned to Charlotte. "What would you like?"

"Do you have that New Zealand sauvignon blanc I like so much?" asked Charlotte, looking up.

"Of course! And you, sir?"

"I'll have a Manhattan please, with Knob Creek. Neat," said Peter, his voice betraying his displeasure at having to wait.

"I'll get those right up," said the hostess. She departed, leaving Peter and Charlotte to settle into the evening.

"I love this place," said Charlotte, ignoring her husband's mood. "It's so cozy and charming. The whole atmosphere has this golden glow and I feel so welcomed. It's almost like being part of a big family."

Peter relaxed and tried to be in the moment. "It is that. And it doesn't hurt that you absolutely love their crab rangoon," he said with a slight smile. "Sometimes I think you could have that every night for dinner."

Charlotte grinned and raised her hand. "Guilty."

Their drinks arrived at the table.

"Cheers, hon," said Peter. "Here's to Friday and our weekend."

"To our weekend," said Charlotte expectantly, and they clinked glasses.

Peter sipped his Manhattan, closed his eyes, and felt himself relax, the strain and stress of the week evaporating. He sighed softly and looked at Charlotte. "This is perfect. They always make the best Manhattans here." He took another sip of his drink and then picked up the menu. "What are you in the mood for tonight?"

"Well, crab rangoon, of course," said Charlotte, smiling. "And that halibut looks really good." The heaviness of the week was lifting under Peter's charm, and for the first time in a month, Charlotte was starting to feel close to him again. "What about you?"

"Hmm, tough choice as always. But, I'll have to start with some chowda," said Peter doing his best Boston accent. "Would you split a Caesar with me?"

"That sounds good."

Peter continued, "Then for my entree, I think I'm going to do the swordfish. I know I get that nearly every time, but it's always so good."

He put his menu down and took another sip of his Manhattan. When the server arrived, they ordered another round of drinks along with their dinner.

Charlotte briefed Peter on their week and the children's various activities. With the arrival of the first course, they put aside discussion for a while and just enjoyed their food. Charlotte wiped her mouth with her napkin and looked at Peter. "Wow, that was delicious! I hope you enjoyed yours as much as I did."

"Absolutely. Although I might have skipped the appetizer and just ordered an extra piece of the swordfish. Some of the best fish I've had in years," said Peter.

They passed on dessert but thought some coffee and a glass of port would be the perfect finish to a lovely meal. After the waitress had poured her coffee, Charlotte looked over at Peter. "Do you remember what we talked about last weekend?"

"Umm, I think so, yes," said Peter nervously.

"It was about the time you spend with that company. You assured me that you would start putting a plan together that would allow you to spend more of that time with us. Don't you remember?"

Peter could feel the hairs on his back bristle, and his natural defensiveness come forward. This trait had served him well at boarding school and hazing during his fraternity rush, but he had learned it wasn't always the best quality in a marriage.

"Yes, I do," said Peter hesitantly.

"And what have you come up with?" asked Charlotte.

Peter was silent as he sipped at his coffee. He looked across the table at Charlotte. "I'm sorry hon, I haven't had a chance to even think about it. This financial issue with the company really caught me off guard and consumed all my time."

Charlotte felt her face redden. "That's so disappointing, Peter. After the way you bailed on us so quickly last Saturday, I thought for sure you would have at least spent a few minutes thinking about it. But clearly, it's not important to you."

"Of course, it's important to me. It's just that the company needed me, and I had to get those issues resolved."

Charlotte looked down at her port, trying her best to control her anger. "I don't know how to say this to you other than we need to be making changes to our marriage if we're going to survive. No more promises. We need to make these changes now."

As if to confirm her point, Peter's cell phone buzzed.

"Who the hell is calling you on a Friday night at 9:00?" demanded Charlotte. "This is our time. Please ignore it."

"I'm sorry I can't." Peter fumbled for his iPhone. "We had a final review of the updated financials today in advance of the release, and I need to know if there were any further issues or questions that they have for me. I'll only be a minute." Peter excused himself and stepped outside to take the call. Charlotte fumed.

A quick minute turned into almost twenty before Peter returned to the table. "I'm so sorry."

Charlotte was clearly upset. "Would you have done that for me? Or one of the kids?" she demanded.

"What do you mean?" asked Peter.

"Would you have stepped out of an important meeting at the office if I or Sophie or Spencer had called? Would you put your colleagues' life on hold for twenty minutes to talk with one of us?"

Peter stared at his coffee and remained silent.

"I didn't think so," said Charlotte. "And that's exactly why we need to be making some changes. I cannot continue living as a second-class citizen in your world."

"That's not the case!" said Peter defensively. "You and the kids are my world!"

"Your company is your world. Spencer, Sophie and I are merely the moons that revolve around it. You just find comfort knowing that we're there, circling around you, and assume as we do of the Earth's moon, that it will always be." Charlotte used her napkin to blot away a tear. "But I'm tired of waiting for you to come into our orbit."

Peter reached out to try and hold her hand, but she pulled it away.

"And since I'm putting my feelings on the table, I need to share something else with you," said Charlotte.

"What's that?" said Peter with concern in his voice. *What more could there be?*

"I want to start a foundation and give back to this island that we both love so much," said Charlotte.

"Give back? But we do give back. We give money all the time for just about every cause that crosses my desk. Just last week, I wrote a check for over a thousand dollars to help with the youth camp."

Charlotte scoffed. "Yes, Peter, we do give back, We give back peanuts. I'm not talking about a hundred here or a thousand there. I'm talking millions. Millions that could make a huge difference for this island for generations to come."

"Um, millions?" stammered Peter. "How many millions are we talking about? One, two…?"

"What's our current net worth?" demanded Charlotte.

Peter paused a minute. "With the current share price of the company, I'd guess around one point three."

"One point three what?"

"Billion," responded Peter.

"Exactly," said Charlotte. "Which is why I want half of it to start a foundation."

"Half?" said Peter, nearly spilling his coffee. "You want half of my money to start some damn foundation where people will come with their hands out looking for a freebie? Seriously?"

"I want half of *our* money to complete valuable work on this island. We're so lucky, and we certainly don't need it all. We could do so much good and make such a difference. People look at this island and think it's just a bunch of one-percenters playing in the sun," Charlotte grimaced at the thought. "But this island really does have some serious needs."

"Like what?" Peter asked.

"Hunger for one," said Charlotte. "And affordable housing, land conservation, and education, to name a few more."

"Why am I not aware of any of these needs?" asked Peter.

"Because you're barely here 48 hours a week! You fly in on Friday afternoon and head out first thing Monday. And as we both know, you aren't really here since you're usually working through email or on the phone. And when was the last time you actually read the paper here?"

"You mean The Inq & M?"

"Yes, the Inquirer & Mirror. When was the last time you actually read it cover to cover?"

"It's been a while," Peter sheepishly admitted.

"Well, if you had been reading it, you'd realize one of the biggest issues this community is facing right now is food insecurity," said Charlotte.

"Food insecurity? Is that when you're worried that your food doesn't like you?" Peter joked, trying to ease the tension.

Charlotte rolled her eyes. "No, Peter. Food insecurity is not knowing when or where your next meal is going to come from. There are literally hundreds of families on this island who have to deal with that every day. And then, of course, there is affordable housing. Not everyone can afford a multi-million dollar house that they only occupy a few months out of the year. All of those people who serve us food, stock the shelves, and clean our homes have to live somewhere. Unfortunately, there are not a lot of options for them. And I really believe we could help."

She paused to catch her breath and take another sip of her wine. "And I don't mean just handing out money. We could help fund research to identify workable solutions and then offer seed money to developers to actually build them," she continued. "We could help give these people an honest place to live that would make them feel welcomed but would also fit into the unique fabric of the island.

"And speaking of the island, all of the new development that has happened the last few years, you know, all those one-percenters building their dream cottages," Charlotte scoffed. "The island is only so big, and we need to help preserve those open spaces and natural areas that make this place so unique," she continued. "Our money could make a huge difference here and help protect what we both love so much."

Peter saw the sparkle in Charlotte's eyes, revealing her real passion for the topic.

"And I know how we can make this all happen, our marriage, and the foundation."

"How's that?" asked Peter.

"As I mentioned last week. Sell the company and retire. Let's start the foundation with you as the CEO." She reached over to take Peter's hand. "You've worked so hard and have been so successful. You've made a wonderful life for us, and we want for nothing. But let's create something together that can help make a wonderful life for others. Not only would it be so enriching for us, but I think it would also be a hell of a lot of fun, giving away money and seeing the positive impact we can have."

Peter was angry now. "I told you last week that there is no fucking way I can retire. I promised you I'd put a plan together so I can be with you and the kids more, and I will. But there is no way in hell I'm going to sell my company and give the money to a bunch of needy people!"

His fiery response startled Charlotte, and she brushed away a few tears. She had optimistically thought that just maybe she had gotten through to him. That he realized what was at stake for him and for their entire family. Charlotte's tears came on more steadily now. "We're not going to make it, Peter. I don't want to force you to make a choice between family or company, but I'm afraid that's where we're headed."

Peter started to protest, but Charlotte held up a hand to silence him. "I don't want to hear anymore. You're not going to win this argument." She wiped the tears from her face. "Let's just go home. I was hoping to get through to you tonight, and to be honest, I'd appreciate a little time to myself. You can sleep in the guest suite again. I know you're comfortable there," she said sarcastically.

Peter reluctantly settled the bill, and they walked back to the car.

The ride home was silent. They passed five more deer, but neither Charlotte nor Peter noticed.

CHAPTER ELEVEN

Peter woke the next morning with an emotional hangover, that heavy feeling that sits low in the gut when you know things didn't go well with someone you love. Charlotte had said she wanted some space, so Peter had slept in the guest cottage telling the kids at breakfast that he had some calls to make to Asia and didn't want to disturb any of the family. Spencer was just seven and accepted the story, but Sophie was old enough to sense what was going on and suspected her parents had been fighting. She had several friends at school who had gotten divorced, so she was well versed in the world of marital disharmony.

"Morning," said Peter as he sat down and slid his chair in at the big table. "How did you guys sleep last night," looking over at Spencer and Sophie.

"I slept great!" said Spencer, his broad smile wrinkling his freckled cheeks. And in fact, he almost always did. He was such a heavy sleeper that a plane could crash through the roof, and he'd sleep right through it. But Sophie, on the other hand, had always been a challenge since she was a baby. She had refused to take naps, even though she'd rub her eyes in exhaustion. They had tried the cry-it-out way to no avail. They knew it was merely a matter of stubbornness and her wanting to be in control. So finally, on a rare day when Peter had been home, he sat her down in her crib and told her she just needed a little quiet time but that she could do whatever she pleased during that hour. He then placed a few books next to her and left the room leaving the door open. Ten minutes later, he and Charlotte snuck up the stairs to peek into her room, and to their astonishment, she was sound asleep. It was a positive turning point, but Sophie remained a challenging sleeper. Although she could get to sleep pretty easily, it was often difficult for her to stay asleep. Calling out to mom or dad in the middle of the night was a fairly common occurrence when she did wake.

Peter turned to her. "What about you, Sophie?" he asked.

"I slept okay. But I had that bad dream again," she replied.

"I'm sorry, hon. Which bad dream?" asked Peter.

"That one where you disappeared," said Sophie.

Peter looked at her with concern. She was undoubtedly a perceptive child but doubted that her dream had anything to do with his fights with Charlotte over his time with them. It was probably the same type of anxiety most kids had about losing a parent and nothing for him to worry about.

He stroked her hair. "I know everything will be okay, honey. Please don't worry, alright?"

Sophie looked up at him, her face still showing concerns from her dream. "Alright, daddy," she said softly.

"Good girl." He turned to Charlotte. "What about you, hon? Sleep, okay?"

Used to the perceptive nature of her children, especially Sophie, she said, "I slept pretty well although I did miss you. I know you had to make those calls last night, but I wish you could have come back to the house when you were done." The little white lie to her children made Charlotte feel dirty.

Peter replied, "Well, they lasted far longer than I expected. We have a major customer meeting coming up, and I needed to make sure the team there was ready for it. Since the last call didn't wrap-up until nearly four, I felt it best to just crash there in the guest house so as not to wake you." Both Sophie and Spencer were too busy with their breakfast to notice the annoyed look in their father's eyes.

Quickly changing the subject, Peter asked, "What do you guys say we go to Great Point today for a picnic?"

"Yay!" shouted Spencer and Sophie, almost simultaneously.

"What do you think, Charlotte?" asked Peter.

"I think that's a great idea," said Charlotte with a forced smile and feigned enthusiasm. "It's a beautiful day and perfect for a picnic."

"Great," said Peter. "I'll get the car packed-up with the beach stuff while you pull together the provisions." With that, Peter pushed back his chair and headed to the garage, happy to escape the tension in the room. He crossed the lawn and noticed a few weeds had sprouted in the grass. "Looks like the landscaping team has dropped the ball again," he muttered to himself. Reaching the carriage house, he entered through the side door and went to work to fit out the Range Rover for the trip to the beach.

After loading the car with all of the necessary beach gear - blankets, beach chairs, sand toys, and umbrella - he added the tackle box and threw a couple of surfcasting rods on the roof. There was nothing more frustrating than seeing a bluefish feeding frenzy close to the beach and not being able to do a thing about it. Finishing up, Peter grabbed his favorite baseball cap off a hook in the garage and jumped in the car.

He drove over to the side entrance by the kitchen and collected Charlotte and the kids. He also packed the cooler along with two boat bags filled with towels, sunscreen, books, magazines, chips, cookies, and water.

They left the house, drove through Sconset, and headed out of the village. Peter and Charlotte were quiet as they drove past the lighthouse and Quidnet. They were silent as they passed through the moors, and then the cranberry bogs, still a month or two away from being flooded and relinquishing their bright red fruit. Finally, Peter turned to Charlotte and said quietly, "Please don't be mad at me."

Charlotte looked at Peter but didn't reply, her usually bright blue eyes dull and lifeless. She turned her attention back to her window and looked out across the moors and scrub pine.

Peter slowed the Rover and made the tight right turn on to Wauwinet Road. They followed this winding road to the end, where they pulled into a small dirt parking lot next to a small gatehouse. Peter opened the center console of the Rover and grabbed his air gauge and a couple of small flat-headed screwdrivers. Having done this dozens of times, everyone knew the drill.

"Can I help you let the air out of the tires, dad?" asked Spencer expectantly.

This was usually a job that Peter preferred to do quickly. But realizing where things stood with Charlotte right now, he took a deep breath. "Of course. Hop out and let me show you how to do it."

Spencer was excited. He jumped out of the Rover and knelt down next to his dad by the front tire.

"The first thing we need to do is remove the small plastic cap from what they call the valve stem," said Peter. He slowly removed the cap and handed it to Spencer for safekeeping. "Then I use the end of this screwdriver to depress the air valve. This allows the air to escape the tire." The air hissed as Peter depressed the valve. "Then, I count to thirty very slowly." He handed Spencer the screwdriver. "Do you think that you can do that?"

Spencer looked up his dad, his bright blue eyes wide with excitement. "Yes, I can," he said responsibly. He depressed the end of the screwdriver on the valve, and the air started to hiss. "One...two...three...four..."

Peter moved over to the opposite side and began the process on the other front tire. He knew it actually took about seventy-five seconds to get the tires down to the targeted pressure of fifteen pounds but wanted to give himself a little leeway with Spencer.

"I'm at thirty, dad!" he heard Spencer shout from over the hood.

Okay, be right there to check," Peter replied. He finished counting, and using the air gauge on his tires confirmed it was at fifteen pounds. He then circled around the front to the car and knelt down next to Spencer. He put his gauge on the stem. "Looks like you have a little farther to go," said Peter. "Why don't you do another thirty seconds."

"Okay', said Spencer. He bit his lip in concentration as he again depressed the valve.

Peter started on the driver's side rear when Spencer called out again. Peter laid the gauge on the valve stem and confirmed that Spencer was at twenty. "Fifteen more seconds, Spencer, and then we should be there." Peter waited while Spencer counted patiently to fifteen and then confirmed the tire was ready. "Perfect," he said to Spencer. Taking the cap from Spencer, he threaded it back onto the valve stem. "Can you do the one in the back too?"

"Yes!" said Spencer, and he sprinted to the back of the car. Peter could hear the hiss of the tire and his son's soft voicing counting out. It made him smile. A few minutes later, they were done. "Thanks for the help, buddy," said Peter, rustling his son's hair. Spencer smiled but didn't reply. It looked to Peter like he was feeling quite good about himself.

"Boy, that seemed to take forever," said Charlotte, as Peter and Spencer climbed back into the car.

"Well, you wanted me to be more involved with the children," Peter replied, somewhat sarcastically.

Charlotte looked at him with cold eyes. "Is that why you wanted his help? To make a point with me?" she said.

Peter paused. "Of course not. I'm sorry, that was uncalled for," he said. "Actually, I just wanted to make him feel some ownership of the process." Peter looked down at his lap. "My father first showed me how to do that when I was his age, and I guess I wanted to keep the cycle going."

Charlotte nodded. "I understand. And I also think they love this island just as much as you do. I don't think you need to worry about that."

Peter smiled faintly and selecting drive, pulled out of the parking lot, and headed past the big hotel, The Wauwinet. The road changed to dirt and became very bumpy. Spencer and Sophie were giggling in the back as the car hit one bump and then another, a couple of them so bad that Peter thought his head would have hit the roof had not had on his seatbelt.

He looked over at Charlotte, who had her arms crossed tightly across her chest. "You okay?" he asked.

"I am, but if I had known it was going to be this rough, I'd have worn my sports bra," she replied.

Peter smiled. "It's only for another quarter mile before we hit the sand, and then it will really smooth out."

True to his prediction, the dirt road turned to very soft sand, and Peter checked the dash to confirm the Rover was in all-wheel-drive mode and also turned off the traction control to avoid confusing the vehicle's computer. His last car had nearly burned out the transmission the first time it had made this trip, and he wanted to avoid that. Satisfied, he slowly accelerated to about twenty miles per hour. With the soft tires, the car floated smoothly on the sand.

They followed the route for a few hundred feet until they came to a fork. "Do you guys want to take the inside route or go along the beach?" asked Peter.

The nearly seven-mile trip could be taken one of two ways. The inner path weaved a course through the moors and low scrub punctuated by several small bodies of water where kestrels, swans, and other waterfowl were residents. Despite its beauty, it was a bit more challenging to navigate as it was a single track that had to accommodate two-way traffic. A pull-out every thousand feet or so was designed to allow oncoming vehicles to pass, but that usually meant that someone would have to back-up to the nearest one. Not only was that cumbersome, but it also slowed down the trip. The other option was to just follow the beach next to the water. Plenty wide enough for two vehicles to pass and had the added benefit of ocean scenery.

"Beach!" said Spencer and Sophie in unison.

"Beach it is," said Peter, taking the right turn and heading out toward the water. Peter followed the path across the dune cresting a small hill and descended down to the beach. The sand here was covered in dozens of vehicle tracks, but things settled down quickly, and Peter found a pretty smooth and uniform track to follow. The car felt good under him, and he nudged the wheel gently to keep it centered in the path.

Going the entire way out was about seven miles. Keeping it as the mandated speed limit of fifteen miles per hour meant a nearly thirty-minute trip. Peter had first driven on this beach over thirty years ago and knew just about every part of it by heart. He accelerated up to about thirty and even increased it to nearly forty in a few sections where the tracks were particularly smooth and consistent. Arriving at an area known as the Galls, for the first time, they could see Nantucket Sound to the left and the Atlantic to the right. This small spit of land was often flooded over during heavy storms and had grown and receded many times over the years.

As the Galls ended and the land widened again, there was a turnoff through the dunes. Peter slowed the car and started to make the turn, giving the Rover more gas to power it through the heavy sand of this challenging section of the beach. Successfully making it through, he eased off the gas and maneuvered the car down a narrow path with a small lake on one side and more dunes on the other. Following this trail for another half mile or so, they eventually emerged onto the beach only to find there were over a dozen vehicles already spread out along the water. Peter sighed, surveyed the scene, and then picked a spot that would give them a nice buffer and a modicum of privacy.

Even in the height of summer, the breeze could be a little chilly, so Peter maneuvered the car to provide a windbreak for their picnic site. Turning off the engine, Peter jumped out and went to the back to open the tailgate. With Spencer and Sophie's help, they spread the blankets, set-up the two beach chairs, and unpacked the cooler. Spencer was excited to see fresh cookies from the Sconset Market and naturally went straight for them. Charlotte caught his hand. "Later," she said, "after you've had your sandwich. Why don't you grab your bucket and go play in the sand." Spencer smiled up at Charlotte. "Okay, mom." He grabbed his toys and ran down to the water's edge.

Peter settled down into a chair and cracked a beer. Donning his cap, he stretched his bare feet out over the blanket and surveyed his small domain. Spencer was building a sandcastle fort with stone turrets and crab shells for guards and could see him making noises with his mouth as the slipper shell army was battling the scallops. Sophie, on the other hand, was making a mosaic in the sand using the multitude of rocks and pebbles on the shore.

"Do you have sunscreen on?" asked Charlotte, breaking his reverie. Ever since Peter had had a skin cancer scare a few years before, she was quite diligent in reminding him of the needed protection from the sun.

"I do," he said with impatience. He didn't like to be treated as a child.

"Good," she said.

He thought about last night's argument and felt it gnawing in his stomach like a bad meal.

Reading his thoughts, Charlotte looked over at him and said, "We need to talk about last night."

Peter glanced over at her, half expecting an apology.

She continued, "I know it was tough to hear, but I meant every word. We need to make some changes."

"Are you serious? We're sitting here at the beach on a beautiful day, and you want to talk about taking half my money?" Peter said testily. "And giving up my company?"

"Peter," Charlotte said, her voice calm and quiet, not wanting the kids to hear. "I'm not asking you to give up your company. I know how important it is to you. And it's not about 'taking' your money but rather investing it here on the island. Think about all the good we could do."

"All the good we could do," Peter muttered. "And what am I to tell all my employees? That we're just closing the doors?" he said angrily. "You know, this company and its hundreds of employees depend on me. And you want me to drop it all so that I can be around more?"

Charlotte sighed and looked intently at Peter. "What I want is for you to be as invested in your children, your family, as you are with that company."

Peter turned and looked out at the water. Usually, the view would soothe him, but he just felt agitated.

"What we want is you," pleaded Charlotte. "We want you home and here with us. I'm not talking one hundred percent of the time, but certainly, a lot more time than you're with us now."

"And what if I can't?" asked Peter, turning back to look at her. "What if I can't commit to spending more time with you and the kids? At least maybe for a few more years."

"Then I think we need to consider going our separate ways," said Charlotte. She lowered her eyes. "If we can't make these changes now, then I think I want a divorce."

Stunned, Peter said, "What? Are you serious? After everything I have given you and the kids?" He was furious. "Where the hell is this coming from?" Sophie and Spencer heard the escalating voices and turned to look at their parents, their faces reflecting concern.

Charlotte's blue eyes blazed. "It's coming from me spending most of my week alone. Your children spend most of their week without their father. And even when you're home, you really aren't there. You're on the computer or your phone. And we have all this money that we don't need or will ever use. I want to do some good in this world. Why won't you let me?"

Peter felt angry at being called on the carpet. He struggled out of his beach chair and stood up.

"Where are you going?" asked Charlotte.

"I'm going for a walk. I need some time to think."

Peter started off, struggling to walk in the heavy sand.

"Where are you going, dad?" yelled Spencer.

Peter turned to look at Spencer. "Just going for a walk," he said tersely.

"Can I come?" asked Spencer expectantly.

"No," said Peter.

Spencer burst into tears and ran to his mom for comfort. Peter turned and started walking up the beach.

CHAPTER TWELVE

P eter was angry. What had he ever done but make the best life for Charlotte and the kids? He couldn't help that the company demanded so much of his time right now. Shimmo had become a large and successful operation because of him. No one else could have done that. Who else could set the strategy, make the critical decisions, and close the deals as he had over the years? This was so like Charlotte, he thought. She was never entirely happy; she has always wanted more.

His anger fueled his walk, and he continued past the other vehicles on the beach. *They are having fun and enjoying the gorgeous day and extraordinary location,* he thought to himself. *They weren't being ambushed by their wives and held hostage for half their money.* He was fuming and muttering about Charlotte and the demand for a divorce. If anyone had seen him, they might have thought him crazy, talking so vigorously as he was to himself.

Peter stopped at a thin rope wire crossing the beach from the dunes to the waterline. Spread across a handful of metal posts, the cable had some red and yellow nylon ties to make it more visible and was low enough that Spencer could have crossed it without too much struggle. Every fifteen feet or so, there were signs warning pedestrians that they were not welcome. It was the line of demarcation between the people's beach and the seals' beach.

He looked over the wire to the very tip of Great Point, the northernmost part of Nantucket. He had known the Point, that tapering of the island where the Atlantic meets Nantucket Sound since he was a child barely out of diapers. He came here with his family for picnics and played in the sand much as Spencer had been doing today. When he had grown up a bit, he was invited to join his father and grandfather on one of their many fishing expeditions to the Point for bluefish and striped bass. His father had patiently shown him how to handle the long surfcasting rod, how to hold the line with your finger, and then how to time it perfectly to get the best throw. His grandfather had explained all of the different lures they used, which to use when sunny, which when cloudy, high tide and low. Some danced along the surface of the water while others dove deep and acted like silver minnows to entice a hungry mouth.

He had listened and learned and caught his first bluefish near dawn on a rainy day the summer of his seventh year. He had selected the lure, a silver sliver of metal known as a Hopkins, attached it to the line, and then threw it well into the surf just ahead of a school of blues. He had hooked one almost immediately, and the fight had been tremendous. He felt as if the fish was going to pull him into the water. But he had fought and landed the blue right on the beach. In Peter's office back at the company, he still had the framed photograph of that fish. His seven-year-old self grinning from ear to ear, hair plastered down from the rain, and struggling to hold up the enormous prize. In reality, it had probably only been nine or ten pounds, but to him, it might as well have been a whale.

Charlotte had caught her first bluefish here as well, the first summer after graduation and just a week after they had been engaged. She had taken to it, well, like a fish to water, and caught her fish on only her fourth cast. Quickly reeling it in and with a heave on the rod, she had managed to surf the fish onto the beach using an incoming wave. Unlike Peter, though, she had no desire or intention to eat it. Peter grabbed the obligatory picture of Charlotte with her fish, and then he released the blue back into the surf.

He had wanted to share that same experience with his own children, but the Point was now closed to people and cars. It was the harbor and gray seals now who had the exclusive right to fish at the Point, and while Peter understood the need for conservation, he bristled at the thought that he was no longer permitted to be at this extraordinary spot. Especially because of the seals. Growing up, seeing a seal was rare and an occasion to note. But with the growth of their population, fishing from the beach had become more and more challenging. It wasn't that the seals would get in the way. In fact, just the opposite. Seals would wait patiently just off the surf until a fish was hooked. Then they would swoop in and snatch the fish off right off the line. Sometimes the fisherman would reel in a bloody head still attached to the hook, but usually, the seal took it all, the fish and the lure. Peter wasn't upset about losing a ten dollar lure, it was more the frustration of hooking a fish and then having it stolen from him just a few feet off the beach. It had gotten to the point where a lot of people had just given up surfcasting entirely.

Peter looked at the sign explaining the different types of seals, and next to it, a person walking with a large red X through it.

"Fuck that," Peter said out loud, and stepped over the wire. He continued on his way north, and based on other footsteps in the sand, it was clear he was not the only outlaw in these parts. Walking along, he noticed quite a bit of flotsam and other debris in the sand; strands of fishing nets, pieces of lobster buoys, tangles of fishing line. A plastic bottle a few feet off to the right caught his eye, and he walked over and picked it up. The cap was missing, and it was partially filled with seawater and sand. He turned it over to read the mark on the bottom and was only partly surprised to see his company's logo neatly imprinted. He dropped the bottle and continued his walk.

His legs tired from the heavy sand; Peter eased over to the more firmly packed area closer to the water. The going was much easier as his feet barely made indentations in the sand. He paused to look out over the water and visually soak in the natural beauty of the spot. A faint breeze tickled his cheek and the sun reflecting off the water warmed his face under the brim of his baseball cap. On the horizon, he could just make out one of the car ferries making its regular trip over from Hyannis. It had been years since he'd taken the boat, the jet was his choice of transportation to the island now. But as a child, he and his family had frequently traveled on a ship called the Uncatena. Just recalling the name made him smile. He'd usually spend the entire two and a half hour trip near the ungainly bow hoping to see dolphins playing in the wake or the dorsal fin of a shark. Although the Uncatena was long gone, maybe it was time to share that experience with Spencer and Sophie.

His daydream of a ferry trip with the kids was rudely interrupted by a horrific stench. A cross between three-day-old fish and a large pile of manure, it was almost enough to make him turn around. "Damn seals," he muttered, holding his hand up to shield his nose. He looked up to see that there were hundreds of them. Some swimming along the shore while others were lying on the beach. Reluctantly, he steered a course back into the heavy sand further inland and gave the seals a wide berth. He doubted very much that they were quick enough to catch him, but he had seen what they could do with their teeth and was in no mood to prove or disprove that theory.

The beach in front of him dropped a few feet, eroded by waves from the recent high tide. He jumped down and found himself at the water's edge at the Point, the Atlantic on the right, and Nantucket Sound on the left, coming together to form a strong rip. It was a confused patch of sea with waves building, cresting and breaking over each other, again and again, and extending out toward the horizon for as far as he could see. It was in this very rip where he had caught so many blues over his life, fishing with his father, his grandfather, even Charlotte. Now, instead of fisherman wading the waters in search of blues and stripers, it was seals. So many seals. And while they may have been after the same fish as Peter had in his time, he felt no allegiance or camaraderie whatsoever with these beasts.

"You fucking things," he said out loud, making sure the seals heard him. "I hope you get eaten by a Great White or a Killer whale!" He doubted that intimidated the seals, but it did make him feel a little better.

Peter looked up and noticed that the rip was getting stronger, the waves breaking more forcefully now. "Must be coming to high tide," he muttered. Slowly he edged toward the surf, getting close enough to let his feet get wet as the bigger waves were breaking onto the shore. Seals were in the water all around him now. They did not appear in the least bit aggressive, just curious as to who this new creature was and if it may be a potential food source.

Charlotte's words kept playing through his head, again and again. *I want a divorce.* That short but immensely powerful sentence rang in his ears like a thunderclap and left a very bitter taste in the back of his mouth. *Fine. If that's what she wants, then that's what she's going to get. But she sure as hell is not going to get half of my money.*

More than anything right now, he just wanted to escape the situation. He wished he could jump back on the plane and head back to Connecticut. Hell, he'd even be happy with one of the old flight attendant's crappy Manhattans.

The more he thought about that plan, the more he liked it. He pulled out his iPhone and saw it was just past two in the afternoon. *If I hustle,* he thought to himself, *we could be wheels-up in a couple of hours, and I could be back home by six. Let Charlotte stay here with the kids on her own for a few weeks, and then maybe she'd change her mind.*

As Peter unlocked his iPhone, a wave, more prominent than those around it, was forming a few hundred yards offshore. Oceanographers call them freak or rogue waves. Waves that are significantly larger than the sea state around them. And for centuries, these phenomena were considered mythical, most likely because anyone that would encounter one often did not survive to tell about it. Thought to be caused by a unique combination of events, scientists now believe that rogues occur several times a day in oceans around the world.

This rogue was not that big, really, at least compared to those that genuinely lived up to their names. But it was nearly three times the size of the waves around it and was advancing toward the eastern edge of the Point. Had Peter looked up and out over the water, he would have noticed its hulking mass approaching the shore and backed away. But he didn't. Instead, his eyes were on his iPhone, pulling up the number to call the charter company to prepare the jet.

As the wave neared the shore, its ability to maintain its height was challenged by the rising of the seabed and decreasing depth of water. About thirty feet offshore, the wave could no longer support its height and began to break. The sound of all that water collapsing on itself was a loud roar that caused Peter to look up quickly. Seeing the mass of breaking water approaching him, he turned and tried to run back up the beach. Had he been on pavement, he might have had a chance. But his feet dug into the soft sand, and he struggled to get his body moving quickly.

The water hit him with such force that he was immediately lifted off his feet, his iPhone ripped from his hands. He became part of the wave and traveled with it across the Point, past the seals and gulls, and a few hundred feet into Nantucket sound where the rogue faded away.

Sputtering and coughing up seawater, Peter tried to get his bearings. It was reasonably shallow here, he probably could have touched his feet to the bottom if he tried, but was so unnerved from the wave that he panicked and immediately started swimming toward shore. But as hard as he swam, he could not make any progress toward the beach. It was then that he felt the first pull of the rip, and a cold stab of fear rushed through him.

His mind immediately flashed to when his friend Jack had saved him from drowning in the rip south of Sconset. But this felt different - it was a much more powerful force, probably caused by the tidal currents. And it was getting stronger, and more powerful. He looked toward the beach desperately for help. But there was no one but the seals and a few gulls who seemed to watch him with bored curiosity.

He started to scream, hoping that someone, maybe even Charlotte, would hear him and come to his rescue. But they were hundreds of yards down the beach. And since he had purposefully strayed into an off-limits area, there was no one else closer. He felt the current strengthening and realized that he was being pulled farther out to sea, toward the Cape. The Great Point rip extended here for several miles and was very popular with the sportfishing boats. Maybe he could keep his head above water long enough to be rescued by a passing fisherman.

Peter was tiring quickly, and the rip started now to pull him under the water as well as out to sea. Panic gave way to fear as it began to register that he was not going to make it. Fear gave way to regret as he realized he'd never see Charlotte, Spencer, or Sophie again. The fight with Charlotte was now just a bad memory. He wished he could have just a few moments with her and tell her how much he loved her, the kids, and the life that they had made together. From his new perspective, the fight last night and again today were just silly and pointless. Charlotte was right. And now he was going to die without ever telling her how important they were to him and just how happy they had made him. As the water closed over him, he thought of the beautiful family he was leaving behind. The faces of Charlotte, Spencer, and Sophie were the last thing he remembered as his world went black.

*It is only through the lens of hindsight that
the whaleman's job becomes malicious or cruel. . .
that whales had to die to provide for life.*

Richard Ellis

CHAPTER THIRTEEN

P eter had hit the deck hard. The pain from the fall radiated through his upper body, and the back of his head pounded. Slowly he regained his senses as bits and pieces of memory flashed through his mind. He remembered being on a picnic with Charlotte and the kids at Great Point. He remembered getting into a fight with Charlotte and stomping away. He remembered ending up at Great Point, where he had been hit by a wave and pulled out into the rip. He remembered the strength of the current and choking on saltwater. As he lay there, he realized that this ship must have seen him go under and come to his rescue.

That thought was rudely interrupted as he suddenly felt nauseous and rolled over to vomit out his breakfast along with a good deal of seawater. He wiped his mouth with the back of his hand as his morning meal lay in a puddle next to him; the taste of vomit still fresh. He rolled back and looked up at a figure who he assumed was the captain. "Thank you for saving me," said Peter. "I honestly thought I was dead."

The figure looked down at him, his bearded face in shadow. "Save you? What are you jabbering about, greenhand? You need to get back to work now."

"Back to work? What the fuck are you saying to me? Didn't you just pull me out of the water?" Peter said. It was then that he propped himself up on his elbows and looked out over the railing of the boat and saw nothing but the ocean from horizon to horizon. There was no land, no Great Point, only blue water as far as the eye could see. *What the fuck?*

Looking down, confused, he saw that his clothes had changed. His bathing suit and polo had been replaced by a heavy cotton shirt and what felt like canvas pants. His once bare feet were now ensconced in dark leather boots with square, black leather laces. His favorite baseball cap was gone, replaced by a broad-brimmed straw hat. He patted what he thought was a pocket for his iPhone but came up empty.

The boot hit him squarely on his hip bone. Peter cried out in pain. He rolled over and looked up at the man. "What the fuck are you doing?" he snarled. "Don't kick me!"

"I'll kick you for as long as I want up until you get your ass up and get back to work," said the man. "We have a whale to process and weather approaching. I cannot waste any more of my time with you, greenhand."

Peter slowly stood up. "A whale to process? What the fuck are you talking about? I'm not a laborer on a fishing boat, I'm the CEO of Shimmo Plastics out of Greenwich, Connecticut. I need you to return me back to Nantucket."

The man looked at Peter and said plainly and forcefully, "I'm Master Nelson and God on this vessel. The sun rises and sets under my authority. If you continue to protest and fail to work, I will have you flogged. We will return to Nantucket when we have a full hold of oil. Now grab a fork and see to it that you feed the tryworks until we're done with this whale."

"I don't know what the fuck you're talking about, Ahab, I will do no such thing," said Peter. "I'm the Chief Executive of a billion-dollar company, and I demand to be taken back to Nantucket immediately. Clearly, I have nearly drowned and am perhaps injured. I need to see a doctor right away!"

"That's it then," said the Captain. He turned toward the first mate. "Gale! Flog this man."

Benjamin Gale, the first mate, showed some uncertainty with this order but knew better than to question the captain. He grabbed Peter's arm and tried to steer him to the mizzenmast. Peter pulled his arm away. "Stop this right now and take me home," he demanded. "I'm not a sailor. I'm not supposed to be here. I need to be back on Nantucket now!" he shouted, showering spittle across the mate. Peter was nearly apoplectic with rage, fueled by confusion and by the treatment from what he thought were barbarians. "Who the fuck do you think you are?" he shouted.

Gale knew this was going to be a bit of a challenge and looked about him for possible assistance. A number of the crewmen had been watching this situation with a great deal of interest and amusement. Life aboard a whaling vessel tended to be short bouts of excitement followed by days, if not weeks, of complete and total boredom. Although they had work to do, they were fascinated by the exchange between the master and the greenhand. Gale called out to a couple of the crewmen who were more than happy to help tie Peter to the mast. Despite his struggles, the three men were able to pull him to the mast and bind his wrists together tightly, forcing his body to hug the mizzen. Gale reached up and pulled Peter's shirt down, exposing his back. The mate turned to the captain for direction.

"Ten lashes, Mr. Gale." He handed the leather whip to the first mate.

"Aye, captain."

Peter was struggling to free himself, his face flushed red with anger and exertion. "Stop this at once! I will have all of you arrested for assault!"

The whip cracked, and the first lash landed on Peter's exposed back. He cried out in pain. The second lash fell. He continued to struggle and protest the abuse. "You can't do this to me. I'm one of the most important men on Nantucket." Two more lashes fell as the whip cracked. "I will have you all jailed and will sue your asses off! I will ruin you all!"

More lashes fell. Peter tried to lower himself and arch his back out of the way, but his bound hands prevented such movement. His face was now wet with tears, from both pain and frustration. He had never been treated this way. Fraternity hazing during his freshman year had been far easier to understand and accept. And even then, it hadn't really been painful - just some sophomoric challenges meant to build a bond with the other pledges. Some had even been fun. But this was far beyond anything he had ever experienced. These men would pay for mistreating and humiliating him.

The tenth and final lash fell on his back. Although the whipping had stopped, the pain continued. His back was burning, and he could feel the blood running down over his waist and settling in the crack of his buttocks. Peter lowered his head against the mast and sobbed quietly. Yes, he'd make these men pay. They would pay for this abusive treatment, this humiliation.

The first mate untied his hands, and Peter collapsed on the deck.

"Now, greenhand," said the captain. "Are you ready to work, or shall we try another ten lashes?"

Peter looked up at the captain through tear laden eyes. He realized that wherever he was, he had little to no control of the situation. He was now at the mercy of this man, at least until he could figure out what was going on and come up with a solution. For now, he realized painfully that he had only two simple choices; work as this man demanded or suffer another ten lashes or more at the hands of the mate. Peter struggled to stand, being careful to avoid the vomit and the blood that puddled at his feet. As he stood, he slowly pulled his shirt up to cover his bloody back. "I will work," said Peter reluctantly.

"Very good," said the captain. He turned to the first mate, "See to it that this greenhand is feeding the tryworks and keeping up with the rest of the crew."

"Aye, captain," replied Gale.

"And how are we progressing on the whale?"

"Nearly forty barrels processed, sir and in the hold. We should be done shortly."

Peter stared at the captain and the first mate in confusion, trying to understand what they were talking about. *What were they doing to this whale, and what was in the barrels?* His mind remained foggy both from his situation and from the lashing. He just couldn't seem to manage a clear thought.

"Excellent. Please let me know as soon as the work is complete. I fear we may have a gale approaching and want to clear the decks in advance."

"Sir," said Gale. He nodded to the captain, turned, and grabbed Peter's arm. "Let's go, greenhand. I need you back to work so we can finish this whale and make ready for the weather." Peter walked reluctantly with Gale until they reached a brick furnace that looked very similar to the large masonry grill Peter had installed in the outdoor kitchen at Sheldon House back in Connecticut. What made this one so different from his were the two large cast-iron pots nestled in cutouts above the firebox, each of which looked like they could handle twenty or thirty gallons. A hot fire raged and was being fed by a crewman with what looked like chunks of fatty meat. Black smoke poured out of a short chimney and followed the breeze over the port side of the ship. The foul smell emanating from this structure made Peter's throat contract. He started to heave, and it was all he could do to not vomit again. "I don't think I'll be grilling some steaks for dinner," he mumbled to himself.

"What was that?" asked the first mate.

"Nothing," replied Peter. "Could you just remind me what I'm supposed to be doing here."

"My God, man. What is wrong with you? First, your insolence to the captain, and now you don't know how to do your job? Maybe it would be easier to put you over the side and be done with it," said the first mate.

Not catching the man's subtle sarcasm, a brief flash of fear spread through Peter at the thought of going into the sea, miles from shore.

The mate took a long fork from the side of the tryworks. He turned to Peter, "Men will be in the blubber room, cutting down the pieces into smaller chunks and heaving them up to you through that hatch," Gale said, pointing to the hatch in the deck just forward of the tryworks. "It's your job to take those chunks and throw them into the kettles." Peter looked into the first kettle and saw boiling oil of some sort. The first kettle was about half full, the second was close to topping its rim. The mate then demonstrated by stabbing the prongs of the blubber fork into a freshly cut piece and then placed it into the pot, being careful to not splash any of the hot oil. "Do you think you can manage that?" he asked Peter.

It was not unlike when he'd fry a turkey at Thanksgiving. Using a large stainless vessel fueled by a propane flame, Peter would fill the pot with peanut oil and then crank the burner to the maximum to get it to boil. Sipping on a Bloody Mary, he'd wait patiently until the temperature was just right and then slowly lower the turkey into the oil. If the bird wasn't properly prepared and dried of all moisture, the oil would bubble and spit and sometimes even overflow the pot. He thought he could manage this, although some bloodies would have made it so much easier.

Peter nodded and took the blubber fork from the mate.

"And be sure to skim the oil frequently - we need to make sure to remove as much of the skin and other solid parts before we put the oil in the barrel. Anything you find in the skimmer should be thrown into the fire to keep it going."

As the mate was showing Peter the skimmer, a phone book size of flesh slid up to his feet. Peter looked down and grimaced. Using the fork, he slowly lifted the piece of fat and carefully deposited it into the first kettle. The oil bubbled and spat. Peter thought sadly that there would be no delicious turkey to enjoy when this was done. As he sighed, another piece of flesh slid up to his feet.

The crew finished up the whale by early afternoon. The last of the oil was scooped from the trypots, and the fire was doused with water. The deck was scrubbed of the blood and flesh. Peter looked at the wooden bucket and old fashioned mop with scorn. Never in his life had he ever mopped the floor, that's what maids were for. But he followed the actions of the crew until their work was done for fear of another lashing. Exhausted, he leaned on his mop and looked out over the water. "What the fuck."

"Starbuck!" someone hissed.

Peter turned and saw Jack Tate staring back at him. That is if Jack Tate was wearing clothing from the nineteenth century. He had the same build, the same flaxen hair, and the same green eyes as his old friend. But that wasn't possible, Jack had died years before. Was this a hallucination? Was this whole thing just a horrible nightmare? How could Jack be looking at him?

"Starbuck!" said the apparition. "I saw what happened. The master has been impatient of late, and was taking some of that out on you. I haven't seen him that angry in a long time."

"Who are you?" asked Peter. The strangeness of the day floating in his mind like a dense fog.

"Who am I? Boy, that pulley block must have really done you a good one," he said, laughing. He even had the same laugh as Jack. "I'm Tris, Tristam Coffin. Don't you remember me, Starbuck? I've been your best friend since we were both lads."

Starbuck?

"I'm sorry, er, Tristam," said Peter unsurely. "I have had an incredibly strange day. I thought I had nearly drowned and then rescued... but this ship and the whale... I really have no idea what the fuck is going on," he stumbled. Peter rubbed his eyes with his knuckles, not believing the sight of the visage in front of him. "I do think I have suffered trauma to my head as my memory seems to have escaped me." He looked at the vision of his old friend intently. "Where the fuck are we?"

Tris looked back at Peter, "What is this word...fuck?"

"What?"

"Sorry, Starbuck, but I've never heard that word before. What does it mean?"

"Oh my god, this isn't happening to me," said Peter. He clasped his hands and started walking agitatedly back and forth between the mast and the rail, losing his balance a couple of times when the ship would encounter a larger swell. After a few minutes, he paused and looked at Tris. "Okay, just tell me where we are right now?"

Tris looked at his friend with concern in his eyes. "Where are we, you ask? Now I know that you must have been knocked about quite strongly. We are on the *Paragon*, one of Nantucket's finest whaling vessels. Currently, we are in the Pacific Ocean a few hundred miles off the coast of Chile at the Archer Ground. The good news, though, is that we're nearing our capacity for oil, so it's likely we will start the return voyage to Nantucket in the next few weeks, God and the whales willing. That small humpback we just finished certainly helps."

"What? Chile? Archer Ground? A whaling vessel? Oh my god, this absolutely can't be happening to me," said Peter, incredulous. "This must be a dream, a nightmare. Take me back to the shore right now."

Tris looked at him with confusion in his eyes. "Are you okay? You seem delirious."

"No, I'm not okay!" he shouted back into Tristram's face. "I was just walking on the beach and was pulled into the water and onto this...what is it...a whaling ship? What the fuck is going on?"

"Come with me, Starbuck." They made their way forward past the brick tryworks to the bow. He sat Peter down on an oak cask and looked into his eyes. "What has come over you?" asked Tris.

Peter had never been more confused in his life. It was like that feeling when you wake up from a nightmare and can't remember where you are or even who you are. With a dream, though, it was just a few seconds before reality slipped back in, and you were able to quickly adjust, and things returned to normal. But not this time. It had been hours, and still, this intense feeling of confusion persisted. If it was a dream, perhaps he just hadn't awoken yet. But yet the pain still radiated from his back and his head. He didn't ever remember feeling pain in a dream.

"What do you mean?" replied Peter.

"What is the talk of nonsense about being on a beach? And of being swept into the water. You've been with us on the Paragon for over three years. I myself convinced Captain Nelson to bring you on. You've gone on the whaleboat with me dozens of times, and together we have harvested many whales."

Peter, his eyes were dazed and glassy, looked back at Tris. Who is this person? And how the hell could I be on a whaling ship? *Please, please let me wake up! Let me get back to our picnic at Great Point.*

Tris looked at him with concern. "You took a hard hit in the head from that pulley block. The crew was trying to winch on a large blanket of blubber when the rope sheared, and the block swung down and caught you squarely on the back of your head. Do you not recall any of that?"

Peter rubbed the back of his head. Clearly, there was a large bump forming where the block had apparently hit. But he remembered none of that. What he remembered was that he had been on a picnic with his family. It was a beautiful day, and the kids were happy playing in the sand. He and Charlotte had a fight, and he had walked up to the tip of Great Point. Then he had been hit with a large wave that knocked him off his feet and pulled him into the rip. Then blackness. Then this. This whaling ship. These people. It is not possible.

"Let's go below and see if Cook has any food ready. I think a meal and some rest may do you good. You need to take care of that head of yours, Starbuck. You've been talking nonsense since you took that blow, and I'm worried for you."

Tris led Peter back toward the stern and below decks to steerage where he found his friend some salt horse, a biscuit, and a wooden cup of water.

CHAPTER FOURTEEN

A s the captain had predicted, the weather had turned, and the Paragon was seeing thirty to forty-knot winds with bands of heavy rain. Sailing with reefed canvas, she was making slow but steady headway against the large waves and angry seas. After a rather disgusting meal of a hard biscuit, some salt horse - which Tris said was actually beef - and a little water, Tris and Peter left the relative comfort of steerage. They climbed the stairs through the main hatch and battled their way forward on the weather deck, their bodies leaning into the wind and doing their best to stay upright as the ship climbed and fell beneath them.

As they reached the forward mast, the Paragon dropped into a deep trough between two huge wave crests. Both Peter and Tris quickly grabbed hold of ropes on the mast as the bow fell through the trough and crashed into the following crest. Water cascaded over the rails and rushed down the deck, soaking the two men with seawater. They shook off the water and stumbled ahead to open the hatch of the forward cabin. Quickly and carefully, they descended the narrow stairs and closed the hatch above them. Water dripped down from the hatch onto the floor.

Peter gazed about the dimly lit and foul-smelling space. The triangular-shaped room was at the bow of the ship and held eight double-decker wooden bunks - four on each side. Under the light of a few candles, he could just make out the shadowy figures of a dozen or so men. The room was moving significantly in the wave action, and every fifteen or twenty seconds, a loud thump would reverberate through the cabin as the Paragon encountered another large swell. The air was humid from the sweat of the men and reeked with the odors of unwashed bodies. The hatch was the only source of fresh air, and with it closed, the air was lifeless and stale. Peter started to feel seasick.

Tristam had called this space the "foke sill", short for forecastle or fo'c's'le, and was the forwardmost cabin on the ship. Peter immediately thought of it as the "fuck sail" as it reflected his feelings on his new world most entirely. For the first time since he landed on the Paragon, he smiled.

"And this is your berth," said Tris motioning toward the top bunk closest to the bow on the port side. Peter looked at the wooden frame, which held a thin mattress with a filthy, stained canvas cover. It was a far cry from his king-size bed back at Fernweh with the thousand thread count Egyptian cotton. And instead of Charlotte sharing the bed with him, he was sharing this claustrophobic and disgustingly dirty space with at least twelve other men. He had only met a handful of them when he was working at the tryworks, and none of them impressed Peter with their cleanliness or a disciplined approach to housekeeping.

"And in case you forgot, this is your sea chest," Tris said, pointing to a rather large wooden crate at the base of the bunks. As

Peter's eyes adjusted to the light, he saw sea chests near or next to every bunk. Each was unique and expressed some of the character and personality of the owner. Some were reasonably compact, others larger. Peter's looked to be made of pine and was quite large, nearly as big as the roller bag that he used for most of his trips, especially the more extended European stays. A number of the crew were sitting on their chests. Some looked like they were whittling while others were removing their boots in preparation for sleep.

He noticed that seven of the bunks were already holding prone bodies. Peter was used to being around men from his early prep school days at Deerfield to fraternity life at college and, of course, the locker room at the club. But in each of those circumstances, he had been around other privileged men from wealthy families. They would tell some off-color jokes, try and make the loudest fart, or speak to their prowess in the bedroom, but at least they all held some level of decorum, a line they wouldn't cross. He didn't feel that same level of comfort here.

"Which is your bunk?" asked Peter.

Tris smiled. "I'm a mate now, Starbuck. With your memory, you probably do not recall this, but on our last voyage, I had to step in to be the boatheader on one of the whaleboats. The prior boatheader was killed when the harpoon line wrapped around his ankle. The whale sounded and pulled him into the deep. We never did find his body. But Captain Nelson was pleased with my performance and promoted me before this trip. Not only do I bunk with the other mates in the stern, but my lay has also increased."

Peter felt a bit uncomfortable at the thought of Tris leaving him here alone. He was the only man on the ship that he had connected with and who had helped guide him through this madness, this strange world so utterly different from his own. But he was strong and determined. If he could survive fucked up financial reports and that sleazebag CEO from Clean Seas Forever, he could survive a night in this room with these men.

"Good night," said Tris. "I hope you rest and your memory returns in the morning. I really would like to have my old friend back." Tris touched Peter's shoulder, turned, and climbed the stairs back to the main deck. As he lifted the hatch, fresh air and some seawater poured into the cabin, giving Peter a brief respite from the foul air. He inhaled deeply. Then he crossed the cabin and climbed up into his bunk. His back was still sore from the lashing, so he lay on his stomach, his head cradled in his arms.

Sleep was difficult to come by, and Peter thought of the life that had been ripped away from him. Yes, Charlotte had infuriated him. But was he really upset with her, or was he mad at himself for being called out on his own failures as a husband and a father? And what the fuck was he doing on this whaling ship? And why were they still whaling using this old ship in the 21st century? Hadn't whaling been made illegal? The questions kept Peter's mind racing until finally, the swaying of the boat, the thump of the waves, and the creak of the ship's frame lulled him into a fitful sleep.

He dreamed of Fernweh. In it, he was grilling a nice steak and enjoying some wine with Charlotte, and like many dreams, the imagery didn't quite match his memory of reality. In this case, Charlotte had longer hair and a bustier figure. The grill he was using looked like the one he had at the Connecticut house, but the steak he was cooking to perfection looked more like a big slab of whale fat. In one hand, he held a wrought iron fork with a ridiculously long wooden handle. So long that he was standing several feet from the grill and was struggling to flip the steak and kept losing his grip. And no matter what he did, the fire kept flaring up as the fat dripped onto the coals. As he cooked, he watched Spencer riding his small bike across the yard and ringing the little bell on the handlebars. But it was louder than a regular bike bell and had a deep resonance that seemed to vibrate inside Peter's head. In his dream, he got madder and madder at Spencer and yelled at him to stop with the incessant bell. Charlotte then grabbed his arm and started to shake him all the while yelling at him that he was a lousy father, and she wanted a divorce. "It's time, Peter," he heard her say. "It's time."

Slowly Peter emerged out of his dream to the sound of a bell clanging. "Stop it, please. Let me sleep." Then Peter realized that someone was indeed tugging on his arm. But it wasn't Charlotte. Through blurry eyes, he could just make out the friendly face of Tristam staring down at him, a smile exposing a full set of teeth. "Starbuck, it's time to get up! You can't afford to upset the captain again today, and he does not tolerate laziness or indolence. Let's go, there is work to do."

Groaning, Peter struggled out of his bunk. He noticed the rest of the crew were already gone, apparently to work. "What am I doing here?" asked Peter.

The smile on Tris's face evaporated. "I guess your memory has not returned?"

Peter looked at him. "I really need your help. I have no idea where I'm and how I got here. Can you please refresh my memory? Maybe that will trigger some recollections."

"Sure," said Tris. "But first, let's get some breakfast and get our morning work done."

Peter and Tris climbed the stairs to the weather deck and were met with a clear, crisp blue sky. The weather had passed, and the seas had calmed significantly. Shaking off the foul air of the "fuck sail", Peter breathed in deeply and relished the sharp, tangy taste of salt. He closed his eyes and let the sun warm his face. All he needed now was a beach chair, an adult beverage, and a few hours to shake the past twenty-four hours from his memory.

"Starbuck!" The captain's yell snatched him from his reverie and plunged him back into the confusing world he had landed in the day before. "I'll have no more of your laziness when there is work to be done. See to it, man, or I'll have you flogged again."

"Yes, sir," he mumbled. He followed Tris down the length of the boat and back to steerage, where they secured another nearly inedible meal of salt horse, hardtack biscuit, and some water. They ate their meager rations on deck, where at least Peter was able to enjoy the fresh air. When they were done, Peter turned to Tris, "So what work do we have to do today, Tris?"

"It's not too much. We need to double-check that the whaleboats are ready to be launched with all of their gear. And that the whale irons are sharp."

"Okay. But can I ask you some questions first?"

"Of course. What would you like to know?"

Peter looked up at all of the sail canvas snapping in the wind and the web of ropes securing them. He looked up and down the boat and finally a long look at Tris. "First of all, can you tell me a little bit more about this ship and our voyage?"

"Sure. This here is the Paragon, one of the finest whaling vessels anywhere. We left Nantucket just a little over three years ago and have harvested about fifty whales. With this last whale, we have over two thousand barrels of oil in our stores. With some greasy luck, we should fill the hold in the next few weeks so we can head back to Nantucket."

"The Paragon?" asked Peter.

Tris smiled. "Yes, the Paragon. She is top of the line and was constructed about ten years ago in New Bedford. She's made of live oak with copper fastenings and just over a hundred and ten feet in length, not counting the bowsprit. This is her second voyage under Master Nelson and has proven herself to be a fine whaling vessel indeed!"

Peter absorbed this quietly but was shocked to learn that this ship had been at sea for over three years. "And what year is it?"

"What year?" said Tris laughing. "It's 1828, you silly fellow."

Peter was dumbstruck. *1828? What the fuck? How the hell was that possible? How could he have traveled back in time nearly two hundred years?* It made his head spin, and he almost lost his balance. "Starbuck, are you okay?" said Tris, grabbing Peter's arm.

Peter simply stood looking out to sea, a dazed expression on his face. *1828! Eighteen fucking twenty fucking eight!* He walked to the rail and leaned on it for support. He was breathing heavily, almost hyperventilating. *Get a hold of yourself! Think!* He ran a billion-dollar company, surely he could figure this out and get back to the Nantucket he knew. The Nantucket, where Charlotte, Sophie, and Spencer were waiting for him. And no doubt panicking at his disappearance. It was then he recalled Sophie's dream from a week ago. Or was it a couple of hundred years in the future? The thought just made his head swim.

"Starbuck?"

Peter calmed his mind and gathered his thoughts. If he was to get home, he first needed to survive, and with that, he needed to know more about this ship. He took a deep breath and looked at Tris. "Could you perhaps take some time and help me remember how things work on this boat? I fear my memory still hasn't recovered, and I recall very little about our work here."

"Of course," said Tris. They were standing on the starboard rail just forward of the mainmast. "Follow me. Let me remind you of the key parts of this ship." They strolled toward the bow as Tris pointed up at the rigging. "If you remember, the Paragon is bark rigged, so she has three masts, the forward two, the foremast and mainmast, are both square-rigged. If you look up, you can see the sails are perpendicular to the hull. The third mast, the mizzenmast, is all the way toward the stern, and you can see the canvas is rigged parallel to the hull."

Tris continued, "Captain Nelson much prefers the bark rig versus a more traditional ship rig as the canvas can be managed with fewer men. That means more money for us, and it's easier to handle when the whaleboats are out." Tris stopped and pointed up to the sails. "This type of rig also allows Captain Nelson to sail closer to the wind, which gives us more navigational options and speeds our voyages out and home."

"Okay. But what if there is no wind. Do you have an engine as well?"

Tris looked back at him with some confusion. "An engine?"

"Oh, never mind. I was thinking of something else," said Peter. He realized that he was going to have to be a lot more careful about what he said and did. He certainly did not want these people to think he was insane. God only knows what they did to the poor bastard who they thought was crazy. Probably just threw him off the side of the ship.

"And you said we catch whales?"

Tris laughed. "We don't catch them, Starbuck. We hunt them down and harpoon them. See here," Tris said, pointing to what Peter thought were the lifeboats. "The Paragon carries six whaleboats, three on davits on the port side between the mizzen and foremast with a fourth on the starboard side near the stern. We also have two additional whaleboats that we store on the deckhouse as back-ups in case any of the whaleboats get damaged.'

"How would they get damaged?"

Tris stopped and took a long look at Peter. Long enough that it made Peter feel uncomfortable. "I'm very concerned about your health. You don't seem to remember anything!"

"I'm sorry," said Peter. "I'm worried too."

Tris reached out and held his friend's shoulder. "It will be okay. We will get through this together." Sighing briefly, Tris continued, "The whaleboats are often damaged or destroyed by the whales.

Sometimes they come up right under us and spill us into the water while they break up the hull. Other times they stove us in but good when they ram us."

Peter's face registered shock at the thought of being in the ocean in these little boats while those massive beasts swam around them. It was a chilling thought, not unlike the fear he felt after he saw *Jaws* for the first time when he was twelve. He hadn't swum in the ocean for weeks. "And unfortunately," said Tris, "sometimes a whaleboat and her crew will harpoon a whale, and we never see them again."

"What? What happens to them?"

"Sometimes they get pulled far away from the ship and disappear in a bank of fog. Sometimes, the weather will sprout up unexpectedly and catch them unawares, and they go down in the rough seas. And sometimes, the whale attacks and sinks them." Tris stood quietly, thinking of the many crews that had been lost at sea over the years. After a few minutes, he continued, "But much of the time, our hunts are successful, and we return to the ship to process the whale."

"Process the whale?" asked Peter.

"Yes. Once the whale has been harpooned and killed, we tow it back here and lash it over to the starboard side of the ship. See here," said Tris pointing to openings in the rails next to the mainmast. "We pull the whale here and use these tools to strip the blubber. Then we render the blubber into oil in the tryworks, like you did yesterday. That oil is put in casks in the hold and kept there until we get back to Nantucket."

They had nearly reached the bow of the ship. The breeze had freshened a bit, and Peter could feel the boat straining under him as it moved through the waves. "And how much money will you make?" Peter asked.

"If it's anything like our last voyage," said Tristam proudly, "I hope to make a thousand dollars or more!"

A thousand dollars? That's all? He had a new appreciation for Tris and the other whalemen on this ship. It was a hard and dangerous life for minimal reward. And it hardened his resolve to get back to his life and his time.

"Let me show you one more thing," said Tris. He led Peter to the bow of the boat and pointed under the bowsprit. "Do you remember our figurehead?"

Peter leaned over the rail to look and saw a beautifully carved woman, her hair flowing, and her arms extended backward as if supporting the bow of the ship. She had large breasts and appeared scantily clad in folds of near translucent material that flowed back from her body. Her face held a defiant set to her jaw and her eyes a piercing stare. If she had been real and not of wood, she would have been drop-dead gorgeous, in this century or in Peter's.

He leaned back up and smiled at his friend. "Oh yes, I absolutely remember her," said Peter laughingly, even though he didn't. Tris smiled back and put his arm over Peter's shoulders. "It's good to have you back, my friend. It's good to have you back."

CHAPTER FIFTEEN

Peter's first full day aboard the Paragon ended with him back in the fo'c's'le shortly after sunset. Although the physical work had not been too strenuous, Peter found that the mental and emotional toll on him had been significant. His mind was still struggling to come to grips with his new situation on the Paragon and the fact that he was now nearly two hundred years in the past. The faces of Charlotte, Sophie, and Spencer, ran through his mind as he lay in his flea-infested bunk, struggling to sleep. The boat was again in heavier swells, and his berth was continually moving with the ship, up and down, side to side.

Sleep finally came, but it was a fitful one. He awoke several times during the night, each time hoping, praying, that this was all just a bad dream, and he'd find himself back at home at Fernweh and snuggled up next to Charlotte. But each time, he awoke to the sound of snores and farts from the men as well as the constant groaning and creaking of the hull. He was awake and staring at the ceiling just inches above his head when the ship's bell clanged six times. There was movement from the other bunks, and the men slowly crawled out of their berths and dressed for the day. Peter got up and laced his boots. Grabbing his hat from his sea chest, he followed the men up the ladder and through the hatch to the weather deck.

For the first time, he was able to get a good look at the rest of his bunkmates and was struck by the sheer diversity of the men. About half were what he'd have called a white man or caucasian, although their skin was tanned deeply, and their English had an accent and a vocabulary that at times was unfamiliar to him. Others appeared to be of Caribbean descent and spoke a dialect of English, which he struggled to understand. He noted two men who appeared to be Native Americans and thought most likely that they were descendants of the Wampanoag tribe that inhabited Nantucket for hundreds of years before the colonials settled on the island. Finally, there were a few men of clearly European heritage based on their language he suspected were from Portugal, Spain, and Ireland. It was a very diverse and eclectic crew that appeared to work well together.

As the CEO and leader of a relatively large company, Peter knew that it was the leadership that set the tone, the direction, and managed the stability of an organization. If he were to survive on this ship - at least until he could figure out how to get home - he'd have to 'network' with the leadership of the Paragon. He knew the captain, of course, Master Nelson, but that relationship had gotten off to a rough start. That was going to take some significant work to rectify. He was also familiar with the first mate, Benjamin Gale, and although his back still ached from the lashing, he held no hard feelings toward the man. He had only been following the master's orders.

From his observations and what Tris had shared with him, he was estimating that there were probably about thirty men on the ship, although he didn't really understand their duties and rank on board. What he really needed was an organizational chart that broke down the positions, responsibilities, and reporting structure. But from his experience and seeing how his bunkmates interacted with the others, it was clear that they were the lowest rung on the ladder with responsibilities that were those of a laborer.

As the men walked down the deck towards the stern, Peter noticed that they had the same grumbles, complaints, and bitching that all workers did when starting their shifts. Hard work here was really no different than hard work in his time. He saw it in his factories whenever he visited them. The men ambled toward the main hatch where the cook had brought up food for them, another meal of hardtack, salt horse, and water. Fortunately, the weather was again fair with a blue sky, white puffy clouds, and a pleasant breeze off the port side. The men grabbed their food and scattered. Some simply sat on the deck while others searched out something to sit on like a cask or chest. Peter grabbed his food and went to the rail, where he struggled to get the food down. The salt horse was like eating a big piece of crappy beef jerky, and he felt the biscuit might break a tooth if he wasn't careful. More than anything, he wanted a good cup of coffee. But he sure as hell wasn't going to ask.

"Starbuck! Good morning"

Peter looked up to see Tris standing in front of him, a big smile on his face. "Morning. Did you get some breakfast?"

"I did," replied Tris. "With my promotion to mate, I now eat with Captain Nelson in his cabin. It's so much better than salt horse and hardtack. We actually had some fresh fruit today."

"Humph," replied Peter, a little jealous at not only the better menu but also, the more civilized environment in which to eat.

"Are you ready to man your watch?"

"My what?" asked Peter.

Tris laughed. "Still the memory problems, eh? Well, my friend, I need to remind you that you are one of the lookouts for the forenoon watch."

"Okay. What does a lookout do, exactly?"

Tris's smile evaporated at the realization that his friend had no idea what he was talking about. Clearly, his memory problems were even more severe than he thought and would need to keep a close eye on him lest he run afoul of the crew by shirking his duties. Tris pointed high up on the mast. "That's the crow's nest. As a lookout, your job is to scan the seas for any sign of whales. You may see flukes or the spout or even their backs. When you do, you call down with the direction so the captain can steer a course to get close enough to release the whaleboats."

Peter, with a fear of heights for as long as he can remember, took one look at the top of the mast and felt the warm rush of adrenaline through his body. "Up there?" he asked, his voice shaky.

"Yes, your watch is at four bells, which," Tris paused to look at the sun's position in the sky, "is in about two hours."

149

Peter did not respond. He had been on this ship for barely two days, had been whipped, eaten really shitty food, slept in a flea-infested rathole, been drenched in seawater, and was now expected to climb a hundred feet up a mast to stand on what looked like a small wooden platform whose only safety feature was a hoop that would circle his chest. *Oh my god*, he thought. *I have got to get out of here.* But he kept his mouth shut and simply nodded to show he understood.

"Tris?" asked Peter. "Could you walk with me a bit?"

"Sure." Peter led Tris away from the men, so he was out of earshot. They walked toward the bow and found a more private area close to the foremast.

"I wanted to thank you for all you're doing for me," said Peter. "I know it probably hasn't been easy for you to deal with me, and I really appreciate it."

Tris smiled. "Of course. You were clearly more injured than we thought from when that block struck you. And given all you and I have been through, it's the least I can do to make sure you're okay."

Peter smiled back, hesitant to ask, but he needed to know. "And why do you call me Starbuck?"

"Because that's your name!" said Tris, smiling. And for the second time that morning, his smile evaporated as he saw the confusion and uncertainty in his friend's eyes.

"I'm sorry, I really am. I should try and understand how difficult this is for you." Tris paused for a minute, unsure of where to start. "You and I grew up together. We've been friends for as

long as I can remember. And our families have been part of
Nantucket for over a hundred years. Do you remember when we
were in school under the master, Cyrus Peirce?"

Peter shook his head.

"Well, there were ten boys in our class, and three of you were
named Peter. So the master started calling each of you by your last
names so as to minimize the confusion. So you became Starbuck,
Peter Macy became Macy, and Peter Folger became Folger. I'm
not sure why but the name stuck outside of the class, but soon
everyone just called you Starbuck. The name just seemed to fit you
really well."

"So, I'm part of the Starbuck family?"

"Of course you are! Just as much as I'm part of the Coffin
family," Tris said, smiling. "And if you want, you can start calling
me Coffin."

Peter smiled. "Thanks, but I think I'll stick with Tris."

His friend smiled back at him. "I'm just sorry you're still
having issues with your memory. If there is anything more I can do
to help, please let me know."

"Well, there is another thing I've been curious about."

"What's that?"

"Why do the captain and some of the crew call me a
greenhand?" asked Peter.

Tris roared with laughter and clapped the shoulder of his
friend. "Oh, that's precious!" When his laughter finally subsided,
he looked at Peter and continued, his eyes sparkling in amusement.

"A greenhand is the nickname for a crewman who is on their first whaling voyage."

"This is my first voyage, then?"

Tris was suddenly serious again. "Yes, this is your first voyage on any ship." He paused before continuing, "You had been working the docks on Nantucket and had complained to me that you weren't making much money. So I convinced the captain to bring you aboard for this trip, and up until your accident, things had been going very well." Tris placed his hand on his friend's shoulder and looked into his eyes. "And they will continue to go well. Just give it a little time, and I'm sure your memory will come back, as good as normal."

"Thanks," replied Peter. "You are a good friend."

Their discussion was interrupted by the ship's bell, which clanged four times. Tris looked at Peter and said, "There's your watch. Greasy luck to you, and we will talk more later." Tris turned and walked back toward the wheelhouse where his watch was to start.

Peter looked up and saw two men descending the rigging and realized that they were actually using rope ladders, one on each side of the mast. The men, having done this hundreds of times, came down quickly and jumped the last few feet onto the deck. Peter looked up and again felt that warm rush of adrenaline through his body. *Be brave,* he thought to himself. *Be brave.* He walked over to the rope ladder on the starboard side and started to climb. He realized that another crewman was on the opposing ladder and was already a third of the way up and climbing very quickly. Peter tried to speed up, but the flexibility of the rope made him feel very insecure with his footing. He tried not to look down and kept his focus by taking one step at a time, slowly and deliberately until finally reaching the platform. He put his hands above his head and carefully pulled himself through the ropes so that he was kneeling on the wooden platform. Then holding the iron hoop for support, he raised himself up, squeezed his chest through, and stood up.

His focus had been so intense that when he looked out, he gasped at how high he was and just how far he could see. It took his breath away. His thoughts immediately went to when he had climbed to the top of Sankaty Head lighthouse. Charlotte had donated money to the Sconset Trust, the group that oversaw the care of the old structure. In a show of appreciation, they had been invited to a cocktail party one warm summer evening. As part of the festivities, they were encouraged to climb the iron stairs and take in the view from the platform just outside the main beacon. Screwing up the courage with help from several drinks, Peter had scaled the old stairs, taking care not to look down, and had made it to the top.

The view had been fantastic. To the north, closest to the lighthouse, he could see the brackish pond, Quident, while way out in the distance, he could just make out the Great Point lighthouse, it's light blinking every twenty seconds or so. Turning to the west, he looked across the lovely golf course and the moors and could just see the church steeples in town, seven miles distant. To the south, he saw all the homes down Baxter Road along with much of Sconset and the south shore beyond. But it was the view east that had impressed him the most, the endless blue ocean stretched out to the horizon with nothing between him and Europe. And it was that view in his memory that he was seeing again, only this time from the top of the mast of a 19th-century whaleship. Unlike the lighthouse, though, his platform was swaying significantly from side to side with the movements of the ship below him. It was more than a little unsettling, and he tried not to think about it.

His reminiscing was interrupted by the crewman standing next to him. "Sure took you long enough." Peter looked over and recognized one of his bunkmates, a man he believed to be from Nantucket. The Nantucket of 1828. Peter replied, "Yes, sorry. I'm still a bit dizzy from the accident this week and wanted to be extra careful."

"Humph," the man acknowledged and turned to look out over the sea.

Seeing that his platform-mate wasn't much of a talker, Peter did what he was supposed to do and focused his eyes out over the water. He was soon captivated by the endless variations and patterns he saw in the waves. They would rise and fall, merge and separate, pause, and accelerate. And with that, the color of the water changed from a deep blue when the sun shone brightly to a grayish-green when a cloud would cross the sun. In his mind, he could also feel waves, waves of confusion, and opacity. Moments of clarity followed by moments of murkiness as if shadowed by this time, from being sent back nearly two hundred years to this ship to the realization that he might be a descendant of the Starbucks.

Could he really be a Starbuck? If he was going to be honest with himself, then it was completely and totally irrelevant. What's in a name that's going to improve his life in any way, make him even more money, or strengthen his frayed relationships with his family? But what it did do was to make him feel even more connected to the island he loved. Being a summer resident for most of his life had always made him feel a bit of a second class citizen. Those that grew up on the island, the true natives, and those who could trace their lineage to the early families held a special place in his mind. And he was excited at the thought that maybe he might be able to count himself among those that for years he had secretly envied.

That all depended, of course, that the Peter Bois of 1828, Starbuck in other words, was the same Peter Bois of his current time. And he'd not be able to answer that question until he returned home and was able to do a little digging in the genealogical records of the island. It wasn't much, but it was the first good news he had heard since landing here.

The two men continued scanning the seas, but neither Peter nor his quiet colleague had seen any sign of whales when the bell clanged eight times to signal the end of their watch. Peter hadn't moved much during his time in the crow's nest and realized he was quite stiff from being stationary. He tried to stretch a bit and then made the mistake of looking straight down toward the deck. Immediately he was hit with a buzz of fear through his gut and started to panic. He closed his eyes and tried to tell himself that he could do it, that it would be alright.

"Let's go," said his colleague, who was already twenty or so feet down the ladder. He waved up at Peter and then continued his descent down to the deck. Peter slowly knelt down on the wooden platform and then extended his leg over the side, trying to engage his foot into the ladder. After wiggling it about, he found the ladder with his left foot and then extended his right foot down as well. With both feet on the ropes, he slowly started down the ladder, reluctantly letting go of the security of the platform. He was about halfway down when he saw another mate across from him on the other ladder, climbing quickly up to the top of the mast. Fearing backlash from his replacement on the watch, he tried to increase his speed and a minute later reached the security of the deck. He let go of the ropes with a long sigh.

Tris was there to meet him. "No whales, eh?"

Peter replied. "Nothing but water and waves."

"Very well," said Tris. "Maybe you'll get lucky on your next watch."

CHAPTER SIXTEEN

W hen Peter had inherited Fernweh, he did nothing for
many years except essential maintenance,
landscaping, and keeping nature from gaining a
foothold. His goal was to preserve the house exactly as his parents
- and his grandfather - had left it. But with the marriage to
Charlotte and the births of Sophie and Spencer, he soon realized
that he needed to make changes that would better accommodate a
21st-century family. He also realized that with the right design, the
changes could be sensitive to the history and character of the
house. That awareness kicked off a multi-year renovation project
that touched every room. Many of the rooms saw little changes,
mostly paint or wallpaper, and in some cases, new electrical and
lighting. But several rooms had been completely gutted and
reimagined with a clean slate.

The kitchen had been one of these with significant revisions to
the layout and flow of the space. When it had been built in the 19th
century, the builder had incorporated a unique circular bump-out
on the west wall of the kitchen that featured large windows looking
out into a garden. It was the perfect spot for a dining table and
chairs, and it was one of their favorite places in the house. And it

was the one part of the kitchen that they kept unchanged. The rest of the room received significant renovations, which included new French doors that opened to the patio, custom-built white cabinetry, marble countertops, and stainless fixtures and commercial appliances.

Another space that had been reimagined was their master bathroom. Originally pretty cramped, they had taken the opportunity to increase the size by annexing a nearby bedroom, which more than tripled the square feet. With that, they were able to add a large walk-in shower - fit for two - a clawfoot soaking tub, and a small steam shower. Custom vanities, quartz countertops, and polished stainless hardware completed the outfitting. Along one wall, four double-hung windows were installed with six over six panes to match the rest of the house, and framed in a lovely floral print window treatment. At the end of this wall of windows resided the toilet, which Peter would never admit, was one of his favorite places in the house. It allowed him to have his morning constitutional while looking out across the beauty of Sconset and the nearby moors. And aside the toilet was a matching bidet that ensured him a clean finish.

That visual was fresh in his mind as Peter sat on the splintery bench near the bow of the Paragon, just after dawn. Relieving oneself onboard was a bit of a challenge. If the weather was suitable and all had one to do was to empty one's bladder, then a crewman or mate simply leaned over the rail of the ship and went straight into the water. If the seas were rough or the weather nasty, they might pee directly on the deck near the scuppers and count on the seawater coming over the rail to flush things away. If the seas were so bad and the ship moving violently, say in a storm, then the crew would utilize a bucket in the fo'c's'le, which would be emptied and flushed with seawater as soon as conditions permitted.

Going number two was very different. If the captain allowed it, some men would hang their backsides off the rail to go, which required not only a lack of a desire for privacy but also perfect balance lest it end with an accidental fall into the water. Captain Nelson frowned on this practice, so the crew of the Paragon, Peter included, were required to use one of the two heads at the bow of the ship. These simple privies, one on each side of the bowsprit, were no more than small wooden shacks that held an oak bench with a couple of holes cut into them. The holes led to chutes designed into the planked sides of the ship where the waste would fall and be washed away by seawater.

But it was nothing like the master bathroom at Fernweh.

Peter had been on board now for nearly a week and suffered from almost constant diarrhea. He attributed it partially to the nerves of being in his new situation but more likely due to the low quality of food and water that he had unavoidably consumed. It had been months since the Paragon had made port, and as a result, the stores were moldy and the water rank.

The diarrhea was physically debilitating, but it was the emotional toll of life aboard the Paragon that was overwhelmingly depressing. Peter Bois was a man who was used to living a life surrounded by nothing but the best from bathrooms to homes to private jets. Aside from splashing some saltwater on himself from a wooden bucket a few times, Peter had not had a shower since before they had left for their picnic at Great Point. He was a man who was used to being clean, and adjustment to this new lower level of personal hygiene was challenging, made more so by the continuing issues with his GI tract.

Peter finished and stepped out of the head. He looked out over the ocean and took a moment to enjoy the sunrise. The sun was just barely breaking the horizon and high, thin clouds were exhibiting a glorious range of colors from light pink to deep red. Peter thought of all the sunrises and sunsets he had watched with Charlotte over the years and felt a deep stab of sadness. He was missing her and the kids tremendously. It felt like it had been years, not days since he had held her in her arms. He wondered what she was doing and how she was handling things on her own. Did she miss him? Was she happy he was gone? Or was she crying herself to sleep every night? He had to figure out how to get home and get back to his old life. And he knew that if he got back, he'd need to be different. He would need to be the husband and father he promised her he would be. Lost in thought, he didn't hear Tris walking up to him.

"Do you have a minute?" his friend asked.

Peter, startled out of his thoughts, looked at Tris, trying to hide the sadness in his eyes. "Of course, Tris, what is it?"

Tris looked at Peter with concern in his eyes. "It's the rest of the men. Since your accident last week they feel that you've changed. You used to be one of the most hardworking men on this ship and earned the respect of everyone from master Nelson, the mates, and all of the crew. Now they feel that you're weak and lazy."

"What? Weak and lazy?" replied Peter. "I feel like I have worked my ass off since I landed here!"

"Landed here?" asked Tris hesitantly.

"I mean my accident - since that block landed on my head," said Peter dancing around his words.

"Well, whatever, the crew, the mates and the captain all feel the same way, that you're no longer the same man you were. You even missed your watch yesterday!"

"I'm sorry, I forgot about it."

"Forgot about it?" said Tris, shaking his head. "That's not like you at all. And it's things like that that are causing concern with the captain and the crew. You need to work to convince them that you haven't changed, that you're still the same Starbuck that everyone respects, especially as a greenhand."

"I appreciate you telling me, and I'll do my best to be that 'old' Starbuck."

"Good," said Tris and placed his hand on Peter's shoulder. "And I'll continue to keep an eye on things."

Peter smiled and was about to respond when he heard a shout from above.

"Thar she blows!"

Peter and Tris looked up to the Crow's Nest and could see a crewman pointing off their port bow. "Thar she blows!" he yelled again.

The next voice he heard was that of Captain Nelson, who shouted up to the men in the hoops. "What kind of whale? And how far out is he?"

Peter strained to hear the man's response. "Looks to be a sperm whale, sir," said the crewman, "and about a half-mile out."

"Very well," said the master. He turned to the mates and the crew that had gathered about him upon hearing the first shouts from above. "To the boats!" he yelled. The men responded as if stung by bees and stormed across the deck.

Peter stood watching, confused, and unsure of what he was supposed to do. As usual, his friend bailed him out. "Starbuck!" shouted Tris, "You're with me!"

The two men sprinted across the deck to the davit off the stern of the Paragon. There were already several of the crew at the boat making preparations to launch. Peter and Tris jumped in the boat with Tris at the stern and Peter settling on the middle bench. Crewmen fore and aft immediately began to let out the ropes lowering the boat to the water. Before he could even get his bearings with this new and rather diminutive craft, Peter felt the hull hit the water. Tris called out, "Pull men! Pull!" Peter watched the four other crewmen dip their oars and start pulling in unison. Tris's comments still fresh in his mind, Peter wrapped his hands around the oar across his lap and began to pull in synch with the others. Tris stood in the stern and used another oar to steer the boat around the back of the Paragon.

Three other whaleboats were also in the water now, their crews rowing hard in the direction of the whale. Peter watched as the Paragon retreated behind them and then looked over his shoulder to see nothing but the expanse of the blue sea and the promise of a large whale somewhere in the distance. He was scared.

* * *

Peter had spent enough time on the water to be comfortable at sea, at least in the confines of a large sport fisherman with modern electronics and safety gear as well as a full refrigerator of beer and snacks. An experienced captain and crew and a reasonably reliable weather forecast also contributed to his sense of security. So equipped, he was quite confident that his personal safety was never in any danger.

But he and five other men had just dropped themselves into the largest body of water on the planet in a craft that would make him feel nervous just cruising around Nantucket harbor. His anxiety further ratcheted up several notches as he realized what was at stake and what he and these men were about to undertake. They were going to attempt to catch, harpoon, and kill one of the largest animals to ever swim in the sea and do it from a fragile-looking, twenty-one-foot whaleboat that looks like it could be cut in half by a dolphin.

It might have seemed fragile, but it was well suited to its purpose. It was lightweight yet sturdy and built for speed and ease of maneuverability. It had also dropped into the water with a significant inventory of items needed to help ensure their hunt was successful. This included harpoons to secure their boat to the whale, nearly two thousand feet of rope coiled in baskets and attached to the harpoon, lances for killing, drinking water, and some hardtack for the men, a compass and lantern, and canvas buckets. In addition to the five oars providing propulsion, the boat could also be wind-powered. A twenty-foot wooden mast could be stepped and sails rigged if favorable air currents were available.

From Peter's seat on the middle bench, he watched as Tris's eyes constantly surveyed the waters ahead for any sign of the whale. He was managing a much longer steering oar off the stern of the boat and was consistently making adjustments to keep the whaleboat's bow pointed in the right direction for the intercept. In the bench closest to Tris sat Eli, a crewman from the Azores who Peter had talked with briefly in the fo'c's'le, mostly about the daily schedules and watches. Behind him, in the next two benches, were a couple of crewmen from New Bedford, John Thain, and Ichabod Alrich, both men on their second voyage aboard the Paragon. It was clear that they had known each other for a long time with their easy banter and familiar nature. He suspected that these two were probably good men to have around if and when things got rough.

At the bow of the boat was another compartment mate from the fo'c's'le named Thomas Pitman, a native Nantucketer. Peter had spent a watch with Thomas and found him to be intelligent, ambitious, and insightful. Peter had peppered him with questions about the boat, the captain, and Nantucket in general, all in the guise of working to regain his memory. Thomas had patiently answered his questions and shared his own story. Although he was just twenty-two, he had spent over six years at sea and truly loved the water in general and whaling in particular. As the two men rocked side by side at the top of the mainmast, Thomas had shared his dream of being the captain of a whaling vessel before he was thirty-five. His success as a harpooner during this trip had him hoping to be promoted to mate for the next. In some ways, Thomas reminded Peter of himself when he was that age, full of ambition, desire, and a plan to make it happen.

The men were rowing steadily and rhythmically, the whaleboat moving quickly through the water. Peter settled into the pace and was managing to keep his oar in sync with the five from the other men. He had heard that the first boat to harpoon the whale received an extra ration of rum, and by looking at the energy the other men expended, he could tell that the race was on. He hoped that this would not last long despite the promise of alcohol. He wasn't in the best of shape and could feel his arms already beginning to tire. The last thing he wanted to do was to reinforce his newfound reputation as lazy and incompetent by letting down the rest of the men.

Tris suddenly pointed and shouted to the men, "thar blows - we're getting close, boys!"

Peter turned to look over his shoulder and saw a plume of spray just a few hundred feet ahead, followed by the broad, gray back of the whale. As it dove back underwater, a massive fluke emerged, easily as big as the whaleboat itself, before it slipped quietly under the waves. *This is fucking insane!* Peter thought. *This beast could kill us in a heartbeat if it tried. All we have is this flimsy little boat to protect us - no life jackets, GPS, emergency beacons, or even a radio to call for help. We're completely and totally fucked if this whale attacks us!*

As these panicked thoughts raced through his mind, he watched Thomas at the bow of the boat, pull his oar from the water, and grab the harpoon. The weapon was about six feet long with an iron rod tipped with twin barbs extending from a thick wooden base. Attached about a third of the way from the sharp end was a sturdy, rough rope that trailed down to the hull where it ended in a large coil in the bottom of a woven tub. Peter realized that this wasn't a dream or a nightmare, they were actually going to throw that barbed weapon into the back of an eighty-foot beast. He turned his head, focused his energy on the oar, and silently said a prayer for his safety.

The men pulled harder to stay ahead of the other boats while Tris adjusted their direction subtly to bring them up from behind and on the right side of the whale. This would minimize the chance of the whale seeing them and give Thomas the best angle for his harpoon and, with it, the greatest opportunity for success. They were catching the whale quickly and had closed to under a hundred feet.

"Ok, quiet now," Tris whispered to the men. They eased their oars out of the water and let the boat glide closer to the whale, keeping as still as possible so as not to spook the beast. The whale surfaced just in front of the boat, and Peter could hear the exhale of air followed by a deep intake before the whale dove under. The fluke again surfaced, this time just in front of the whaleboat. Peter watched as the huge tail towered up and over their boat before descending back into the water with a splash of water. *Holy shit!* thought Peter. He could only imagine what he looked like right now if Tris or one of the other crew had seen him. But their attention was focused elsewhere, Peter's shocked expression was missed by all.

Tris motioned to Thomas to be ready and maneuvered the boat to where he expected the whale was going to surface next. Thomas stood up at the bow, his leg braced against the railing and held the harpoon high up with his right arm as if he was getting ready to throw a fastball. Peter watched incredulously, the memory of a Yankees game in his head when he heard Tris shout out. "Now!"

The whale broke the surface just as Thomas jumped up in the air and threw the weapon at the gray back with all his might. He let the harpoon fly, its black dagger glinting in the sun. The tip pierced the flesh and penetrated deeply into the blubber, the barbed weapon secured in the whale's back. Peter thought he heard it bellow in pain and in rage.

The whale spasmed, bringing up its powerful tail and dropping the fluke onto the whaleboat. The blow slammed the back of the boat, knocking Tris into the sea and swamping the boat with seawater. Eli, the crewman just ahead of Tris, had taken the tip of the fluke directly on top of his head and slumped across his bench unconscious.

All thoughts about the dangers of what they were doing vanished from Peter's mind, and his natural leadership abilities took over. He shouted to the other men, "Bail! We must bail for our lives!" John and Ichabod went to work immediately, grabbing the canvas buckets from under the gunwales and scooping and tossing water out of the hull. Peter then jumped up and moved quickly to the stern of the boat, stepping over the prone body of Eli. Grabbing an oar, he extended it out to Tris, who was floating in the water but seemed confused as to what was going on around him. The whale gave a powerful thrust of it's tail and took off, the coil of rope in the hull quickly playing out. Peter instinctively knew he didn't have much time. "Tris! Grab the oar now!" he shouted. Tris looked up at the shout, startled out of his confusion, and reached for the oar. It was just inches out of reach. "Swim!" shouted Peter. He knew that when they ran out of rope, the whaleboat was going to be pulled behind the whale, leaving Tris in the water, alone, to fend for himself.

Tris struggled to move forward, clearly never having any formal swim lessons, but made enough progress to gain the few inches he needed. He wrapped his hand around the end of the oar and hung on as Peter pulled him closer to the boat. At the bow of the boat, Thomas was struggling to manage the rapid release of the rope. He had wrapped it round the loggerhead, but it was moving out so quickly it was smoking. The whale was still diving and taking more and more line. All Thomas could do was keep the rope cool with seawater and hope that the whale returned to the surface to breathe before the coil ran out. If not, they risked losing the whale and all of the hard work they had invested.

Using the oar, Peter was able to pull Tris to the stern of the boat and turned to yell at Ichabod, "Help me get him on board!" Ichabod stumbled to the stern, and together they were able to grab Tris under his arms and pull him into the whaleboat where he collapsed in the bottom of the hull, still partially full of seawater despite their bailing efforts. Tris was vomiting and gasping for breath, clearly in no condition to direct the boat.

Peter shouted forward to Thomas, "Where is the whale?"

The rope had finally stopped playing out, and Thomas had just secured it to a cleat at the bow. Thomas called back, "He's surfacing now!" A few moments later, they saw the spout, it's edges tinged with pink, and heard the whale take a deep breath. The whaleboat had started to move, being pulled behind the giant beast as it tried to run from its pain. When Peter was a child, his grandfather had taken him to the Whaling Museum, where he had learned about the "Nantucket Sleigh Ride" remembering, in particular, one imaginative painting of a whaleboat flying through the waves seemingly faster than a speedboat. As their whaleboat accelerated, Peter realized that he was now living out that image and was on the ride of his life. "Hang on men!" he shouted as they sped across the waves.

The sleigh ride was as exciting as Peter imagined it would be with the whaleboat being pulled further and further from the Paragon. At times moving so quickly, it jumped over waves and showered the men with seawater. Then the boat would slow, and all aboard would hope the whale had finally tired, and they could move in for the kill. But then the whale would surface, take another deep breath, and swim off again, with the prayers of six men following. Before long, the other whaleboats were specks on the horizon with the tops of masts of the Paragon just barely visible. Fortunately, the weather had remained fair, and the seas calm, so it remained a game of patience for the crew.

Tris had regained his composure and was sitting on the bench just forward of Peter, who had been handling the steering oar throughout the ride doing his best to keep the boat as steady as possible as the whale pulled them ever and ever faster. Peter looked down at his friend through a spray of water. "Tris, good to see you back. We almost lost you there," he said with a smile.

Tris smiled back, "I have had far worse encounters with whales, Starbuck. I'm certainly not going to go that easily!"

Peter looked up to check on their progress and satisfied the boat was stable, turned again to Tris, "Can you check on Eli? I'm afraid he took a massive blow from the fluke," he said. Eli remained slumped backward over the center bench with his head on the gunwale, not having moved since the tail had crashed down.

Tris leaned forward and slapped him on the face a couple of times to wake him. He then grabbed his shoulders to shake him awake. Eli's head flopped about as Tris moved him from side to side. "I fear he is dead," said Tris, sadness in his voice. "His neck is broken."

Peter had never seen a dead body before, let alone witnessed a death. Eli had been just a few feet from him. Had that fluke been a little further right, it might be him lying dead in the bilge instead of this young man. The thought ran chills through his body and brought all the dangers they had faced in this hunt clearly to the forefront of his mind. *God, I need to get home!* he thought to himself. *I need to get back to Charlotte and the kids.*

Finally, the whaleboat slowed, the whale tiring. The men stowed the oars as Thomas, Ichabod, and John grabbed the line and began to pull themselves to the whale. The whale was still breathing but moving very slowly. Carefully, they brought the boat up on the left side of the whale this time. Tris fully recovered now, swapped positions with Thomas, and pulled a long lance from under the gunwale. Securing himself at the bow of the boat, he used the long lance to plunge into the whale, again and again, trying to hit the heart and lungs. The water turned red with blood and brown with vomit. It was dying.

The whale, who just hours before had been one of the most powerful animals in the Pacific, expelled a blood-red plume from its blowhole. Tris knew he had been successful in finding the critical organs and shouted out, "He's showing the flag, men! Let's back off." John, Ichabod, and Peter remounted their oars and slowly rowed, backing themselves away from the whale. Once they were a hundred feet or so, they stopped, watched, and waited.

The whale was clearly struggling, and death was near. Peter sat in the whaleboat incredulous that he, along with five other men had caught, harpooned and killed this massive animal. But he also felt a deep sense of sadness and remorse at participating in the death of this magnificent creature.

As they watched, the whale began to swim slowly in circles, it's lifeblood trailing behind it, another plume from the blowhole, bright red with blood. The fluke raised in the air one final time slowly paused, and then came crashing down on the water. The whale rolled onto its side, its flipper in the air, and was still. It was at long last, dead.

CHAPTER SEVENTEEN

T he whale lay still in the water. "Great job, men!" Tris
yelled out. "Well done." The men smiled and laughed,
their ordeal over, and knowing that this whale, with its
valuable oil, would put them that much closer to returning home to
Nantucket. Tris reached down and grabbed the tub of water, and
took a deep drink. He passed it down the boat with each of the men
taking a long swallow. The weather had been fair but warm, and
the men were soaked through with perspiration and seawater.

The good mood was short-lived as the realization of Eli's death
hit them. Tris stood solemnly at the stern and mumbled a brief
prayer. Ichabod and John moved his body to the center of the boat
and covered him with a piece of canvas. Then they turned to the
next challenge, getting this massive, dead animal back to be
processed.

The men regained their positions at the oars, and Tris
maneuvered the boat to the whale's once hazardous fluke, the
weapon of death for poor Eli. That danger gone, Thomas secured a
rope around the tail and passed the line to Tris, who fastened it to a
cleat in the stern. "Okay, men!" Tris commanded. "Without Eli, we
will need to work ever harder." The men dipped their oars in the

water and began to pull. Slowly, ever so slowly, they began to move, the whale following them fluke first back toward the Paragon.

Peter dipped his oar in the water, pulled hard, lifted, pushed back, and then repeated. He was in sync with the other men but completely and totally exhausted. Every stroke of the oar sent pain through his back and burning through his lungs. *Was it really just a couple of weeks ago that I told myself I needed to start exercising?* he thought to himself. Dip, pull, lift, back, repeat. He and four other men were towing tens of thousands of pounds of dead whale using nothing more than five wooden oars. It was no wonder he hurt so much. Peter looked down at his hands and saw blood trickling down the oar handle, the rough wood finish had blistered both his hands. "Pull, men! We're making great progress!" shouted Tris, encouraging the crew. "I can see the Paragon. It won't be much longer now." Peter stole a glance over his shoulder and could see the ship sailing towards them, all canvas flying. It was a beautiful sight. Peter sighed a breath of relief, knowing that he soon would be back on the Paragon and could give his body some rest. He'd be happy as well to get out of this little craft, the experience of being in this boat had been physically demanding and emotionally unnerving.

They closed the distance to the Paragon quickly and maneuvered the carcass to the starboard side of the ship. Tris untied the rope and tossed it up to the mate, Benjamin Gale, who was standing at the rail. He and another half dozen men pulled on the line to bring the whale amidships and then began to fasten the body to the hull with chains.

Peter sat on his bench, exhausted, but relieved to be back to the Paragon. By the height of the sun, Peter guessed it was well into the afternoon, he'd been on the whaleboat for hours. He looked up to see Captain Nelson standing on the rail, looking over their catch. He seemed very pleased. "Great job, boys. Now let's get to work!"

Get... to... work...? Thought Peter. *What the hell do you call what we just did?*

Peter looked back at Tris for guidance. Tris was attaching the ropes from the davit to the stern of the boat while Thomas managed the same at the bow. Then Peter heard the rattle of pulley blocks and felt himself being slowly lifted up, the boat tilting back and forth as it climbed up the side of the Paragon.

With the whaleboat secured on the davits, Peter climbed out slowly and forced himself to stand, his back and body protesting every move. He turned to see Thomas and John lifting Eli's prone body from the bottom of the hull. They carefully maneuvered him over the rail of the boat and laid him down on the deck. Had he not known any better, he'd have thought Eli was just sleeping, his face was so peaceful.

He pulled his eyes away and staggered over to Tris, who was engaged in conversation with the cooper, William Smythe, a short, stocky man who resembled the product he made. Tris said to him, "It's a big whale, and I'm guessing we will need at least a hundred barrels or more!"

"A hundred barrels! That would be a record for this voyage! I best get started then." William turned and headed below decks to grab staves and irons to start making barrels. He knew he'd need a head start.

Tris turned and saw Peter next to him. He placed a hand on his shoulder, his blue eyes sparkling with success. "Well done, today, Starbuck! Thank you for saving me and for taking over the boat. I'll be sure to share the story with the master."

"Of course," said Peter. "But what will be done with him?" nodding to Eli's body.

"Death on a voyage is not an uncommon occurrence, unfortunately," replied Tris, sadly. "We will wrap the body well in an old sail and then bury him."

"Bury him?" asked Peter.

"Yes. At sea, that is. Tradition dictates that we will have a simple ceremony at sunset, Master Nelson will say a few words, then we will commit his body to the deep."

Peter stood silently.

"Try not to let it bother you, Starbuck. We can be thankful it wasn't either of us, and we live to whale another day."

"Of course."

Tris, anxious to change the subject, pointed down to the carcass of the whale where the crew was busy laying a wooden framework down the length of the body. "That's the biggest whale we have landed this voyage! The captain is pleased and promises extra rations of rum once all the oil is stowed."

As they watched, two men stepped out onto the wooden planks over the carcass carrying what looked like long-handled spades, reminding Peter of what the landscapers used at Fernweh to edge a garden bed. They plunged the spades into the body of the whale and began turning the flesh into long, thick strips of blubber almost a man wide. Blood poured from the wound and into the water. Peter's stomach turned, and he struggled not to vomit. Barely maintaining control of his stomach, he turned to Tris. "What's next?" he asked.

Tris looked at his friend with understanding. "The men here," Tris pointed at the whale, "will use those cutting spades to remove large pieces of blubber. The mates and I will man the windless, and we will hoist those pieces on board. At the same time, we will work to sever the head and bring that aboard whole. Although I must admit I'm not sure the windlass will be able to manage a head so big," Tris said with a bit of a chuckle. "But when the carcass is stripped, and the blubber all put away, we will then light the tryworks and boil off the oil. You remember that job, don't you?"

Peter thought about his first few hours on the Paragon and recalled the lashing he received and then being forced to feed the raw flesh into the boiling oil. And the godawful stench. Suppressing the heaving of his stomach at the thought, he looked at Tris and said, "I do remember. I think I can handle that."

"Very well then, Starbuck. While the men are stripping the pieces, I'd suggest you go and help Thomas with the head. There will be a lot of spermaceti to capture, and it's quite valuable, as you know. We need to get it on board without problem." Peter nodded and went to look for Thomas. He found him coming from the bow and heading toward the staging platform. "Thomas!" Peter cried out. "I'm to help you with the head." Thomas smiled. "That's good news. I can certainly use the help with this one, it's huge!" said the young man, spreading his arms wide. "Follow me, Starbuck."

They walked nearly to the stern of the boat to get to the head of the whale. Peter looked over and saw the toothy jaw of the giant beast slightly open. He turned to Thomas, "What do we do first?"

"The first thing we want to do is get the jaw off," replied Thomas. He pulled an ax from his waistband, jumped down onto the staging, and began to hack at the base of the whale's jaw. It was no easy feat. He raised the ax and brought it down repeatedly as if he were trying to cut down a small tree. For the third time in the last few minutes, Peter's stomach heaved. He turned away to settle things down but couldn't avoid Thomas's eyes. "Feeling a little nauseous, Starbuck?" said Thomas teasingly. Two more blows from the ax took care of the last bits of connective tissue, and Thomas grabbed the nearly fifteen-foot long jaw and wrenched it from the carcass. "Starbuck, be ready!" he shouted out. Struggling a bit with his prize, Thomas lifted the jaw nearly vertical and dropped the pointed end on the rail above him. Peter was able to grab hold and pull the jaw onto the deck, careful not to look at the ragged bits of flesh on the other end. Laying there on the planking, thin and long, it was an impressive sight with two rows of enormous teeth.

Thomas called up to Peter. "Grab a hammer and a bucket. You need to remove all those teeth before we strip the flesh."

Peter went and found a hammer and a bucket and began the unpleasant business of removing the sixty or so teeth from the bony, narrow jaw. It was not physically difficult work, but it was emotionally challenging for Peter, and it took him a while to desensitize himself from what he was doing. Once he had numbed himself to the task, he was able to complete the removals pretty quickly and had even developed a rhythm. A horizontal hit from the hammer on the tooth would break it from the root, twist the tooth to sever the remaining flesh, and drop in the bucket. Repeat. He was nearing the last few rows of teeth when he heard Thomas call for him. He put down the hammer and walked over to the rail. "Yes, Thomas, what is it?" he shouted down.

"How are you making with those teeth?"

"Nearly done," said Peter. "Just a few more to go."

"Outstanding!" said Thomas. "Please come down here and help me with the head when you're done."

"Oh, okay," said Peter, more than a little nervous at the thought of being on that flimsy wooden scaffolding just a few feet from the water. He turned to finish with the jaw when he heard Thomas call out, "and bring a cutting spade with you!"

The jaw denticulated, Peter took the bucket, now brimming with teeth and weighing close to fifty pounds, and handed it to another of the crew who carried it down to the hold. Peter secured a spade from one of the mates and carefully proceeded down to the staging to help Thomas remove the head. The wood was slick with blood and oil, and it was all Peter could do to maintain his balance. He noticed that Thomas had nearly managed to sever the large head of the whale and was working now to cut the neck vertebrae of the animal.

"Starbuck," said Thomas. "Help me cut this bone. It's so thick, and my blade is dulled and my arms tired."

Peter looked at Thomas but remained quiet. He turned and stared at the body of the whale, it's neck's exposed by a huge incision several feet across. At the bottom of the wound, he could make out the white of two of the vertebrae, the size of basketballs, and a gap between. He lifted his spade and tried to bring it down on the gap but lost his balance as he started to thrust. Fortunately, Thomas was quick to grab his arm and keep him from falling off the plank.

"Careful there, Starbuck," said Thomas. "You know there are sharks down there that would love to have you for dinner."

"Sharks?" asked Peter with a bit of hysteria in his voice.

"Yes, sharks," said Thomas. "In fact, there's one right there," he said, pointing past Peter.

Peter turned to look and saw the large fin of a shark circling just feet from the whale's carcass. It was twenty or thirty yards away but still brought an electric jolt of adrenaline through Peter's body. He turned back to Thomas, fear in his eyes. Thomas grabbed his shoulder. "It's alright. Let's get this done so we can get back on deck."

Peter nodded and once again lifted his spade. This time he was far more deliberate, taking careful aim and settling his feet before ramming the spade into the wound. The tool bounced off the bone and plunged into the flesh. He pulled the blade out and tried again. This time he was more successful and managed to chip off a large piece of bone as well as cut through some of the ligaments between them. After several more attempts, the blade sailed through the last of the tissue and bone, leaving the head attached with only a few feet of flesh.

"Good job. I think we're ready to hoist it aboard," said Thomas. He called up the deck. "Gale! Send down some rope.

We're ready to bring the head aboard." The mate peered over the rail, acknowledged the request, and disappeared. A few minutes went by before he reappeared with the rope, which he threw down to the two men. Thomas caught it and turned to Peter, "Help me get this rope around it and secure for the windlass."

They passed the rope around the head multiple times and worked together for nearly fifteen minutes to complete their handmade harness. After taking a brief rest to catch their breath, Thomas assessed the work again to ensure it was secure. Satisfied, he called back up the mate. "Gale, we're ready!" he shouted.

The mate appeared again over the rail and touched his hand to his head. Once again, he turned and disappeared. Peter heard a creak and looked up to see a large wooden boom swinging over the rail toward them. Gale reappeared at the rail with the end of the rope attached to a large hook. It, in turn, was attached via block & tackle to the wooden beam above. Thomas grabbed the hook as it was lowered and secured it to their harness. "Let's go, Starbuck," said Thomas and led them down the plank to where they could climb back on deck.

The rope followed a series of pulleys to the windlass, which was being worked by four of the crew. Using poles, they slowly started turning the windless, taking the slack out of the ropes. Thomas and Peter watched as the head began to lift, and all of its tremendous weight was now suspended from the hook. Gale yelled, "Hold!" and the men at the windless stopped. Thomas grabbed his spade and jumped back down on the blanking to cut through the remaining bits of flesh and fully separate the head from the rest of the body. Divorced from the body, the head rocked slowly side to side following the motions of the Paragon and the waves below her.

"Pull!" yelled Gale to the men at the windless. The men again began to turn the windless, their bodies and shoulders leaning against the poles to provide maximum torque. Slowly amid creaking ropes, the head started to rise again, and Peter could feel the boat listing over from the sheer weight. It took several minutes for the head to clear the rail. Gale paused the men at the windless, and he, along with a number of the crew, grabbed the harness and pulled on it to swing the head over the deck.

"Back off now, slowly!" Gale yelled to the men at the windless. Gradually the windless reversed and the severed head of the whale descended gently onto the deck, balanced on the cavity that was once its mouth, grayish eyes casting an accusing stare at the men around it.

Peter stared incredulously at the car-sized object in front of him. *What the hell are we going to do with this?*

"Starbuck!" yelled Thomas from across the deck, as if reading his mind. "Help me empty the case!"

Empty the what?

The cooper had rolled over a few barrels next to the head. "I have more coming," he said to Thomas and headed to the hatch to go below. Thomas had pulled a small wooden stage next to the head and climbed on top. Using his ax, he broke a hole through the top of the skull and widened it enough that he could have squeezed in if he tried. Putting aside the ax, he extended his arm toward Peter, "Hand me that bucket, will you Starbuck?" Peter looked down and saw a large wooden bucket on the deck. He grabbed it and handed it to Thomas.

Thomas dropped it in the hole and pulled it out, filled to the brim with a clear liquid. He handed that down to Peter. "Dump that in the barrel, will you," said Thomas. "And then hand it back." Peter did as instructed, dumping the now whitening liquid into a new oak barrel fresh from the cooper. He handed the empty back to Thomas, who dipped it in the skull and returned it to Peter, who emptied it into the cask. They repeated this until the barrel was full. A crewman brought a circular piece of wood and a wooden hammer and sealed the barrel while a second man rolled a new, empty barrel up to Peter.

This continued for several hours and well into the evening before Thomas, who was now working inside the skull, had popped his head up and said they had gotten the last of it. Peter nearly cried in relief. His day had started with the sun, in the whaleboat until afternoon, and now hours of disgusting, backbreaking work emptying the skull of a sperm whale. He was covered in blood, whale vomit, and oil. He thought a ragged, smelly, flea-infested mattress was never going to feel so good.

"Starbuck," said Thomas. "Great work today. Best get some rest as we will be trying out the blubber at dawn."

"Yes, Thomas," said Peter. He turned and headed toward his bunk in the bow. His legs were tired, and his body weak from the long day, and he was ready for sleep. But he paused at the foremast and gazed up at the stars. It was a beautiful, clear evening and the stars were bright. It reminded him of the many walks he and Charlotte used to take through Sconset at night, holding hands and listening to the sounds of the ocean. Looking up at the stars, he realized that they hadn't been on one of those evening walks in years. *God, could I really be that awful of a man and husband to not want to walk with my wife? Was work that damn important?* Suddenly the reality of the day and the pain at what he had lost came bursting through his exhaustion. "Charlotte," he said to the wind, a tear trailing down his cheek. "I will find my way back to you."

He took one last look at the stars as he wiped the tear away. He turned and descended down into the fo'c's'le, the sounds and smells of the exhausted men greeting him.

CHAPTER EIGHTEEN

A s he had done every night aboard the Paragon, Peter was dreaming.

He was at the beach with Charlotte, Sophie, and Spencer. He was playing in the sand with the kids and making a castle using rocks to decorate the edges and shells to stand in as a protective army. Charlotte was on a beach chair up by the car, reading a book, and enjoying the sun. He turned away from the sandcastle and smiled at Charlotte. She smiled back at him, looking radiant. A deep sense of well-being enveloped him, and he felt that all was right with his world. He turned back to the sandcastle and saw with horror that the shells and pebbles had been replaced by bits of whale. Bloody teeth lined the top of the sides while pieces of flesh flanked the walls. Everything seems to be covered in oil, and the whole castle was surrounded by a moat of whale blood. But Sophie and Spencer didn't seem to notice. They kept on playing, marching the teeth as soldiers and splashing the blood on each other, their faces freckled in red. Peter was horrified. *No! Get back! This is not for you!*

But Sophie and Spencer kept playing. And Charlotte kept smiling and waving to him. Frantically, he tried to stand up, but his body wouldn't respond. His feet were flailing in the sand, but the more he moved, the more he seemed to be sinking. He was trying to turn and yank his legs from the sand when he saw a wave. It was only a foot or two high but advancing quickly toward him. *Run kids. Run!* He shouted at his kids, but they didn't move, absorbed in their play with the dead whale bits.

The wave enveloped him, and he felt the cold rush of water. But it didn't push him forward. Instead, it was as if two hands had circled his legs and started pulling him from the sand, out to sea and away from his family. He clawed desperately with his hands trying to halt his movement but managed little more than creating grooves in the sand. The force was relentless. He watched helplessly as he was dragged away from his family and pulled under the water. He saw Spencer laughing and playing with a whale tooth just before his head went under.

Peter woke up and sat up quickly enough to slam his forehead on the beam above his bunk. Holding his forehead, he lay back down and thought about the dream. Thank God it was just that. Relieved, he rested on his bunk, wondering again how Charlotte was making out in his absence. Was she doing okay? How were the kids? Did they miss him as much as he missed them? Seeing the other men getting up, he resigned himself to commit to another day on the Paragon. Slowly he swung his legs over the bunk and jumped down to the floor. He saw with disgust that he was still in the same blood and whale oil-soaked clothes from the day before. Much of the blood had dried and starched his heavy cloth trousers making those first few steps a little awkward. His mood was foul with the knowledge of another long day of work ahead of him. They were going to try out the whale.

He climbed the stairs to the weather deck and was relieved to see that at least the weather had remained fair and calm. Cook had brought out the food, and he grabbed some hardtack and salt horse. He sat on a tub by the rail and tried to eat the foul-smelling provisions. He noticed movement and took a closer look at his hardtack. A small maggot had crawled about halfway out of where Peter had just taken a bite. He struggled not to vomit and threw the biscuit into the sea. "Disgusting," he said out loud. John Thain, who had been on the whaleboat with him the day before, saw what happened and smiled. "What is it, Starbuck? Don't you like maggots?" he said and burst into laughter. Peter smiled wanly, stood, and headed towards the stern.

He arrived at the tryworks as they were being lit. A small bundle of wood and kindling was under each and just starting to burn. The tangy, sharp smell reminded Peter of Fernweh and the fires they would have during the cold, fall days. He thought of his dream, and of Fernweh. *God, I want to go home.*

Tris came up next to him. "How are you feeling this morning, Starbuck?" he asked. "A bit tired from our adventures yesterday, perhaps?" and smiled.

Peter looked into the green eyes of his friend. "I am a bit tired, but ready to work." *Anything to get me closer to home and take my mind off this situation.* "What do you need me to do?"

"The same as you did before, Starbuck," said Tris. "The men below in the blubber room will cut those large blankets of flesh into pieces about the size of a book - some men call them Bible pieces - and then they'll toss them up to you. Drop them in the pots and boil them off. Thain and Ichabod will use buckets to empty the pots into barrels," he concluded.

Peter nodded and grabbed one of the long forks.

"Oh, and make sure you skim the top frequently for pieces, then feed those to the fire to keep it burning hot." Tris smiled and turned, seeking out the cooper to ensure enough barrels were prepared.

As Peter watched his friend walk away, he heard a swishing sound. He looked down to see a small piece of flesh slide up to his feet. *And so it starts,* he thought.

For a man that had never done any hard, manual labor in his life, save a couple summers of construction during college, he worked as if he were a machine taking breaks only to relieve himself and have some water to stay hydrated. The sun was advancing across the sky as the pieces of flesh continued to arrive at his feet, one every twenty seconds or so. As Peter steadily fed the pots, barrels were filled, sealed, and rolled down to the hold. Tris was back early in the afternoon and walked up to the tryworks. "How are you doing?"

Peter dropped a piece into one of the pots and then leaned against his long fork. Wiping sweat from his eyes, he replied, "I'm okay, Tris. But I have to admit this is foul work. The stench from this oil is enough to make me vomit."

"That's true!" Tris laughed. "They say you smell a whaling ship approaching long before you see it!" He paused for a minute and then asked in a serious tone, "I know your watch is over now, but are you able to continue for a while?"

"Of course."

Tris nodded solemnly. "Thank you. It was Eli who was to relieve you and since the incident yesterday..." his voice trailed off.

Peter looked at Tris, "I will take his watch. You can count on me."

"Thank you, Starbuck," said Tris and slowly walked away.

Peter returned to the task at hand and was startled to see a half dozen pieces had arrived at his feet during his brief conversation with Tris. He fed them into the pots and got back into the rhythm of feeding and skimming. Thain and Ichabod had been replaced by two crew from the fo'c's'le, Stephen Wood and Caleb Lynch, who talked incessantly as they transferred the oil from the pots to the barrels. Women, money, going home, the mates and captain, and when they would see their next whale. They tried to engage Peter several times in conversation, but he was in no mood. He just wanted to get the work done.

They worked tirelessly throughout the afternoon and evening until it was too dark to do any more. The fires were snuffed, and the tools laid aside until morning. Peter was so exhausted that he headed straight for his berth, climbed in, and was instantly asleep. For the first time on the Paragon, he did not dream.

He slept through the night, disturbed only by the occasional itch from a flea bite. The stirring of the men in the bunks around him woke Peter just after sunrise. His first few movements were met with sharp and painful muscle aches from yesterday's work. Thinking about the day, he was somewhat surprised to feel a sense of accomplishment and satisfaction almost as if he had proven something to himself.

The year before, a well known financial magazine had done a profile piece about him and Shimmo Plastics. They had spent a couple of days interviewing him at his office and trying to understand what made him tick and how he had achieved such tremendous success. Flattered by the attention, Peter was very candid about what it had taken, even sharing the firing of his prep school friend Chuck Thompson, positioning it as a challenging but brave thing to do.

When the article was published, it featured a photograph of Peter astride his desk, his arms crossed, with what Charlotte would later call "an arrogantly smug expression" on his face. Peter had been happy with the piece and thought the article had accurately reflected what it took to make Shimmo the success it was. Charlotte had thought he had come across as a son-of-a-bitch who would do anything to make himself and the company successful. She hadn't felt the piece flattering.

He could only imagine what an interview about him now would look like. Covered in blood and filth, working in monotonous and dangerous conditions, and being a simple cog in the production of a commodity that kept the world alight and lubricated. He was no longer the CEO, didn't make the decisions, didn't have any authority. Yet he felt strangely at ease with that. If a photograph were taken now, he'd probably still appear smugly confident.

He smiled at the thought and climbed down from his bunk. His clothes had gone from bad to worse, now thoroughly soaked through with foul-smelling oil. Surprisingly though, his stomach didn't heave. *Maybe I'm getting used to this.*

He climbed through the hatch and up onto the weather deck. He did have some salt horse but skipped the hardtack, the thought of the maggot still fresh in his mind. Finishing with a deep drink of stale water, he headed down to the tryworks. He hoped that they would finish this whale today.

Peter arrived as the fires were being lit and grabbed his fork. He had to wait a few minutes before the first pieces of flesh appeared, but within a half-hour, the pots were full and boiling away. As with yesterday, Peter worked his shift and was well into another when the pieces no longer appeared at his feet. They had finished, finally, the remaining parts of the whale. The last bits were rendered, the pots emptied, and the barrels taken down to the hold.

Tris appeared at his side. "Well done, Starbuck! You've worked hard. Let's get this ship clean, so we can ready ourselves for the next whale."

The next whale? Peter thought. *You've got to be kidding me. We're going to do this again? Watching for spouts, launching the boats, catching the whale, and then this disgusting, bloody, awful work of butchering this beautiful beast?* His sense of satisfaction had disappeared, replaced by a feeling of dread and futility.

Peter worked with the rest of the crew to scrub every part of the boat. They used mops, brushes, and seawater to remove as much of the blood, vomit, and filth as they could. When they had last finished, they were able to turn their attention to their own hygiene. Despite scrubbing himself sore and rinsing himself with bucket after bucket of saltwater, Peter found he could not fully get the stench of oil off his body. But he was delighted to see a second set of clothes in his sea chest and was nearly giddy putting them on.

As he was preparing to climb the ropes and take his shift atop the mast, he heard the voice of Captain Nelson call out. "Mates, assemble the men!"

The mates gathered everyone and all grouped around the mainmast, anxious to hear the captain's words. He didn't often talk directly with the entire crew.

"Men," said Captain Nelson. "This whale yielded one hundred and two barrels, including over twenty-five of spermaceti!" The crew cheered, smiles all around. Peter watched confused and not understanding the significance of the statement or the financial implications for the crew. "And the hold is full!" Another round of cheers went up from the men, and a few threw their hats in the air. The captain yielded a rare smile, "Now, we sail for Nantucket!"

More cheers and smiling faces. Peter looked out across the water. He might not understand a lot of what happened on the Paragon, but he understood this. He was returning home to the island he loved. Sadly, he wondered what and who would be waiting for him when he arrived.

CHAPTER NINETEEN

T he captain's words still ringing in his ear, Peter watched
happily as the men celebrated the end of their hunt and
their return to home. True to his promise, the captain had
broken out the rum, and a few of the crew had pulled out
instruments and started to play some music. The men drank, sang,
and danced well into the night. Even the mates participated in the
celebration, although the captain had returned to his cabin to plot
out their return voyage.

Tris was enjoying the evening, but as a mate, he was careful to
not imbibe too much as he had a watch in a few hours. Peter had
decided that he deserved to get a little drunk and was more than a
bit surprised at the quality of the rum. If he had been back in his
time, it would have definitely been top shelf and premium-priced.
He had just finished his third cup when Tris cozied up to him and
put his arm around his shoulder. "You've been amazing the last
few days, Starbuck," said Tris. "The way you took over the
whaleboat when I was knocked into the sea and Eli killed. That
showed tremendous courage and leadership. And the last two days?
You've worked tirelessly and without stop to help us process the
whale. Thank you," Tris concluded.

Peter was not used to receiving such praise. Usually, he was on the giving end of such a conversation, although he rarely handed out approvals or compliments. The old business adage of 'commend in public, condemn in private' he felt was old fashioned and he believed in the exact opposite. He didn't hesitate to call out members of his team at Shimmo when they screwed up and was equally happy doing it in front of the entire organization if need be. It certainly hadn't made him a popular leader, but he really didn't care about any of that. He just wanted the business to be successful.

Yet here he was, almost bashful at being called out for the great work he had done. *Oh my God, am I really blushing?* But as Tris's words sank in, he had to admit he did feel a deep sense of satisfaction, that he had proven something to himself and to the other men aboard this ship. Just over a week ago, he had been sent back through time and dropped down onto the deck of this vessel; arrogant, confused, and completely disoriented. Since then he had been flogged, suffered terrible diarrhea, held watch at the top of the mast, was nearly killed chasing an eighty-foot sperm whale, been covered in blood, guts and vomit butchering that same whale, and all while having to learn and adapt to a new and strange life nearly two hundred years in the past from his own.

"Thank you," said Peter. "That means a lot coming from you."

"Well, it's not just me," Tris continued. The rest of the crew and the mates have noticed as well, including Master Nelson."

"Master Nelson?" asked Peter.

"Yes, even Captain Nelson. In fact, he even made mention of promoting you for the next voyage."

Peter was taken aback at the thought. *Promoted?* He hadn't been recognized like that since his first job out of college when he had advanced quickly though his first Wall Street firm. Some of his colleagues would say that he advanced all right, on, and over the backs of others. And those promotions hadn't meant much to him other than for the financial rewards they brought with increased salaries and bigger bonuses. But the thought of securing this promotion was significantly different. He had encountered tremendous personal challenges and, through sheer determination and force of will, had succeeded in overcoming them. And perhaps more importantly, he now felt like he was part of the crew of the Paragon. He had earned their respect. But the sense of satisfaction could not overcome his desire to be back home, back in his own time, and back with Charlotte and the kids.

"That would be great if it happens," said Peter smiling. "And if so, I would owe a lot of the thanks to you. You really helped me after my accident and helped me get back my bearings. Thank you for being there and for being so patient with me."

"Of course!" said Tris, slapping his hand on Peter's back. "Isn't that what friends are for?"

Peter looked deeply into Tris's green eyes and was struck at just how close his friendship had developed with this man over the past week. He realized that the connection must have been built on the foundation of his close relationship with Jack Tate. Even though he was not directly responsible, he had never forgiven himself for Jack's death, and his absence from his life still left a void that he felt almost daily. And that friendship had never been replaced. He was close to Charlotte and considered her his best friend, but he never had another like Jack. Sure, lots of acquaintances, some he thought might have even liked him, but he had never allowed himself to get close to another man until now. Tris had worked his way into Peter's heart and started to fill the void Jack had left.

"Yes, that's what friends are for," and smiled warmly. They watched as the men danced and celebrated the start of their voyage home. Peter said, "Can I get you some more rum?"

Tris looked down at his nearly empty cup and thought for a minute. "Perhaps, but just a little. I have a watch coming up and need full control of my senses."

"Great," said Peter. He grabbed Tris's cup and went to the barrel by the mast. Returning to Tris, he handed him his half-filled mug and asked expectantly, "So how long to home?"

Tris took a sip of rum and thought about the question for a minute. "There are a few variables that play into that. Winds and weather, of course, but also the weight of oil in the hold. The Paragon sails a little slower when she is so full." He thought some more. "But if I had to estimate, I'd say twelve to fourteen weeks."

"Twelve to fourteen weeks!" said Peter, surprised.

"Yes, if we get good weather and fair winds. And the Horn, of course. The weather there is so unpredictable. Some ships take weeks just waiting for the right conditions to make that rounding."

"The Horn?" asked Peter.

"Yes, Cape Horn. One of the most dangerous spots for sailing vessels on earth," replied Tris. "If you don't remember, on our voyage out, it took us nearly ten weeks before we were able to round the Horn. The winds were constantly blowing hard from the west and northwest, and we had to wait for them to diminish before we could recommence our journey."

Tris saw the shocked look on Peter's face and smiled, "But don't worry. The voyage eastbound is usually much easier though we will still need to worry about the storms and waves."

As Tris was describing their last rounding, Peter started to understand what lay ahead for this ship and her crew. They were to sail from the Pacific ocean off the coast of Chile, down and around Cape Horn at the tip of South America, up the coast of Brazil, and then across thousands of miles of the North Atlantic to that little speck of sand out in the Atlantic. All at the mercy of prevailing winds and without GPS, radar, radio, or any way of knowing what lay ahead of them beyond what they could see with their own eyes. *Holy shit!* An electric stab of fear radiated through his body.

"But don't worry. Captain Nelson has been at sea for over twenty years and has proven himself time and time again. And the Paragon is a fine and sturdy vessel. The biggest challenge for the crew tends to be boredom as there isn't much to do other than attend the sails," said Tris.

Ready to change the subject and take his mind off what lay ahead for them, Peter looked at Tris and asked, "What is the first thing you're going to do when we get home?"

Tris laughed. "I'll go and see my Abigail, of course. I miss her terribly. And you know what?"

"What's that?"

"I'm going to ask her to marry me."

"Really? That's wonderful!" said Peter and cuffed his shoulder. "Does that mean you'll stop whaling?"

"Oh, no. I will continue to whale. It's all I really know, and I love to do it so. And the financial prospects will allow me to provide nicely for Abigail."

"But what will she do while you're at sea?"

"Oh, she'll do what all the whaling wives do on Nantucket. She will run our household, raise our children," Tris paused to wink at Peter, "and manage our affairs until I return."

Although he hadn't met her, Peter felt a sense of sadness at the thought of Abigail on her own for years at a time when Tris was out at sea. All that time, not knowing how he was, what he was doing, and whether or not he'd even come home. His thoughts immediately went to Charlotte and the idea that in some ways, he had done the same to her. He wasn't going to sea to hunt whales but instead going to work to run a business. And although he wasn't physically gone as Tris would be, he accepted that he had been gone emotionally. Running Shimmo, he was no closer to Charlotte then Tris would be to Abigail when he was out to sea.

"You know, whaling would not be possible were it not for amazing women like Abigail who can do the work of men when we're gone," said Tris. "And I'm lucky and thankful to have her. I want her by my side for the rest of my life."

Peter noticed a tear forming in Tris's eye and smiled at his friend. "I understand, probably more than you realize."

"And I want you to be the best man, of course!"

"I'd be honored!" said Peter and slapped him on the back heartily. "There is nothing that would make me happier."

Tris pulled away and looked at Peter, "What about you? What is the first thing you're going to do?"

Peter thought for a minute, careful not to let the confusion he felt show in his eyes. He had no idea what or who was waiting for him and was hesitant to ask Tris. "I'm really not sure. But I know it will feel good to be back, if only for a while."

"Yes it will, Starbuck, yes it will. And if you'll excuse me, I need to take my watch at the wheel."

"Of course. I'll see you in the morning," said Peter. Tris nodded, smiled, and turned, walking briskly to the stern.

Peter continued into the evening celebrating their return home while nervous about the journey and the prospects waiting for him back on Nantucket. But the rum was excellent, both in taste and in effect, and soon he was good and pleasantly drunk. He took his leave from the rest of the crew, still celebrating, and staggered his way forward. The air was crisp, and the skies were again laden with stars.

He decided that he was not going back to his flea-infested bunk but instead would sleep on deck under the stars. He and Charlotte had done that many times when they were just married and had relished the experience so much that they built a sleeping porch at Fernweh. Initially, they had taken advantage of it frequently, even, Peter suspected, conceiving both of their children there. He smiled at the memory.

But that smile evaporated as Peter sat and looked at the stars. He could not recall one time that they had slept on the porch in the last few years. So many things had changed in his life, it seemed, and for the worse, because of the company. Was he any different than these men, gone for months at a time, hunting and butchering whales? And despite Tris's claim, would he really continue whaling if he didn't need to? Would he stay home with Abigail and be with her always if he had the resources to do so? Given the love he saw on Tris's face when he talked about her, he suspected that the answer was yes.

He closed his eyes and slowly drifted off to sleep, the faces of Charlotte, Sophie, and Spencer, smiling and laughing in his mind. He was ready to be home. He was ready to stop whaling.

CHAPTER TWENTY

D awn broke on the Paragon to a dull and breezy day, the wind gusty from the northwest and accompanied by light rain. Peter awoke wet, cold, and hungover. It had definitely been some good rum, and he was now questioning the wisdom of his intake quantity as well as spending the night on deck. Rubbing his eyes, he tried to sit-up, but his body protested. Unlike the sleeping porch at Fernweh, there had been no bed for him to enjoy, so he had slept curled up on the hard deck with only a coil of ropes as a pillow. His body ached, and his head pounded, aggravated even further by the clanging of the ship's bell calling the watch.

He slowly stood up and made his way to the rail, where he relieved himself of some of that rum. Feeling a little better, he headed to the stern where he found Tris at the wheel, his right hand on one of the rim's handles while he leaned forward to view the compass set under a small greenhouse-like structure. Peter noted that Tris could see very little ahead and certainly nothing even remotely close to the bow of the ship. He was completely reliant on the men above in the hoops to warn him of any potential dangers in their path.

"Good morning. Lovely day, isn't it?" Peter said sarcastically, trying to stretch out his back.

Tris chuckled. "Yes indeed, a lovely day! I trust you enjoyed your evening?" he said with a wry smile.

"I did, but not sure sleeping on deck was my best idea," replied Peter, rubbing his lower back.

Tris chuckled. "I understand that. But glad you had fun and appreciated the celebration. You certainly deserved it."

Peter smiled. "So, how are we progressing?""Very well," Tris replied. "We are under full sail and making over ten knots. If we can maintain this speed, we should round the Horn within the week."

"That's great news!" said Peter. "But I'm curious, how do you know which way to head?"

Tris checked the compass again and made a slight adjustment to the wheel, bringing the bow of the boat ever so slightly to starboard. He looked at Peter. "Captain Nelson has plotted our journey. I just need to follow the heading he has given me. He will reassess hourly to track our progress and adjust as necessary."

"Really?" said Peter. He was fascinated at the intelligence of Captain Nelson and his ability to navigate the broad expanse of the ocean using only a map, compass, and sextant. Peter had become, like much of his modern world, dependent on the mapping apps on his phone and the GPS systems they utilized to accurately determine his location. He knew he'd be hard-pressed to even read a paper map and correctly orient himself on land, let alone negotiate an ocean barren of any landmarks.

Tris smiled. "Really. The captain has years of experience at sea and knows the route home like the back of his hand." Tris checked the compass and made another slight adjustment with the wheel. "Let's just pray for fair weather and following winds. I want to get home to Abigail."

Peter nodded and felt the churn of nerves in his stomach. He looked out across the expanse of the ocean, the water a dull gray and covered in whitecaps from the wind. What and who was waiting for him back on Nantucket? *Am I doomed to live in the past*, he thought. *Or can I find the way home to Charlotte and the kids?*

A snap of canvas startled Peter out of his thoughts. "Starbuck," said Tris, "would you please adjust the topsail? It's leaking the wind and needs a trim."

Peter looked at Tris as if he had just spoken Greek to him. He stammered out, "I'm sorry, but not sure I remember how to do that."

"It's okay, I'll show you," said Tris kindly. He turned and called out to the first mate, "Gale! Do me a favor and take the wheel for a moment. I have to see to something."

Gale strode back to the wheel quickly. "Right. What's our course?"

"Southeast by South"

The mate nodded, "Very well."

"Starbuck! With me, please," said Tris, and he headed forward. They walked to the mainmast and stopped. Tris pointed up at the large sail just below the Crow's Nest. "That is the main topsail," he said patiently. "And as you can see, the canvas is flapping loosely and not fully capturing the wind. To adjust it, you need to climb the main rigging here," he paused, pointing at the rope ladder, "up to the main topsail yard and trim the sail a little tighter with the ropes there."

Peter looked up and understood precisely what Tris was saying. A week ago, he'd have been completely lost and confused and afraid to proceed. But he was comfortable now and able to climb the rigging as good as any of the crew. "Got it, Tris. Thanks." He quickly ascended the rigging, found the right rope among the many secured there, and carefully trimmed the canvas until it filled with wind. He paused for a minute to take advantage of his perch and stared in wonder at the sheer complexity of the sails, spars, and rigging of the Paragon. When he had first landed on the ship, it was a baffling maze of ropes and canvas that made no sense to him. But his time on the Paragon and his experience on watch had shown him the system behind it all. His confusion had been replaced by awe and respect on how this crew, these mates, and this captain managed to sail this vessel so efficiently and quickly through the waters. Checking again on the trim of the topsail, Peter descended down to the deck, satisfied in his work.

With a little time before his watch, Peter walked toward the bow and down into the fo'c's'le to get out of the weather. While he still found the space dark and smelly, it was a respite from the wind and the light rain on deck. As his eyes adjusted to the dim light, he could make out a number of the crew in their bunks. He also noticed Thomas sitting on his chest with what looked like a whale tooth in one hand and a long needle in the other.

"Thomas. What are you doing there?"

Thomas looked up at Peter. "Oh, hello," he replied. He turned his attention back to the tooth and eyed the surface in the dim candlelight. "I'm scrimshandering."

"Scrimshandering?" asked Peter, confused.

"Yes. I'm documenting our voyage in this tooth."

"Really," replied Peter. "Can I see?"

"Sure," said Thomas and handed him the tooth.

Peter held the tooth in his hands and angled the surface to the light. He was amazed to see a near-perfect carving of the Paragon at sea, her sails flying. Off her bow, the back of a large whale was clearly visible with a whaleboat and her crew approaching from behind. The detail was complete down to the rigging in the sails and the whale iron in the hand of the harpooner. It was extraordinary.

"This is beautiful."

Thomas looked pleased. "Thank you. I find it really helps pass the time, especially when we're heading home, and there is little to do but attend to the watch."

Peter reluctantly handed the tooth back to Thomas. "Well, you certainly have a talent for it. That piece is exquisite."

Thomas took the tooth and smiled. He held it to the light, and using the long needle continued his work. Peter watched fascinated for a few minutes as Thomas worked slowly and deliberately on his scrimshaw. Yawning, Peter turned away and climbed into his bunk to catch a little rest. His hangover had abated somewhat, but he was still tired from his long evening and a tad too much rum.

And he was hungry. Once again, breakfast had proven a challenge for him, and he just couldn't bring himself to eat all his rations, as usual, getting nauseous after only a few bites. Finding a few more maggots in the hardtack didn't help things either. The one positive of this whole adventure, he thought, was that he was losing weight and getting into better shape. *Maybe I can start a new weight-loss trend*, he thought. *The whaleman's diet of stagnant water, salt horse, and maggot-infested hardtack.* He smiled at the thought and drifted into sleep.

* * *

The weather and the winds had cooperated, allowing the Paragon to move even faster in the water, at times approaching twelve knots. And sooner than Tris had predicted, the Paragon found herself nearing the Horn in unusually fair weather and calm seas. She crossed the fifty-sixth parallel in the twilight of a southern hemisphere winter with a moderate westerly wind making for exceptionally easy progress. Clearing the Drake passage at the tip of the Tierra del Fuego, she turned north, and for the first time in over three years, the Paragon was closing the distance to Nantucket.

With the turn to the north, the dozens of sails hung across three masts needed to be adjusted to their new heading. Most of the crew went aloft to manage the hundreds of ropes, spars, and blocks required to trim the canvas and capture the wind. The entire process took well over an hour under the watchful eye of Captain Nelson. Once he was satisfied with the set, he turned to Tris and said, "Now, Mr. Coffin." Tris nodded, turned, and walked forward.

He found Peter near the bow of the ship nursing a wounded hand. While comfortable aloft, Peter still lacked the practical experience of managing the canvas and the dangers that it posed. He had been in the rigging of the foremast, managing the trim of the fore topgallant sail when the wind caught the canvas unexpectedly, whipping the rope through and out of his hands. Peter recovered the rope and trimmed the sail but was left with a nasty burn across his palm.

Tris greeted him, "How are you?"

Peter looked up from his palm and gave Tris a grimaced smile. "I'm fine. Just got caught up in an unexpected gust."

Tris looked at Peter's hand. "I've seen far worse. I think you will be fine. Just bathe it in saltwater several times a day and keep a bandage on it. It will heal in no time."

"Thanks," said Peter. "Did you need me for something?"

"Yes, I do," said Tris, smiling broadly. "I was sent to bring you back to the captain."

Peter suddenly felt nervous. "The captain wants to see me?"

Tris continued smiling. "Yes, he does. Please come with me."

Peter's last interaction with Captain Nelson had resulted in a flogging. Since then, Peter had made a concerted effort to avoid the man at all costs preferring to work directly with the mates, particularly Tris. Nervously Peter followed Tris down the length of the boat to the stern where they were met by the captain, the mates, and a number of the crew. Captain Nelson greeted him warmly by name, and Peter partially relaxed.

All were quiet as the captain spoke, "Starbuck, you are here to be celebrated as a whaleman."

The men cheered, and all smiled at Peter, who stood confused and not understanding the milestone celebration that was occurring.

The captain continued, "As our tradition holds, when a greenhand on a whaling ship crosses the Horn from west to east, then he has earned the honor to be called a whaler. He will no longer be known or referred to as a greenhand." He turned to the crew. "Men."

The crew had filled a couple of buckets with seawater. One represented the water of the Atlantic, the other from the Pacific. Two of the men from his whaleboat, John and Ichabod, grabbed the wooden buckets and proceeded to pour them over the head of the unsuspecting Peter, drenching him in the cold water.

The captain called out, "Three cheers for this whaleman!"

The crowd replied, "Hoozah!... Hoozah!... Hoozah!"

I'm a whaleman? Holy crap.

The captain reached out to shake his hand. "Well done, Starbuck. I had my concerns about you after your accident, but you've proven yourself more than worthy time and time again."

"Thank you, sir," replied Peter.

The captain smiled and walked back to his stateroom to check the map and their progress home.

The mates and the crew surrounded Peter, slapping him on his back and offering words of congratulations. For the first time in his life, he felt that he was part of a team. Part of something far bigger than himself. He wasn't the lone man on top of the organizational chart, the CEO telling everyone what to do. He was just a cog in the wheel of this whaleship, part of the crew that did dangerous, exciting, and amazing things in their pursuit of oil. And even more surprising, he found that he liked being part of the team, preferred it in fact, to that of the sole leader.

As the praise rained down, Peter couldn't help but smile with satisfaction, pride, and a sense of belonging. He looked around at the assembled men and marveled at what he had been through with them and what they had taught him about himself. He realized that he had probably learned more about life and leadership from these men in the last few weeks than he had in his two years at business school and all of his experience in the working world.

The men slowly drifted away, all but Tris, who remained, smiling at Peter.

"Congratulations."

"Thank you," Peter said warmly. "Thank you for being such a great friend and helping me through some challenging times."

"Of course. And I look forward to many more times together! We make a great team, and I think we could even have our own whaleship someday. Think of the money we could make!"

Own a whaleship? The thought made Peter feel sad. All that time away from families and loved ones. All of the death and destruction to those beautiful animals. All that sacrifice, all that loss, and for what? So machines could be lubricated, and houses lit at night? And was Shimmo really any different? Churning out plastic bottles and containers by the millions so people could take their food and drink wherever they wanted? *There has to be a better way*, he thought.

"Why so sad?" asked Tris.

Peter replied, "Oh, I'm sorry. I was just thinking of home."

Tris but his arm around Peter's shoulders. "We will be there soon, my friend! But for now, let's celebrate. The captain has allowed us to open another cask of rum, and I don't have a watch until tomorrow. So let's enjoy some drink tonight!"

Peter looked at his friend and smiled. There had been a void in his life since Jack's death so many years ago. A void that was far more pronounced and painful than he realized. He had tried to fill that empty chasm by working like a madman, hoping that wealth and success could overcome the sense of loss. But he had also insulated himself from others, even Charlotte, keeping them at arm's length and not letting them into his heart.

In just the span of a few weeks, Tris had filled that void left empty for over twenty years. And filled it to overflowing.

"Let's go get some rum!" said Peter, and clamped an arm around his friend's shoulder.

* * *

As the Paragon continued sailing north for Nantucket, a squall line was moving westward off the coast of Africa and out into the Atlantic ocean. Many times these storms fall apart, but this one held together as it traveled, gaining strength from the warm water and humid air. It continued westward riding on the African jetstream building in size and power. A hurricane was being born.

CHAPTER TWENTY-ONE

The winds and weather continued to be favorable, allowing the Paragon to make substantial progress homeward. A day after rounding the Horn, the winds shifted to the south-southwest, permitting Captain Nelson to steer a nearly direct course north. And the winds speeds remained moderate, enabling the Paragon to average almost two hundred and fifty miles a day.

Initially, Peter monitored their progress constantly through Tris, asking him multiple times during the day how they were progressing. Tris would patiently update him with each query, but Peter could sense the patience running out. He felt like he was the little kid in the back of the car that was always asking, "Are we there yet?" and Tris was the parent in the front seat tired of the nagging. For the sake of his friendship, he decided he'd only inquire once a day, usually at sunset.

He tried to stay busy to ease the boredom, but there was only so much to do on a whaling ship that wasn't actively whaling. He manned his daily watches, helped in ship repairs, learned to splice rope, and even tried his hand at scrimshandering. Thomas had patiently sat with him and explained the basics of the art form and how to effectively etch the tooth to create an image. Despite the training, the best that Peter had been able to do was to depict a crude stick figure on a poorly rendered ship. It was, he thought, a sad end to a sperm whale tooth, and he tossed the ruined bone overboard in frustration.

Much of his free time was spent socializing with the rest of the crew, especially the blacksmith, the cooper, and the carpenter. Peter had always thought of himself as handy and had completed some simple projects at Fernweh - building a trellis for the climbing roses and some shelving in the library. The confidence in his abilities quickly waned when he saw the skilled trades at work on the Paragon and their ability to create something from nothing, such as a barrel, a harpoon or a spar, all in the confines of the ship and without access to a local hardware store or lumberyard.

Peter most enjoyed his time with the carpenter, Zaccheus Folger. Known as Zack on the ship, the native Nantucketer took pity on Peter and his limited skills and showed him the basics of his trade. Together they had repaired a whaleboat, refashioned deck planking by the wheelhouse, and even crafted a new spar for the mainmast.

Try as he might, though, Peter couldn't fill every waking hour with activities which left him a lot of free time to think and wonder what waited for him ahead in the Nantucket of 1828 and how those he had left behind were faring in his absence. By his reckoning, he had been gone now over a month and imagined the worst for his family. *Do they think I'm dead? Did they find my body in the surf at Great Point? Is anyone even looking for me?* These thoughts regularly assailed his idle mind, and the lack of understanding of his situation deeply frustrated him. How exactly had he traveled back in time, and what, if anything, had remained of him back home? His thoughts also occasionally drifted to that of Shimmo Plastics and how the company was doing without him. Like most CEOs, Peter thought the company would be lost without him and drift aimlessly without his leadership. *Who was making the decisions? Who was watching the financials? How did his employees react to his disappearance? Was there grief or were there celebrations?*

Peter did his best to push these thoughts out of his mind, knowing there was nothing he could do about them now. He suspected that the answers to all these questions lay ahead.

"Starbuck!" shouted Tris, walking towards him from the stern, his smile wide and his green eyes sparkling in the late afternoon sunshine.

"Tris," said Peter. "How are you?"

"I'm fine," he replied. "And I'll save you the trouble of asking, we've made over 200 miles today!"

Peter smiled sheepishly, "That's great. Thanks for the update."

"It is good progress. At this rate, we should make Nantucket before October is out."

Charlotte's favorite time on the island.

"Are you okay?" asked Tris.

Peter looked at him with watery eyes, "Yes, I'm okay, just feeling a little sad all of a sudden."

Tris placed a hand on his friend's shoulder. "I'm sorry. Anything you want to talk about?"

Peter paused, wondering what Tris would think of him if he shared the real story. That he has traveled back in time. That he has a wife and family nearly two centuries in the future. That if he were in his Gulfstream, he could be landing on Nantucket in a matter of hours. Instead, he looked at Tris kindly and said, "Thanks, but I'm okay."

"Well, I'm here if you need to," said Tris. "And it's time for the crossing celebration. I'd like you to join us."

"The crossing celebration?" Peter asked.

"Crossing the equator, Starbuck! It's a tradition that we honor to give a word of thanks to God for a good voyage and our safety."

Peter looked toward the stern and saw the crew gathering near the mizzen mast. "Oh, okay."

Tris and Peter joined the rest of the mates and the crew and gathered around Captain Nelson. The men bowed their heads as the master, a Bible in his right hand, said a prayer of thanks for their success and continued safety. When he finished, they all mumbled 'Amen' and dispersed across the ship.

* * *

As the men returned to their duties, a thousand miles to the northeast, the squall line had developed into a tropical storm and was moving over warmer water. It had become a convective engine, sucking in the warm moist air and propelling it upward where it condensed and released heat and energy. The lowering pressure at the base of the storm sucked in more warm, moist air creating a feedback loop that quickly strengthened the storm. Within hours an eye had formed, and the entire powerhouse of clouds and thunderstorms was moving northwestward rapidly and directly into the path of the Paragon.

* * *

Two weeks passed uneventfully. They had encountered a gale shortly after crossing the equator, but the winds were not even strong enough to force the captain to reduce sail. Instead, he leveraged the stronger winds to drive their speeds ever higher and, at one point, exceeding over three hundred miles in a single day. The mood aboard among the crew remained positive, almost celebratory, as their voyage continued to be blessed. They had a full hold of oil and were going to dock in Nantucket days or weeks earlier than they had initially thought when they had left the whaling grounds. The crew looked forward to time back at home with pockets full of money.

It was a sunny, mid-October day just before noon. Peter had been working with the carpenter, Zack, since breakfast, and they were at the bow of the boat addressing some damage to the fo'c's'le companionway. It was a fairly minor repair that Peter could handle by himself and was happy to show the ship's carpenter how far his skills had progressed under his tutelage. He was just hammering in the last few nails to a trim piece when he heard Zack exclaim, "Oh my god."

"What is it?" asked Peter, setting the final nail. He lowered his hammer and looked at Zack. Zack's eyes were focused over the bow at something in the distance.

"Look for yourself," replied Zach with a tinge of fear in his voice.

"What?" Peter turned and looked out over the bow. While there was blue sky and fair weather over the Paragon, on the horizon stood the black smudge of a massive and powerful storm. He felt the warmth of adrenaline course through his body. "What the hell is that?" he asked, alarmed.

"That my friend looks to be a hurricane," Zach said seriously. "We need to finish this up as I'm sure the captain will have orders for us."

Peter nodded and nervously cleaned-up his work, gathered the tools, and took them to the storeroom. With everything put away, he went to find out what was going on and what they were going to do. Tris and the other mates were already meeting with Captain Nelson, and he didn't interrupt, waiting for the captain to dismiss the men before approaching Tris. It was all he could do not to tug at the man's sleeve.

"Tris, what's going on? Please tell me we're not going to sail into that," Peter said, pointing at the storm on the horizon.

"Don't worry, the Paragon has been through many storms and will get through this one as well. The captain has given the mates orders to prepare the ship, and we will spend the rest of the day making her ready."

Peter was frightened but also knew he didn't have any other options. There was no way that he'd be able to talk Tris or Captain Nelson into waiting things out and let the storm pass. Steeling himself, he knew that keeping busy would help distract his mind from any dire thoughts. "What can I do?" he asked Tris.

"I need you to get a team together to scour the deck and stow away any loose items - tools, ropes, casks. Anything not essential needs to be stored below. I have another crew working to lash down the whaleboats and a third working below to secure the barrels and prevent the cargo from shifting. We will be ready," Tris finished confidently.

"You can count on me." Peter turned and went to round up the crew from his whaleboat; Thomas, John, and Ichabod, to help him execute their orders.

The crew worked tirelessly to prepare the Paragon, and by nightfall, nothing remained to be done. The Paragon and her men were as ready as they were ever going to be. Peter went to bed under a full moon and a sky full of stars. The black smudge on the horizon continued to get bigger, blotting out stars as the storm and the Paragon edged ever closer. The captain was estimating that the gale would hit sometime the following day, and the crew should be prepared to stay below and ride it out. Only those with essential duties were expected on deck. Peter lay in his bunk, listening to the sounds of waves lapping the hull and the soft creak of the hull timbers as the boat swayed gently. He was afraid of what lay ahead and whether or not they would survive the storm. Charlotte would never know what had happened to him. He would die alone.

He fell into a fitful sleep and once again dreamed of being with Charlotte and the kids. They were back at the beach although he couldn't sense where. He was playing with Sophie and Spencer near the water and building sandcastles. Charlotte was in her chair, reading, and smiling down at them. Everyone was happy and enjoying the day. As he was laying a quahog shell on one wall, Spencer jumped up and pointed over him. *Daddy. Look!* Peter turned to see a black wall approaching them quickly. The wall was made of storm clouds that were rolling and seething as if alive. The belly of the wall was filled with lightning, and the sound of thunder exploded over them. Spencer and Sophie both screamed, and he looked up to see Charlotte jump out of her chair in a panic. She was trying to run to them, but the wind was so strong it was blowing her backward. And then the wall hit. Sophie and Spencer's screams were immediately silenced, and his world went black. He felt as if he was swimming in mud, his arms and legs weighed down as he struggled to get to the surface. He called out for Charlotte and the kids but couldn't get his mouth to form the words. Despite his efforts, he felt himself falling deeper and deeper into the blackness. He tried to scream. Nothing.

A loud crash against the hull woke Peter from his dream. His heart was beating quickly, and he was sweating profusely. He sat up on his elbows and tried to get his bearings. *Thank god it was just a dream,* he thought relieved. As he started to calm down, he noticed that the ship was rocking more than usual. The groans and creaks from the hull were far more pronounced, and every so often, there was a tremendous thump from the bow, just below his bunk. Peter turned and tried not to think of his dream or the storm.

Instead, he thought of the happy memories he had with Charlotte and the kids. And of the happy times, he hoped would come.

Dawn came with a full gale lashing at the Paragon. Peter woke to the shriek of the rigging in the wind as if it were in pain. *This must be it*, he thought. His bunk was leaning heavily, and he could hear the men's sea chests sliding around the floor. He propped himself up and let his eyes adjust to the dim light. He surveyed the other bunks and was surprised to see a number of the men still asleep while others were awake but clearly feeling the effects of the storm. Two were seasick and vomiting while three others sat quietly in their bunks, mumbling prayers.

Peter could make out Ichabod across the way, looking back at him.

"Ichabod," Peter whispered loudly, "what's going on?"

"We're in the storm. And it's a bad one."

Peter felt a surge of adrenaline through his body, his fear ratcheting up. "Have you ever been in a storm like this?" he asked nervously.

Ichabod replied, "Only once, and we barely survived. The storm lasted for several days, and the ship took a horrendous beating. On the third day, the hull opened up in the forehold, and the water started coming in. We had to bail for our lives while the ship's carpenter and the mates were able to make repairs to stop the water."

Peter's eyes went wide, and Ichabod could see his fear even across the dim room. "It's okay," he said, "Master Nelson is the best captain I have ever sailed with."

"I hope so," replied Peter. "But if you don't mind, I need to go and see for myself."

"I wouldn't do that," said another voice. Peter looked down to see Thomas staring back at him. "The captain has given orders for us to stay below. Ichabod is right, Captain Nelson will see us through this safely. We just need to stay here and wait it out."

There were many traits that Peter could claim about himself, but patience and ignorance were not among them. He looked at Thomas, "I'm sorry, but I need to know what is going on." With that, he swung his legs over his bunk and jumped down to the floor, almost falling flat on his face as the Paragon was hit by another large wave. He caught himself and made his way over to the ladder. He grabbed the rung, looked over his shoulder to Thomas and Ichabod, and started to climb. The boat was rocking so heavily that Peter nearly fell off halfway up, his body dangling from one arm. Regaining his foothold, he was able to climb the last few rungs and make his way on deck. Clearing the hatch, he was met with the full force of the storm. He stepped out into the weather and started making his way to the stern. It was tough going as the deck was rising and falling beneath him; the wind was whipping his clothes, and a fierce rain assaulted his face.

He paused by the leeward side of the foremast, the massive piece of timber providing some shelter from the wind and the rain. He squinted through the deluge and looked out over the water. The ocean was in a rage. Seas were thirty feet high and breaking, the wind whipping foam across the crests. The water had the appearance of a fine sirloin that had been left in the sun to spoil, a green-gray color with white veining. Peter could see that the deck was awash in water, from the sea and the sky, and knew getting to the stern was going to be a challenge.

The Paragon was struggling through the waves and was flying very little canvas. Captain Nelson had ordered only the mainsail, the spanker off the mizzen, and a jib on the bow be raised, just enough to maintain steerage in the storm. Every thirty seconds or so, the bow of the Paragon would drop precipitously into a trough and then slam into the face of the oncoming wave, sending a shudder through the entire ship and huge sprays of water over the bow and down the deck. Peter felt his bowels loosen but would rather soil his clothes than try and use the head right now. He put it out of his mind and continued astern.

He paused again at the mainmast when an unusually large wave crashed over the windward rail, flooding the deck in several feet of water. Peter was knocked off his feet, carried across the deck and slammed into the leeward rail. Gasping for air and spitting out seawater, he struggled to his feet and stumbled back to the lee side of the mainmast. He was breathing heavily and soaked through but knew he had to get to the stern and check with Tris. Steeling himself, he took a deep breath and started back to the wheelhouse, leaning on the windward rail and struggling to maintain his balance on the pitching deck, slick with water.

Peter pulled himself along the rail, pausing to duck under it each time a wave would crash over the side of the Paragon. Exhausted and drenched, he finally made his way into the wheelhouse. Tris was at the wheel, his feet spread wide, and doing all he could to maintain his balance and keep the bow pointed into the waves. The wheelhouse on the Paragon was little more than a roof and sides and open to the bow and stern. In a storm of this magnitude, it provided minimal shelter for the crew from the wind and rain.

Peter braced himself against the wall of the wheelhouse and shouted to Tris, struggling to be heard above the roar of the wind and waves, "Do you need me to take the wheel?"

Tris was about to respond when a massive wave hit the Paragon broadside and rolled her slowly on her beam, nearly putting the masts in the water. That same wave sent thousands of gallons of water down the deck and directly into the wheelhouse. Tris lost his grip on the wheel and was carried across the deck and over the rail. Arms flailing, his hand fell on the davit for the stern whaleboat, and he held tight. The whaleboat was swept overboard and into the Atlantic. Tris was about to follow.

"Tris!" shouted Peter and scrambled across the deck. He could see his friend was hanging on for dear life and didn't have much time. One more wave would wash him into the ocean with no hope for rescue. Peter slid himself across the nearly vertical deck, locked his feet against the rail, and leaned forward. "Grab my other hand!"

Tris released his grip on the davit and grabbed Peter's outstretched hand. Fingers locked together, Peter used all his strength to pull Tris back onboard. They collapsed in a pile on the deck just as another wave came over the windward rail. The rush of water pinned them down.

Captain Nelson had come bursting out of his cabin when the first wave hit and immediately grabbed the unmanned wheel. He spun the helm, trying to get her bow pointed back into the waves.

Slowly the Paragon started to right herself and regain her trim. The captain had witnessed Tris's rescue and shouted at Peter, "Take him to my cabin!"

They struggled to their feet, and Peter half-led, half-carried Tris to the master's cabin. It was warm and dry, but the entire room was moving from side to side and up and down. He helped Tris sit down in a chair at the table. "Are you okay?" asked Peter.

Spitting out seawater, Tris said, "I'm okay, I think."

"Good," replied Peter. "But, I need to get back out and help Captain Nelson."

"Very well, but be careful. And thank you for saving my life. Again." Tris smiled faintly.

Peter smiled back. "Anything for you, Tris." He paused, putting his hand on Tris's shoulder, before turning and heading back on deck and into the storm.

* * *

The Paragon struggled for most of the day. Captain Nelson, Benjamin Gale and Peter all took turns at the wheel, working to keep the bow into the waves and minimizing the impacts to the ship as much as possible. It was mid-afternoon when Peter realized that the sky had brightened, and he could see shadows across the deck. He looked up to a pure blue sky and realized they were in the eye.

"Captain."

"Yes, Starbuck." replied the Master.

"I believe we're in the eye of the hurricane. I'd recommend that we quickly survey the ship and assess any damage before the eyewall approaches," he paused, "in case any immediate repairs are needed."

Captain Nelson looked at Peter with admiration at the man's resilience. "Very well. Perhaps Mr. Coffin will have recovered sufficiently to assist you."

Peter smiled and went down to the captain's cabin. Tris had made his way to the couch and looked as if he had just woken from a nap.

"How are you?" asked Peter.

Tris sat up on the couch and rubbed his eyes. "I'm fine now. All that seawater I ingested made me feel quite ill, but that has passed."

"Excellent," replied Peter. "We're in a lull in the storm, and the captain has asked us to gather the crew and assess any damage to the ship. Are you up for it?"

Tris stood up. "Absolutely!"

Peter smiled at his friend. "Very well, you gather the mates, and I'll get the crew from the fo'c's'le. We will scour the holds and the hull. I suggest you focus on the rigging and the deck."

Tris smiled at Peter. "Now which one of us is the mate, and which one of us was just a greenhand?"

Peter blushed. "Sorry, I didn't mean to overstep."

Tris slapped Peter's back and laughed. "Not at all, not at all! I think you could even captain this ship if we needed you to!"

Exiting the cabin, they separated to complete their plan. Tris went below to gather the mates and the carpenter while Peter went forward and rustled the crew from their bunks in the bow. They completed their assessment and were back at the captain's table in under an hour. Captain Nelson, Tris, and the first mate, Gale, sat in chairs at the table. The other mate, George Henry, was handling the wheel. Peter stood, leaning against the wall, trying to maintain his balance. Despite the lull, the waves were still significant, and the ship continued to roll and pitch heavily.

Captain Nelson looked at Tris and said, "What is your assessment?"

"Sir, we have lost all but one of the whaleboats. The main mast has a significant crack at the base and runs about ten feet up from the deck. The sails are torn, and we do have some tangled rigging as well as two spars missing from the foremast and one on the mainmast. Only the mizzen is in good shape," Tris finished.

The captain stared down at the table, absorbing the news. He looked up and turned his attention to the ship's carpenter. "Zaccheus, what is your assessment on the mast?"

"It's quite serious, sir. I've asked the blacksmith to fashion some hoops that we can use to reinforce the base. Unfortunately, he will need to wait until the seas settle before he can light the forge."

"Hmm," said the Master. He turned to the first mate. "Mr. Gale, I'd suggest we lower the canvas on the mainmast to reduce the stress. Can we add additional sail on the mizzen or foremast to compensate? We need to maintain sufficient speed for steerage."

Gale replied. "Yes, captain. I will add a topsail to the mizzen."

"Excellent," replied the captain. He turned to Peter. "And you, Starbuck? How are things below?"

Peter replied, "Sir. We're in good shape overall. We had some shifting of barrels in the lower main hold, but the crew has added additional ropes to secure them fully. As for the hull, it appears to be sound and in good shape. No damage was visible."

"Very good," replied the captain. He looked around the table. "Men, the worst of the storm is ahead of us, and nightfall is fast approaching. We will be facing the most dangerous part of the hurricane in the black of night," he paused. "May God watch over us."

The men dispersed, and Peter started walking toward the door.

"Starbuck," said the captain.

Peter stopped and turned. "Yes, sir?"

"I'd like you to stay here with me," said the captain. "I may need your help before the night is out."

Peter was taken aback. "Of course, sir. I'm at your service."

The captain smiled and nodded.

Outside, the eyewall was approaching, and with it, the most violent quadrant of the storm. The sun began to set just as it crossed the Paragon.

CHAPTER TWENTY-TWO

Peter had never been more terrified in his life. The Paragon entered the strongest part of the storm in complete and total darkness. Robbed of any visual cues, it was all Peter could do to not imagine the worst; towering waves that would hit and sink the boat, being pushed onto a rocky coastline where they would break up, or that he was going to be swept off the deck and into the water to drown and die alone. He pushed those fears from his mind and tried to focus on the job at hand. Captain Nelson had requested his presence, and he directed his energies into helping out the master as best as he could.

Initially, one of his responsibilities had been to keep the candle lit above the compass. It was meager light but enough for the master to see their heading and adjust as needed. But the rain and wind had other ideas, constantly snuffing the candle and pitching them back into darkness in the wheelhouse. Peter did his best, but eventually, everything was too wet to even try. The only light in their vicinity was a soft glow from the skylight of the captain's cabin. Strangely, it made Peter think of Christmas.

"I'm sorry, captain," Peter shouted over the roar of wind and waves. "I can't keep it lit, it's too wet to take the flame."

The captain shouted back, "I can manage without the compass."

"But how will you know the heading?"

"I can feel it," the captain replied. "The pitch of the deck, the way the ship labors, the vibrations through the hull, the sound of the wind in the rigging..." the captain's voice trailed away, muffled by the roar of a breaking wave.

Ichabod had been right about the captain. He was entirely in control of the ship and was steering her masterfully through the storm even though he couldn't see a thing. Peter didn't sense any fear from the man, only a steeled resolve and determination to see them through. This man is a true leader, thought Peter. What a CEO I could be if I only had a fraction of his composure.

The rise of the moon had helped bring some relief from the darkness. Nearly full, it penetrated the storm clouds sufficiently to allow Peter to discern basic shapes and give him some idea of what was going on around him as if seeing through a dense fog. He could just make out the frame of the captain at the wheel, the rise of the mizzen mast, the galley hatch, and a seething gray mass of ocean.

He felt a body saddle up next to him and could just make out the face of his good friend. "How are we doing?" shouted Tris, struggling to be heard above the roar of the wind.

Before Peter could even answer, a huge wave hit the boat, forcing her over and nearly putting her masts in the water. Peter lost his grip on the frame and fell into Tris, slamming both men into the other side of the wheelhouse. Captain Nelson spun the wheel, using the turn to try and right the ship. As the Paragon started to recover, they heard a tremendous crack and suddenly felt the ship slow and veer further to port, putting her nearly beam-to in the high seas.

"I think we have lost the mainmast!" shouted the captain.

Peter and Tris scrambled to their feet and made their way back to the wheel. "What?" Tris shouted to the captain.

"We've lost the mainmast! The helm is not responding, it must be in the water. We need to clear the decks if we're to survive!"

Tris nodded at the captain. "We will take care of it." He turned to Peter, "Let's go!"

Together, Tris and Peter stumbled up the deck, slowly making their way forward. The ship was rolling violently now from side to side making it very difficult to even stand up, let alone walk on deck. Her beam nearly to the waves, she was getting battered and in danger of being rolled over. If that were to happen, the water would flood her hold and send her to the depths in a matter of minutes. With all but one of the whaleboats gone and the immense waves around them, there would be no hope of survival for the crew.

Tris knew the urgency and pulled Peter forward. They reached the mainmast only to find that it had snapped off just a few feet above the deck and was now laying in the water on the port side, held fast to the Paragon by all of the rigging. The mast acted like an anchor, slowing the Paragon to a crawl and pulling her further to leeward. They had to clear the wreckage, or the ship would be destroyed.

"Starbuck!" shouted Tris. "We need to cut the rigging and free the mast. One of us must go below to the stores and get a hatchet or a knife."

Peter, his hair plastered to his head and water streaming down his face, looked at his friend, "I'll go. I know exactly where they are."

Tris nodded. Peter left, and knowing the main hatch was battened down, he made his way to the galley hatch near the stern. He pounded on the hatch until it opened and Gale's face appeared. "What is it?" he yelled.

Peter shouted, "We've lost the mainmast and need to cut it free. Get me a hatchet or a knife!"

The hatch closed, and the mate disappeared. *What? Has that bastard wimped out on us? He was happy to flog my ass, but now when we need him most, he bails?* Just as he was about to pound on the hatch again, it opened fully, and Gale climbed out, a hatchet in one hand and a knife in his belt. He held out another knife to Peter.

Relieved, Peter led Gale back to the mainmast, and they started cutting. Tris was feeling around for any ropes they may have missed when a huge wave crashed over the side and knocked all three of them off their feet and slammed them into the rail. The water had pushed Tris on top of Peter and the two lay in a splayed pile of arms and legs. "Are you okay?" asked Peter.

Tris grumbled something, but Peter couldn't understand what. He reached up to Tris and could feel a gash in his head, his hand coming back dark with blood. He wriggled out from under Tris and knelt beside him for a closer look.

"What is it?" shouted Gale.

"He's been badly injured. I think he hit his head on the rail!" shouted Peter. "We need to get him below!"

"Not yet!" screamed Gale, the roar of wind and waves nearly drowning out his words. "We need to clear the mast. And now!"

Peter nodded and leaned Tris against the rail. He lowered his head and shouted into his ear. "I'll be right back."

Peter joined Gale, and the two cut the remaining ropes. Just as they worked through the final one, another wave flooded over the deck pinning both of them against the rail in a heap of rigging. The mass of water spilled over the leeward side sweeping the remainder of the mast and rigging off the deck and into the Atlantic. Gale, his feet wrapped up in the tangled web of rope, was swept off the deck right behind it. Peter, rubbing his eyes against the saltwater, could just make out the splintered end of the mast as it disappeared into the inky blackness. "Yeah!" Peter shouted and looked for Gale to celebrate but the mate wasn't to be seen. Peter looked about frantically and shouted the mate's name several times. And then he saw Tris.

The wave had slammed into Tris and pinned him between the rail and the deck. His face was flat to the floor, and he wasn't moving. Peter rushed to him and rolled him over.

"Tris, Tris," he shouted, slapping his face. Tris grumbled incoherently.

Peter struggled up and spread his feet. He grabbed Tris under the arms and began to pull him to the stern to the galley hatch. He could only manage a few feet before another wave would hit the ship and slam them to the deck. Each time he'd struggle back to his feet, grab Tris and try to get as far as possible before the next wave hit. Finally, they made the hatch, and Peter banged on it with his boot. Zack opened the hatch and nervously looked up, the rain and seawater cascading down onto his face. Peter leaned Tris forward and dropped him headfirst into the opening, holding his lower body to prevent him from falling.

"Take him to the captain's cabin!" shouted Peter.

Zach nodded and wrapped his arms around Tris's chest and pulled him down the ladder. With Tris taken care of, he turned and headed back to the wheelhouse to inform the captain.

Captain Nelson had been fighting the wheel for hours. He was exhausted. Peter came up next to him. "We're free of the mast, sir!"

"Very good," replied the captain.

"But we lost Gale, sir. I think his feet tangled in the ropes, and he was swept over the rail with the mast."

The captain turned to Peter, his eyes wide. "I'm sorry, sir," said Peter. "There was nothing we could do."

Peter paused, giving the captain time to absorb the news. Then he continued, "And Tris took a blow to the head. He has a large gash on his scalp and is bleeding badly. I had him taken to your cabin."

He looked at Peter. "Take the wheel. I'll see to Mr. Coffin. Keep the bow pointed as close to the wind as she will manage."

Peter nodded to the captain and took the wheel. He spread his feet wide for balance and squinted through the rain and wind to find a path through the raging ocean. The wind was still roaring, but the screams of the rigging seemed to be diminishing. Soon he noticed that the sky was starting to lighten, and dark shapes emerged into greater detail. It was almost dawn.

With the coming light, Peter could see that the worst of the storm was behind them. The wind gusts had dropped significantly, and the rain reduced to just a drizzle. The waves were still high, and the ship continued to pound into them, but the larger waves were fewer and farther between.

We are going to make it, thought Peter, and he began to cry. His mind turned to Charlotte and the kids, the night of terror that he experienced, the loss of Gale, and the injury to Tris. The tears flowed. I have made it through that hell, and I will make it home. I will make it back to Charlotte and the kids if it's the last thing I do.

He heard the hatch slam and saw Captain Nelson approaching, weaving across the deck as if drunk as the ship continued to pitch. Peter quickly wiped his eyes and looked at the captain. "How is Tris?" he asked.

"He has a nasty gash across his scalp, but I was able to stop the bleeding and get a few stitches in. He's resting now, and I think he will be okay."

Peter let out a sigh of relief. It was all he could do to not start crying again.

* * *

By the afternoon, the Paragon was once again sailing under blue skies and a light wind. The seas remained choppy with large swells, but the waves were no longer breaking, and the danger to the ship had passed. From the side, the Paragon looked like the loser in a bar fight. There was a large gap amidships from the loss of the mainmast, and her davits were empty, the last remaining whaleboat had been lost overnight.

Captain Nelson gathered the mates and the crew at the stump of the mainmast. Most of the men looked like they had been to hell and back, their eyes bloodshot and their faces pale. Many had been violently seasick and spent the night vomiting and wallowing in their own pity. Tris stood tall next to the captain, his head bandaged, and with a black eye. The captain surveyed the men before speaking. "We lost one of our own last night, Mr. Benjamin Gale. He was a fine man who died while trying to save this ship and his fellow crewmen. Remember his soul in your prayers and keep his memory close to your hearts." The men bowed their heads for a moment of silence. Waves lapped at the hull, and the call of gulls could be heard in the distance.

The captain paused, letting the men alone with their thoughts. When all eyes were back on him, he continued, "And because of his outstanding bravery and leadership in the face of tremendous challenges, I hereby promote Mr. Starbuck to third mate."

All faces turned to Peter, and the men cheered. News of his heroics during the night had spread through the ship like wildfire. The man once flogged for insolence and thought lazy by the crew had likely saved the ship and everyone aboard her. Peter was shocked at the recognition and the unexpected promotion. More unexpectedly, he felt strangely whole and proud of who he had become on the Paragon. I am a whaleman, he thought. And an officer on this ship.

The captain waited until the cheers subsided before continuing. "Now, men. We must again assess this ship and identify any repairs needed for us to get home. Of most importance is rigging a new mainmast. Mr. Folger, what are our options?"

The carpenter replied, "As you know, we don't have a spare, sir, but I believe we can fabricate something that will hold sail. If you agree, I'd like to request that Mr. Starbuck work with me."

The captain smiled and looked at his new mate. "Of course."

* * *

Peter and Zack started immediately to rig a fix for the mainmast. Without that canvas, the Paragon would be significantly slower and make less than a hundred or so miles a day. At that rate, it would take them at least four more weeks to make port in Nantucket, assuming, of course, that they didn't run into another storm.

"Do we have any wood below that we could use?" asked Peter.

"Nothing suitable for a mainmast," replied Zack. "Only sufficient to make replacement spars."

An idea started to form in Peter's head. "How many spars could we make?"

Zack thought about it and did some quick mental calculations. "Probably four to five."

"What if we made as many spars as possible and then lashed them together lengthwise," said Peter.

The carpenter shook his head. "They would not be strong enough."

"Yes, but what if," said Peter, "we used rope to secure the top and middle of our new mast to the foremast and the mizzen?" He took a piece of charcoal and drew out his plan on a flat piece of wood. He finished and held it up for Zack to see. "Like this."

Zack examined the drawing, and his eyes lit up with understanding. "I do think that might work. It will be ugly and won't hold as much canvas as the mainmast. But I think we will be able to fly enough sail to improve our speed." He looked at Peter. "Well done. Let's review our plan with the captain and then get to work."

Captain Nelson was once again impressed with his new mate and approved the idea immediately, freeing Peter and Zack to get to work. Enlisting help from the crew, they had the new spars created and fastened together by the end of the day and laid out on the deck. The next morning they proceeded with stepping their new mast into place. They started by sawing the splintered ends off the stump of the old mainmast before boring a hole suitably wide and deep to accept the new mast. Using a thick rope, they connected the top of the new mast to the windless via pulleys.

The crew turned the winch, and the top of the new mast rose off the deck. It was spindly and bending at each joint but slowly made its way up. Four crew held guide ropes, two on each side, to keep it straight. They were nearing the top when the bottom end of the mast slipped into the hole in the base with a loud thump. The new mast was fully vertical seconds later. Those watching cheered.

Ichabod grabbed the end of the rope from the winch and made his way up the rigging to the foremast. When he was parallel to the top of the new mast, he pulled the rope tight and secured it around the large timber of the foremast. John Thain did the same but connected the end of the line to the mizzen mast at the stern. Lastly, the four guide ropes were secured, two on each side. The rigging in place, the new mast was remarkably stiff and secure.

Captain Nelson appeared and inspected the work. He was visibly pleased, a smile crossing his weathered face. "Well done, men!" he exclaimed. "Now let's hang some sail!"

The men quickly obliged and pulled on the ropes to raise a large piece of canvas, which was once the main topsail but turned vertically. The sail reached the top, and Peter pulled the sail tight below and tied it off. There was a whump as the sail filled, and the Paragon accelerated noticeably. The men cheered and congratulated Peter and Zack on their solution. Thanks to Peter's innovative idea and their hard work, they would likely be home in Nantucket by the end of the month.

* * *

The last day of October 1828, was unusually warm. The Paragon was sailing under a clear blue sky with a fresh breeze.

Nantucket was clearly visible off the bow, and the mood on the ship was celebratory. They would be in port before the day was out, hugging those they loved, and hearing what had happened in their world over the last three years.

Tris and Peter were on the windward rail, just aft of the bow, and soaking in the sight in front of them. Already Peter could just make out the mouth of the harbor entrance. He turned to Tris, "Happy to be home?"

Tris was beaming. "Of course! I can't wait to see Abigail and ask for her hand. It's been a long voyage."

"How do you do it?" asked Peter.

"Do what?"

"Put your life on hold for three years."

Tris looked pensive for a moment. "I don't know. It's just the way things have always been. I sailed my first voyage as a cabin boy when I was fourteen, and honestly, I don't know any differently."

"Is it worth it?"

Tris looked at him, quizzically, "Worth what?"

Peter stared back at his friend intently. "Whaling. Is three years of your life at sea hunting whales worth the money that you will earn on this voyage? Three years away from Nantucket, from Abigail, from the people you love. Is it worth it?"

Tris looked out across the water at Nantucket, closer now. He remained silent.

"Or do you think when you marry Abigail, you may give up this life? Settle down, have a family," said Peter. "Give up the risk, the danger. I'm hoping you will say yes."

"I wish I could. But there is no job on this island that will pay as well. If I want to take care of Abigail, and maybe a family, then I need to go whaling. It's the only way for me to earn enough to support her."

Peter turned and looked back at Nantucket. Had he not made that same decision with Shimmo Plastics? And was it the only way?

And was anything or anybody waiting for him here?

Sadly, he put his arm over Tris's shoulders and looked out over the water. "Welcome home, Tris."

CHAPTER TWENTY-THREE

The sun was just setting as the Paragon entered Nantucket harbor. All aboard agreed it was a spectacular sunset with the western sky alight in purples, reds, and oranges. A pale last quarter moon was rising to the east, her ghostly white body a vivid counterpoint to the frenzy of color in the opposing sky. Not to be outdone, the land was ablaze, the maples bursting in reds, yellows, and oranges. It was a show of natural fireworks celebrating her safe return.

All were on deck, joyful and happy to be safely home, made more so by the beautiful day, and her late arrival in the season. It would take weeks to offload her cargo and several more to refit the mainmast and address the other needed repairs from the storm damage. With winter fast approaching, her next voyage would likely wait until March, the thought of which brought added celebrations for the men. Home for over four months.

Traveling down the channel, the Paragon passed just to the west of Black Flats, a very shallow area of water just outside the harbor, rounded Brant Point, and proceeded to the North Wharf. Captain Nelson ordered all canvas lowered, and she gracefully eased up the dock. The crew finished tying her off just after 7:00 p.m. The Paragon was, at last, home.

She had departed Nantucket the morning of June 25th, 1825, and had been at sea for one thousand, two hundred and twenty-six days. Collectively, the twenty-eight men of the Paragon who had survived the voyage had spent ninety-five years - nearly a century - of their lives at sea. And in that time, she had traveled over thirty thousand miles, killed and processed over fifty whales, encountered a hurricane and lost two men, both buried at sea. She had also picked-up a traveler, Peter Bois, who stood nervously at the top of the gangplank, Tris by his side.

"Are you okay?" asked Tris.

Peter turned to him. "Not really. I don't remember who, if anyone, is waiting here for me or even where to go."

"I was afraid of that," said Tris. "But, I can probably help you remember a few things."

"Like what?"

"This is going to be hard to hear, but you have no family left on the island. Your parents passed away the year before we set sail on this voyage. And your two brothers are out to sea. Benjamin is on the Washington, and Hadwin is on the Plough Boy."

Tris could see the pain in his friend's eyes. "I'm sorry to have to remind you of this."

"I know, and I appreciate it. Do I have any friends, like you here?" asked Peter expectedly. "Or a woman?"

Tris smiled wanly. "You were fond of Eliza Swain, but she told you she would never marry a whaler and accepted the hand of Thomas Folger. He's a lawyer."

"And friends?"

Tris shook his head. "You've never been one for close friends, just acquaintances. And I'm sure you'll see many of them in the coming weeks."

Peter stared over the wharf and to the town beyond. "So I'm alone?"

"Of course not! You will always be my friend, Peter Starbuck. And I think you earned the respect of every man on this ship," he said, his arm sweeping the length of the Paragon. "Any one of them would be happy to call you a friend."

Peter smiled faintly.

"Where are you staying tonight?" asked Tris.

Peter looked at Tris. "I'm sure I could find lodging at an inn or boarding house."

"No. You need to come with me. We have plenty of room."

"Are you sure?"

"I wouldn't have it any other way. Besides, I know your memory is still shaky and I'm not sure I can trust you on your own," Tris replied and chuckled. "Besides I don't want to see you get in any trouble."

"Thank you."

"Of course. Are you ready?"

"I believe so." Tris and Peter descended the gangplank and onto the wharf. It was the first time they had been on solid ground in months.

* * *

Peter and Tris spent the evening celebrating their safe return and catching up. They walked from the Paragon to Tris's family home just off Center Street. Peter recognized the building from the 21st century, although, in that time, it was split between apartments on the second floor and retail spaces below. It was a classic Greek revival with the temple-like gable end facing the street. It's light gray clapboards were offset by white double-hung windows, eight over eight, and framed by black louvered shutters. Offset to the right of the facade, the front entry was flanked by two fluted columns that supported an elaborately trimmed porch roof. A brick walkway led through a gate in the white picket fence to five wide stone steps. The first floor of the house was nearly six feet above street level.

While they had been at sea, they did keep abreast of news and developments from Nantucket when they spoke with other whaling vessels. When the Paragon docked after her long voyage, the captain and the crew were pretty well aware of the state of the industry, price of whale oil, island politics, and other significant developments. But they had no idea about the nuances and changes in the daily life of their family and friends that had occurred in their three years at sea. Who had died, who had married, who had prospered, who had faltered, new homes and businesses, fires and bankruptcies, and the myriad of other components that make up our communal lives.

That evening the conversation had flowed as easily as the wine with a near-constant chatter of the news of the day and updates over the past few years. Tris's family welcomed Peter as one of their own and made him feel instantly comfortable. In addition to his mother and father, Tris's younger brother and sister were there, as was his older sister, Annabell. She was married to a whaleman who had departed Nantucket over two years before on the Independence. Hence, she, of course, was most interested in any news of his ship and her voyage, and any thread of information of his return on which she could cling.

The highlight of Peter's evening was meeting Abigail. Since Tris had first shared his fondness for her and his plans to wed, he had talked incessantly about her, his dreams, and the life he planned for them funded well by his career in whaling. Peter had found her lovely, charming, and intelligent and could see why Tris was so fond of her. He knew they would make a wonderful couple and secretly wished them a long life together.

The night ended far too soon, and Peter retired to an upstairs bedroom. It was small by his standards but clean, airy, and free of the stench of a dozen other men. He cracked a window to let in the crisp fall air, sat on the edge of the bed, and cried. Meeting and talking with Abigail brought all of his feelings about Charlotte to the surface and made his life feel farther away than ever before. Was he doomed to live in this time, or could he find his way home to her? *I just want to hold her in my arms*, thought Peter. *And tell her I love her with all of my heart and soul.*

He dried his eyes and curled up on the bed. Despite having a clean and comfortable bed for the first time since landing on the Paragon, Peter struggled to sleep. He was accustomed to the groans and creaks of the ship, the sound of waves on the hull, and constant rocking. The quiet and stillness made adjusting difficult. Gradually his body relaxed, and he fell into a deep sleep.

* * *

Peter woke to the sounds of birds chirping outside, and feelings of hope and happiness. He had dreamed of Charlotte and the kids again, and for the first time, it had been a happy dream. In this dream, Charlotte and Peter had been on the patio at Fernweh and watching the kids play on the lawn with someone's dog. It was a yellow lab, smiling and jumping for joy. Spencer and Sophie were taking turns throwing a tennis ball that the dog would eagerly chase down, return, and bark for more. He turned to Charlotte, and her face lit up as if seeing him for the first time in years. He felt her fingers slide into his and grip his hand.

Dressing, he was sad that his dream was over but feeling the warm afterglow. *We need to get a dog,* he thought. He descended to the kitchen and enjoyed the best breakfast he had had since leaving the twenty-first century; fresh eggs, coffee, ham, and bread still warm from the oven, a far cry from the hardtack and salt horse he had eaten on board. Tris joined him at the table, looking refreshed, content, and happy to be home.

"Morning!" he said.

"Good morning," replied Peter.

"Breakfast okay?"

Peter smiled widely, "The best I've had in months!"

Pleased, Tris replied, "Good to hear. You'll need your strength today. After breakfast, we need to head back to the ship and oversee the start of the unloading process. Captain Nelson will also be meeting this morning with the brokerage house to sell our cargo, so I expect we will know how greasy our voyage was by the end of the day."

Peter enjoyed another round of eggs and bread as Tris finished up his breakfast. Satisfied, they slid back their chairs from the table, walked through the front door and down the steps, out onto the brick sidewalk.

"What did you think of Abigail?" asked Tris.

"She is lovely. I'm sorry that I don't remember her from earlier, but I can certainly see why you're so fond of her."

Tris smiled, "I'm going to ask her tonight."

"That's wonderful! What are your plans?"

"We are going to dinner at Market Hall. And then I thought we would walk down Main Street to the harbor. She loves the sight of the ships on the water, and we have enjoyed many fine walks there together."

"Sounds lovely," said Peter.

"Yes, I think it will be. And if she says yes, we will need to celebrate!"

"I wouldn't miss that for the world!"

Tris smiled. "Isn't it wonderful to be alive right now?"

For you, maybe, thought Peter. *You have the woman you love.*

"It is," replied Peter, a hint of sadness in his voice.

* * *

The Paragon had indeed had a greasy voyage. In fact, the most lucrative she had enjoyed under the command of Captain Nelson. In total, her cargo of whale oil, sperm oil, whalebone, and a small amount of ambergris was sold for just over eighty thousand dollars. After deducting for expenses and repairs, the total profit for her voyage was just under seventy-five thousand dollars to be distributed among the owners of the Paragon, the captain, the mates, and finally, the crew.

This distribution was based on an individual's lay for the voyage, that is, a percentage of the total profits earned by the ship. The owners had the shortest lay, as would be expected for they assumed the greatest financial risk, and pocketed seventy percent of the profit. Captain Nelson received a little over six percent, earning him nearly five thousand dollars, a substantial sum in 1828, and why whaling was such an attractive pursuit for many men. Benjamin Gale, the first mate, earned just over three thousand dollars, which Captain Nelson directed to his widow, Judith.

Had the voyage been a typical one, Peter's lay, as a greenhand, would have been one half of one percent or four-hundred and thirty dollars, for over three years of his life at sea. But with his promotion to third mate, the captain had increased his lay to nearly two percent, in line with Tris's, which earned him over twelve hundred dollars.

For a twenty-first century billionaire, Peter was quite underwhelmed when told the news. *Twelve hundred dollars? Seriously? I make that in an hour back home.* But he kept those thoughts to himself as he could see that Tris was tremendously pleased. "This is by far the most I have ever earned!" exclaimed Tris. "And will allow me to buy a home for Abigail."

"I'm so happy for you. And exciting news to share with her tonight. Not that she needs another reason to marry you," said Peter teasingly, nudging Tris with his elbow.

Tris smiled. "It's a risk marrying a whaleman, but I hope she will see it can provide a good life for us."

Peter nodded and wondered if Charlotte, knowing what she knows now about him, would have said yes to him when he asked her back in 1999. Probably not.

"We need to get going," said Tris. "Otherwise I'm going to be late for Abigail."

They walked briskly back to the house, stopping only for Tris to pick some late-season purple aster flowers to give to Abigail. Tris hurried into the house, climbing the stairs by twos, to get ready for his evening. Peter went to the kitchen for some dinner, and a little while later was startled to see a stranger appear in the doorway. "Tris?"

"Do I look okay?" Tris stood in the doorway dressed in pressed woolen slacks, a white cotton shirt, a gray vest, and a long black coat tailored to fit his physique. A gray felt hat was in one hand and a pair of black leather gloves in the other.

"You look terrific!" said Peter. "Nervous?"

"I am. What if she refuses me?"

"She won't. Trust me. I saw how she looked at you last night. You two were made for each other."

"Wish me luck, then."

"Good luck!" said Peter, reaching out to embrace his friend. "And please come straight to my room and let me know how it goes, okay?"

"Done. And thank you for your encouragement," said Tris. He turned, the flowers in a bunch in his hand and left.

* * *

Several hours later, Peter was sound asleep in bed. Only his second night on shore, he had already grown used to having his own clean and quiet space. Not quite Fernweh but far, far better than the fo'c's'le on the Paragon.

He woke in the middle of the night, the bed shaking violently. Drowsy, his first thought was he was back in the hurricane aboard the ship. But as the haze lifted, he realized it was Tris, shaking him and the bed.

"Starbuck! Wake up!"

Peter opened his eyes and looked into the beaming face of his friend. "Tris?"

"She said yes!"

It took a minute for the words to settle in, but as they did, the smile on Peter's face spread wide. "Congratulations!" and reached up to hug his friend. "That's wonderful."

"Yes, it is. And we need to celebrate. Come join me for some rum!"

Peter got up and put on his clothes and joined Tris in the kitchen, where he had refreshed the fire in the hearth and opened a bottle of rum. Tris poured two glasses and handed one to Peter, who turned to him, glass raised, and said, "To Tris and Abigail! A long and healthy life together!" They clinked glasses and downed the spicy, dark liquid.

Tris refilled the glasses and raised his to Peter. "And to you, Starbuck. For your leadership on the Paragon, to your promotion, and to your friendship. May we grow old and wealthy together."

Peter smiled and clinked his glass to Tris's. He looked at the amber liquid, the flames from the fire dancing over the glass, and thought about home. *I want to grow old with Charlotte, wealthy or not.*

Peter put his glass down and reached for the nearly half-empty bottle. He refilled the two glasses, raised his and said, "To the Paragon, and all who sail on her. May her next voyage be safe and greasy."

"To the Paragon," said Tris. They clinked glasses and drank.

Peter wiped his mouth and looked at Tris. "Wow, this is great rum. Do you have any more of this?" asked Peter.

Tris replied, laughing heartily, "A whole case!"

"Hmm," said Peter, chuckling, "I think we may be in for a long night!"

CHAPTER TWENTY-FOUR

P eter and Tris celebrated well into the early hours and nearly finished off half the case of rum. As they drank, Tris shared more and more of his plans for Abigail and his future. He also floated the idea again of the two of them going in on the purchase of a whaleship.

"Think about the money we could make," said Tris. "The owners of the Paragon split over fifty thousand dollars for just this one voyage. I think we could make enough in a couple of voyages to allow us to retire and hire a captain to continue."

"Perhaps," replied Peter. "But do you really want to spend seven or eight years at sea, away from Abigail?"

"Well, no, not really. But I don't see another way to do it." He looked at Peter, "Promise me you'll at least think about it."

"I promise," replied Peter. "And I think we need to be getting to bed. The sky is lightening, and it will soon be dawn."

"Ugh. Very well."

"And please tell me that we don't need to be down at the ship today," asked Peter.

Tris chortled. "No, we are good. Sleep as late as you like. The day is ours."

Peter, heavily drunk, stood up quickly and nearly fell into the hearth. Regaining his balance, he looked at Tris with bloodshot eyes and slurring his words, "Excellent, then, I shall bid you goodnight, my friend."

Tris tried to stand up but lost his balance and collapsed back on the couch. "I think I will stay here."

"A wise idea." Peter turned and walked toward the stairs as if he were on the pitching deck of the Paragon during the hurricane. He weaved left, then right, nearly knocking over a side table, before he made it to the foot of the stairs. He climbed the stairs slowly, using his hands on the treads to stabilize himself. Slowly he made it to the top, walked into his room, and collapsed on his bed, fully dressed.

* * *

The day was nearing noon, and the sunlight streamed through the window, landing directly on Peter's face. He grumbled and pulled the sheets over his eyes to shield them. But the damage was done, he was awake and suffering from a terrific hangover and a throbbing headache. *I'm not sure I'll be able to find any Advil in 1828.* Slowly he raised up and swung his feet over the edge of the bed. His balance off, he stood and carefully started toward the stairs, fearful of a face plant on the wide chestnut floors.

He navigated the steps without falling and made it into the kitchen without incident. The room was empty, and a low fire burned in the hearth. Peter grabbed a couple of logs, freshened the fire, then half sat, half fell into a chair at the table. He crossed his arms on the table, cradled his head, and let out a long, low groan. He heard the floorboards creak and raised his head to see Tris shuffling his way into the kitchen. His eyes were bloodshot, his clothes wrinkled, and his hair stood nearly straight up. If he didn't feel so crappy, Peter probably would have laughed out loud at the sight.

"Morning," grumbled Tris.

"Morning," whispered Peter. "God, I feel awful. Do you have anything that could help this hangover?"

Tris shuffled over to the pantry. "Actually, I do." He reached down into a wooden crate and brought out a bottle of rum. He grabbed two mugs and sat at the table opposite Peter. Uncorking the bottle, he poured a generous amount into each and handed one to Peter. "Hair of the dog," he said and drank the rum.

"Hair of the dog," replied Peter and took a long swig.

Feeling a little better, Tris stood and said, "Let me make some coffee. That will also help."

"Please," said Peter.

Tris made the coffee, topping off the mugs, and found some day-old bread which he put on the table along with some butter. "I'm sorry we don't have any jam," he said.

Peter ripped a piece off the loaf and wolfed it down. "Quite alright. I just need something to soak up all that alcohol we drank last night," Peter said with a laugh and continued, "I'm so happy for you and Abigail. Are you going to see her today?"

"Yes, definitely. We need to start planning our wedding. Lots of decisions to make, including the big date. I'd like to do it before Christmas if we can so we can have a few months together before we sail again."

"A few months isn't very long," said Peter. "And then you'll be gone for a few years."

"I know it will be tough on us. But she's agreeable. And she's strong. With the money from this voyage, we will have plenty to settle down and keep her until my return." Tris nodded at the mug. "Are you ready for some more?"

"Coffee or rum?" asked Peter.

"Yes," replied Tris.

Peter smiled, "Sure."

Tris poured a generous amount of rum in each mug and then topped them off with coffee. He looked at Peter, "What about you? What do you think you'll do today?"

Peter thought for a minute. "I think I'm going to ride out to Siasconset."

Surprised, Tris replied, "Siasconset? Why on earth would you want to go way out there?"

Hiding his true intentions, Peter fabricated a story. "I'm kind of in the mood to explore. And I have some fond memories of a trip there as a child. I'd like to see it again."

"Very well. Enjoy your time."

* * *

After finishing another mug of rum and coffee, Peter dressed, left the house and walked toward Main Street. Tris had suggested it would be easy to find a horse and carriage there to take him to Siasconset. It was a relatively short walk, and he quickly located a carriage and driver at the base of Main Street, almost the exact spot where Peter would hire a taxi in the 21st century. The carriage was black with four, closely spaced large wooden wheels and seating for two, including the driver. It was pulled by a brown and white spotted horse who eyed Peter with curiosity. "Her name is Bea," said the driver, who was standing by her flank. He was older, with gray hair and a bushy beard, and dressed in all black.

Peter stroked her muzzle and looked at the driver. "Can you take me to Siasconset?"

The driver thought for a minute. "Sure. It will take us a couple of hours if that's acceptable."

"That's fine," replied Peter.

The driver placed a foot on the floor of the buggy and pulled himself up. "Climb on in."

Peter did and assumed the space next to the driver. It was cozy.

The driver, reins in his hands, clucked his tongue and gently slapped the horse's back. Bea started walking, and the buggy surged forward, the wooden frame softly creaking. He then tugged lightly at the left rein and guided the horse to turn left onto Washington Street. He looked over at Peter and held out his hand, "Caleb Lynch."

Peter shook his hand. "Peter Starbuck."

"Ah, you're a Starbuck? I know many of your family."

"I'm sure you do, there are quite a few of us on the island!" chuckled Peter.

Caleb smiled. "So, what do you do?"

"I just returned on the Paragon."

"Ah, I know the Paragon. Captain Nelson is the master, isn't he?"

"He is. And an outstanding captain at that."

"Hmm," said Caleb. "So tell me, why would a whaleman want to go to Siasconset? Especially on a chilly November day like this."

"I have family there," Peter lied.

Caleb acknowledged him with a grunt and guided Bea to turn onto Sconset Road, what Peter knew as Milestone Road. The road was about fifteen feet wide, a mixture of clay and sand with deep ruts in the surface, making for a bumpy ride. The driver remained silent, allowing Peter to take in the surroundings. He found it difficult to believe that just a few months ago - and nearly two hundred years in the future - he drove over this spot in the Range Rover on the way to dinner in town. And what an idiot he had been with Charlotte. All she had wanted from him was more of him, his time, and he got mad and impatient. *What a complete and total jerk I was to her*, thought Peter. *When I get back, things will be different*, he promised himself.

"Hmm," said Peter.

"What is it?" asked Caleb.

"Oh, I just noticed the stone marker there. I didn't realize they had put them in already."

"Already?" responded Caleb, a bit confused. "They installed those about five years ago to better time the horse races between Sconset and Town."

"Interesting," said Peter. "Well, if I'm reading that marker correctly, then it looks like we're about halfway there."

"Yes, you read that right. Where should I take you in Siasconset?"

"You can drop me off at the old well."

"The 'old' well?"

"Oh, sorry. I mean, the town pump."

Caleb eyed Peter suspiciously but remained silent. Bea's hooves clopped softly in the road.

A few minutes passed before Caleb spoke again, "I was a whaleman once."

"Really?" asked Peter.

"Yes," replied Caleb. "But, I only went on a single voyage."

"What happened?" asked Peter.

Caleb paused, gathering his thoughts, and then responded, "I had just married, and we were poor. I didn't have a trade and was just doing some odd jobs here and there. A friend encouraged me to sign on with a whaleship and that I could make pretty good money. So I did and was at sea for almost four years. It was a bad voyage from the start, the ship was caught in a couple of storms. We lost weeks making repairs, and even when we finally did get to the Pacific, we struggled to find any whales." Bea had started to slow, the driver clucked his tongue and slapped her back gently with the reins. The horse picked up her pace.

The driver continued, "We spent three Christmases in the Pacific, and in those three years of hunting, the hold was barely a third full. We made port at Valparaíso and a handful of the men, knowing that the voyage was going to be a bust, deserted the ship. We couldn't find replacements, so the captain decided to return to Nantucket."

Peter looked over at Caleb, but the driver wouldn't meet his eye. "When we finally made port back here, I learned that my wife had passed away from a fever. And my lay? It was about ten dollars. Ten dollars for four years of my life!" he said angrily. "That was the end of whaling for me. I hope you have done better."

"I'm sorry," said Peter. "That must have been horrible for you."

Caleb just grunted and nodded his head.

Without the familiar landmarks he was accustomed to seeing on Milestone Road, Peter was surprised to see that they had started to climb the long, shallow hill into Sconset. And unusual for him, he was nervous. What would he find waiting for him here?

Caleb deftly maneuvered Bea through the village and soon had pulled up at the small square with the town well. Peter stepped down and turned to Caleb. "Thank you, Caleb. And thank you for sharing your story with me." Peter handed Caleb payment along with a generous tip.

The driver took the money and looked Peter in the eyes and said, "May you find what you are looking for here." He clucked his tongue, and Bea pulled him away. Peter watched the back of the carriage briefly and then turned to survey the area.

He and Charlotte walked through here frequently, and he was surprised at how many of the cottages he recognized. The significant differences he noted were much more green space and very few trees. Instead of the cozy and quaint village he remembered, Siaconset of 1828 was more windswept, more precarious, as if it was struggling to maintain its foothold on the edge of the Atlantic ocean.

The fog had started to roll in, and with it, a chill in the air. Peter fastened his wool coat to his chin and started to walk. He made his way up the hill, not sure what to expect. If his memory was correct, the construction of Fernweh would be underway. At the top of the hill, he turned left down a narrow lane and continued until he reached what he thought to be his driveway. At least it would be after nearly two hundred years would pass. He paused, the butterflies in his stomach busier than ever.

Then he heard the telltale sounds of construction; men shouting orders, hammers hitting nails, and the whish-whish of lumber being sawn. Taking a deep breath, he walked down the dirt lane, his eyes down and shoulders hunched. When he reached a clearing, he stopped and locked up.

Fernweh.

But it wasn't the Fernweh he knew. It was little more than a stone foundation and the basic framing for the first floor. A lot more work remained before she'd even closely resemble the home he loved. But he could see the bones of her, and a warm rush flowed through him.

"Can I help you?"

Peter turned and looked into the eyes of a bear-like man, tall, broad, and with dark brown hair. He was wearing a wide-brimmed hat and carried a large wooden hammer in his hand.

"Oh, I've just been walking in Sconset and saw the construction, I thought I would take a look." Peter reached out his hand, "Peter Starbuck."

The man took his hand warily. "Joshua Woolley. I'm the builder here."

"It looks like it's going to be a lovely home. Is it for sale? I have a family friend who I think would be interested."

"I'm building this for a whaling captain. He is looking to escape town with his family during the summer. I'm quite certain that he would have no interest in selling."

"Hmm," said Peter, looking over Joshua's shoulder.

"What is it?" said Joshua.

"I see you haven't yet framed the kitchen off the back."

"Excuse me?"

"The kitchen, off the back. The bump-out has a distinct shape, almost circular."

Joshua's eyes went wide. "Who are you?"

"What do you mean?"

"That idea for the kitchen. I have only thought of that design. I have not put it to paper or shared it with anyone. How do you know about it?"

Peter stammered, unsure of how to respond. "Um, I don't know."

Joshua, eyes locked on Peter's, took a few steps back. "Are you a witch?"

"What? No! Of course not."

"Then you must be a traveler," said the builder, his voice trembling.

"A what?"

Joshua replied, his voice still shaky, "Nantucket is a diverse community. We welcome people from all places....and times."

A shock of adrenalin flushed through Peter, the warmth spreading up his chest and into his neck. "Times?"

"Yes," replied Joshua, his voice more confident. "You need to go and see a man named Isaiah."

"Isaiah?"

"Yes. He lives in a small cottage called The Shanty, near the bluff. It's old, uneven and covered in shingles." With that, Joshua turned and walked quickly away.

Peter, shocked by the man's response, took one last look at Fernweh being built, and then turned and walked back down the dirt lane. *All times. How did Joshua know I was from a different time?* Peter quickened his step. It was late afternoon, and the fog was getting thicker. For the first time since he landed on the Paragon, he felt a strange sense of hope. Could this Isaiah have any answers for him?

CHAPTER TWENTY-FIVE

Joshua's words still rang in his head. "Nantucket is a diverse community. We welcome people from all places....and times."

"All times?" Peter whispered to himself. Did that mean what he thought it meant? That maybe he wasn't the only person who had traveled back in time on Nantucket. Enough of them had at least for Joshua to be able to recognize him as one. And Isaiah? Who was he? Was he also a traveler, or was he a witch?

The sun was nearing the horizon, and the light was low and dull. The fog had gotten thick enough that Peter struggled to make out the outlines of cottages, and his woolen coat was heavy with the damp. He had made his way to the bluff and walked slowly down the street, looking for a small, uneven, and shingle covered cottage as described by him by Joshua.

Nearly every house fit that description, and Peter had to pause at each cottage to seek out the nameplate, which many owners cleverly placed in different parts of the front facade so as to be unique and different from the other houses on the street. Some were well worn, making the name difficult to decipher while others had old roses or vines covering many of the letters making it more of a child's spelling game.

The next cottage he approached didn't sport a straight line anywhere he could see. The roof peak wobbled as if the designer had been drunk when he laid out the design, and the walls were all leaning, some precariously so. The door was smack in the center and flanked by two small windows. Above the door, in a very logical place, stood the nameplate.

The Shanty

"This is it," Peter said softly to himself. "But can this man help me?"

He stepped through a well-worn gate in the picket fence and peered through the window on the left side. He could make out a small table and chair set just off from a large brick fireplace. Sconces on each side of the hearth held three candles apiece, each burning brightly to bring a little light into the small space. Although he couldn't make out a fire directly, the smoke from the chimney and the sharp tang of burning wood suggested warmth inside.

He stepped back from the window and approached the door. Two rusty hinges held it askew within its frame, and it looked as if it had been repaired many times over. Its dark green paint was flaking, and a large black iron latch was accompanied by a small brass knocker in the shape of a whale fluke, well worn and green with age.

Peter took a deep breath, reached up to the fluke, and knocked twice.

Inside he could clearly hear some movement and shuffling feet. After a few seconds, he heard the sharp clack of the latch, and the squeaking protest of the rusty hinges as the door opened, revealing an older man with long gray hair, a sun wrinkled face, and intense gray eyes. He was fit, about Peter's height, and carried himself with an air of confidence.

"May I help you," he asked.

"Are you Isaiah?" Peter asked.

"I am," the man replied. "And who are you?"

"My name is Peter. Peter Boi…, er Peter Starbuck. I was told that you might be able to help me."

"Hmm," the man said, looking Peter up and down. "Well, I don't know about that, but please come in." Isaiah motioned for Peter to come in and then closed the door behind him, the hinges protesting a second time.

"Please have a seat," said Isaiah. "I don't often get visitors, so I'm not well versed in hospitality. But I do have some coffee on the hearth if you like," he said.

"That would be great, thank you," replied Peter, who sat down at one of the wooden chairs by the table. "I've been walking for the better part of an hour and am chilled through. Coffee would be appreciated."

Isaiah took a mug from the cupboard in the corner and walked to the fireplace. He swung the kettle away from the fire, lifted the pot off the hook, and poured the steaming coffee into the cup. He walked over to the table and handed it to Peter.

"Thank you," said Peter. He grabbed the mug with both hands and held it to his face, inhaling the warm aroma deeply. He took a sip and settled the cup in his lap, still holding it with both hands.

"So tell me, Peter Starbuck. Where are you from?"

Peter looked down at his coffee. "Nantucket. Well, not really. I was born and raised in Connecticut but prefer to call the island my home."

Isaiah stared intently at Peter, assessing the man before him.

"And when are you from?" asked Isaiah.

Peter's face opened in surprise. "When am I from?" He paused. He hadn't told anyone about the truth of his arrival here, even Tris. He had been tempted, especially last night with a belly full of rum, but knew, in the end, it was not the right thing to do. Tris would probably have thought him crazy and may have even ended their friendship, or even had him locked up for being insane. Cautiously he spoke. "Why do you think I'm not from this time?"

Isaiah smiled faintly, "Because you remind me of me."

"Of you?" said Peter, somewhat confused.

"Yes. Of me," said Isaiah. He stood up from the table and walked over to the hearth. He looked into the fire while he rested his hand on the mantle. He turned back to Peter.

"You see, I once lived in the 'future' such as yourself. For me, it was the year 2001 when I traveled back to this time," said Isaiah.

Peter stared intensely at the man, grateful to meet someone such as himself. "I have so many questions."

264

"I'm sure you do," replied Isaiah, "and I will do my best to answer them. But I'm afraid I don't have all the answers. Some of those have to come from within you."

"Do you know how I can get back to my time?" asked Peter expectantly.

"I do. Or at least, I've been shown how it's done but have never tried myself," replied Isaiah.

"Who told you?"

"It was in a dream, shortly after I arrived here."

"A dream?"

"Yes. I know it sounds strange, but that's where I first learned of travelers and that there have been many on this island and probably more all over the world."

"Really?" said Peter. "How many have you met?"

"Well, perhaps a few dozen in total, at least here on Nantucket. Most went back, or at least I think they went back. They disappeared from here so I just assumed they made it back to their original time. A couple, like myself, decided to stay," said Isaiah.

Peter was too busy absorbing and processing this new information to speak. He stared out the window and into the fog, letting Isaiah's words sink in. After a few moments, he turned back to Isaiah. "You said some disappeared from here, and you assumed they went back to their original time."

"Yes."

"But you don't know for certain where...I mean when... they went?"

"No, I don't know for certain that they went back to their original time. But I think it's safe to assume so because that's how it's supposed to be."

"Supposed to be?" asked Peter, his mouth agape. "What do you mean? That this is all planned?"

Isaiah's eyes sparkled. "Planned is probably too strong a word. But there does seem to be a process at work."

Peter sat back in his chair, his mind reeling. Had he been sent back in time on purpose? And if so, for what? He looked at Isaiah and said hopefully, "Can you tell me why I was sent back to this time?"

"No, that must come from you. All the travelers I have met were sent back for a reason, usually something in their life that they needed to learn or accept. Can you tell me more about your experience here? What have you been doing and what have you learned?"

"I landed on a whaling ship, the Paragon. I'll spare you all the details but it was traumatic, especially the first few days."

"I can imagine," said Isaiah with a knowing smile.

"And I learned a lot about myself, and who I really am. Perhaps that is why I was sent back?" said Peter hopefully.

"I don't know. As I said, that must come from you."

Peter thought for a minute and then said, "Why didn't you go back?"

"It's a long story, Peter Starbuck."

"Actually my last name is Bois. Apparently, I'm a descendant of the Starbuck family from here on Nantucket. I decided to keep that name while I'm here to avoid confusion. And questions," he said. Peter paused for a minute. "And I have all the time in the world. I'd love to hear your story."

"Very well then," said Isaiah. "Let me first stoke the fire and freshen the coffee. This will take a little while."

* * *

Isaiah pulled a few split logs from the woodbox to the right of the hearth and threw them on the andirons. There was a shower of sparks, and then the dry wood crackled and lit almost immediately. The new flames cast a golden light into the room, allowing Peter to better assess the face of his host. His skin was leathery with deep wrinkles across the forehead and around his narrow, gray eyes. He was thin-lipped, and his face was framed by long, graying hair that looked very much in need of a good wash. Peter was not the best judge of age, but with Isaiah, he thought him well into his fifties.

Swinging the crane out from the fire, Isaiah removed the kettle from the hook and poured fresh, hot coffee into Peter's mug. He then filled his, replaced the pot on the hook, and swung the crane back over the flames to keep the coffee hot. He sat down across from Peter and took a sip of coffee. He paused a few minutes to gather his thoughts and then looked intently at Peter.

"Actually my original name is Joseph Chamberlain," said Isaiah. He looked down at the cup in his hands and spoke in barely a whisper. "It has been years since I have spoken that name out loud." Isaiah stopped and stared deeply into his coffee. Peter thought he could make out a slight tear forming in one eye and was about to speak when Isaiah continued, "When I 'arrived' here," Isaiah held up his fingers for air quotations, "I apparently looked like a local man named Isaiah. Given my confusion at the time and fearful of the possible reaction should I protest, I went along with that name. And kept it. To be honest, I feel I have grown into it well, and that name better reflects the man I'm here.

"I was born and raised in New York City. My family and I came to Nantucket for a few weeks every summer and like you, came to feel that this was where I belonged, my real home. This is where I felt whole and at peace with myself. After graduating from college in 1986, I had hoped to get a job on the island and live here full time but my family would have none of that. My father arranged a position for me with a friend of his that owned a small chain of department stores. I started on the floor in the men's department but quickly worked my way off the floor and into management. Within a couple of years, I was in Human Resources and found I had a real talent for disciplining people and letting them go." Isaiah paused and chuckled softly. "Can you believe that some people call that a special talent?" He looked at Peter shaking his head, "But apparently it was, and I was comfortable doing it. Of course, I never gave much thought as to what impact my words were having on those poor people or the damage I was doing to their lives. To me, they were just an issue that needed to be addressed, whether it was poor performance, customer relation issues, unreliability, or termination. I was comfortable, regardless.

"I was progressing well at work and managed to build a good life for myself in the City. I met Brenda in '88, on a blind date no less, and we were married in '90. It was a wonderful ceremony and we spent our honeymoon here on Nantucket. Two weeks! I had never been happier. Brenda had never been to the island so I was able to introduce the woman of my dreams to my true second love. It was early October and we rented this very house, *The Shanty*. Of course, it was a little different then and a hell of a lot more expensive!" Isaiah chuckled. "We had electricity for one - how I really do miss that - and the furniture was far more comfortable and luxurious. And the outside was in much better repair than it is today. But beyond that, this house is much the same as it is a hundred and eighty years from now."

Peter struggled mentally placing Isaiah and his bride in this cottage nearly two centuries into the future. It made his mind spin.

"I know what you're thinking," said Isaiah. "And it can be a lot to get your head around. But think of it this way, Sconset really hasn't changed much between now and your time, which is what, 2012?", asked Isaiah.

"2019," replied Peter.

"Hmm," said Isaiah. "I guess I was close. But picture yourself walking through Sconset in 2019. Is it really all that different? I mean, take away the power poles and street lights, the cars, and the pavement, and you could be in 1919. Or even 1828 like we are today. Of course, there have been some new houses built, and we've lost some others to the ocean down in Codfish Park. But in the end, these gray shingled cottages are still much the same as they have ever been. And perhaps one of the reasons why you and I both love this island so much. Consistency. The continuity. The connection to the past." Isaiah stopped and took a sip of coffee. His eyes wandered to the window, and he looked out on the darkening gloom as evening approached.

"Isaiah?"

"Oh, sorry. I was just remembering that time with Brenda here. We were both so happy and we had our whole lives together spread out in front of us. And things went well for us, at least for the first few years. We had both wanted children but struggled to get pregnant. It was frustrating for us but we worked through it together. We had our physicals, talked to our doctors, and even spent some time with a specialist. But in the end, nature took its course, and we had Jill in '92 and Elizabeth - we called her Liza - in '94. Life was good, and we were happy." Isaiah paused to take another sip of coffee and then continued.

"The company had been doing fairly well and remained nicely profitable, but growth was stagnant. And as a result, our stock price languished staying mostly flat through the early '90s. Then a new CEO came in to shake things up and we had a major strategy shift. No longer were we going to be a small regional player. We were going to become a national presence and dominate the channel. Our little retail operation then went on a debt-fueled buying frenzy and acquired dozens of other local and regional department store chains. And while we kept the retail floors of these businesses mostly unchanged, we had huge consolidation in the back office - operations, purchasing, HR, accounts payable, etc. You get the drift. And who do you think had the pleasure of laying off all those people for the cost efficiencies we promised our stockholders?" Isaiah smiled grimly and tapped his chest. "That's right. It was me."

"In fact, I did it so often that my colleagues started calling me 'the terminator' after that movie from the early 1980s. But we were growing so rapidly! Our stock price nearly doubled over the next few years, and things were looking good, at least from the business front. And financially it was good for us too. We made some decent money from our stock options, and my success as the terminator earned me several promotions, finally making it to VP by 2000." Isaiah paused, a sadness washing over his face.

"But that success cost me more than you could ever know. You see, the job required me to travel extensively to oversee the consolidations. Each new acquisition would send me on the road for months at a time often only returning home on weekends. And with that, I'd usually need to fly out on Sunday afternoon, which meant I barely had enough time to say hello to Brenda, do some laundry, and get caught up on the kids."

"You know, I pretty much missed every major milestone for both Jill and Liza; first steps, first words, the first day of kindergarten, first day of school. The list is endless. And the time away from Brenda put a huge strain on our relationship. Yes, we had financial security but I wasn't there to share the load. We went from being madly in love to being roommates. That's what the job did to us. But I was too busy firing people to notice."

Isaiah used a calloused finger to wipe a tear from his face, his gray eyes brimming.

"She tried to talk to me, but I was too busy with work and travel. I just kept putting her off with false promises that we could talk things out the next time I'm home. Tired of my promises, she started to think about separation and divorce. Sadly, I don't even remember if she told me what she was thinking or not. You'd think I'd remember if she did. But I was all consumed with my job." Isaiah paused. He tapped the side of his mug with his finger before he continued, "So she went ahead and made an early morning appointment with a lawyer on Tuesday, September 11, 2001. Her office was on the seventy-fifth floor of the South Tower of the World Trade Center."

Peter's eyes went wide, "Oh, Isaiah; I'm so sorry."

Isaiah choked back a cry, "Thank you. But even worse was that Brenda was not alone. Both Jill and Liza were out of school, some teacher training day thing, and rather than find a babysitter, Brenda brought them with her to the appointment. I'd like to think that she had plans for them when they were done - maybe hit The Met or catch a movie or perhaps spend the day at the Central Park Zoo. But instead, all three were on the seventy-fifth floor when that United plane impacted the building." Tears flowed down Isaiah's cheeks now, and he sobbed. Peter reached over and held his shoulder.

After a few minutes, Isaiah was able to gather himself. "But you know what is really sad? What makes this story so totally tragic? I was leading a meeting with our newest acquisition in a hotel ballroom in Denver. I was with the management team and advising them of the consolidation timeline - essentially how many people were to be let go and what the termination packages were going to be. Shortly after the meeting started, a few people got calls on their cellphones, and soon we knew that there was an attack underway. One of the hotel employees wheeled in a television, and we all stopped to see what was going on. This was about 7:45 central time. And as you know, it was just fifteen minutes later that the South Tower was hit."

Isaiah dropped his face into his hands, "I saw that plane hit the South Tower. On live TV! My entire family wiped out, and I didn't even know it." He leaned up in his chair and rubbed his face. He looked over at Peter, his eyes moist, "I saw the plane hit and my family killed, and I didn't even know it because I was too goddamn busy with work."

Peter looked at Isaiah and tried to imagine the pain he must be feeling. Yes, things were strained right now with Charlotte, but she and the kids were at least alive. They were all healthy, and while they might not be as happy as they could be, he could at least change that if he could get back to them. But there was no hope of that for Isaiah. His family was gone.

"And do you know what I did next?" asked Isaiah incredulously. "I told everyone in that meeting that we had to get back to work. Can you believe that? Here is our country being attacked, our citizens killed, and I'm telling people to get back to work? I was such a jerk. Needless to say, they all ignored me and rushed home to check on their loved ones, if only to assure themselves that their worlds were still together. Me? I typed out my notes and emailed them to my boss. I didn't even bother to call Brenda to make sure she was okay."

"So how did you find out that they were in the Tower?" asked Peter.

"My sister-in-law called me later that morning. I guess Brenda had been talking with her about things and knew she had the meeting set-up. She had talked to Brenda while she was waiting for the lawyer - I guess Brenda was having some second thoughts about it. While they were talking, Brenda mentioned the amazing views she had of the city from the attorney's office. Amazing views," scoffed Isaiah. "If only I had listened to her, had talked to her, she never would have been there." He paused and looked into the fire. "I killed them. I killed the woman of my dreams and my two beautiful and sweet daughters." Isaiah lapsed into silence. The fire was slowly dying, and the room chilled. Peter stood up and grabbed a few logs from the woodbox. He stirred the embers with the tip of one of the logs and then laid the three onto the andirons. He knelt down and blew onto the embers. They glowed orange, and then the fresh wood caught with a burst of flame. Peter stood and turned to Isaiah, "Can I get you some coffee? Or anything else for that matter?"

"No, thank you," said Isaiah. He sniffled and sat up in his chair. His cheeks were dry and his eyes had cleared. "I think I need to finish this."

Peter sat down in his chair and looked over at Isaiah.

"After I got the call, I had no idea what to do. If you remember, all air traffic was grounded but I had to get back to the City as quickly as I could. I was holding onto a shred of hope that perhaps they really had not been there. Or maybe by some miracle they had all survived. A colleague and I were able to rent a car - one of the last available - and we drove non-stop back to New York. I got back to the apartment late Wednesday afternoon and of course, Brenda and the girls were not there. That's when it hit me. It really hit me that they were gone.

"I literally cried for three straight days. It was not just to mourn their loss. It was also because of my complete and total failure as a father and a husband. The guilt and pain from that realization led to some very black days, indeed. After a week, I had recovered enough to go to the office. By then, I saw the job and the company as the reason for my loss. That Brenda, Jill, and Liza would still be here if it weren't for that company and that goddamn job. So I gave it to our CEO with both barrels. In fact, I gave it to anybody and everybody I saw. The terminator self-destructed in front of the entire company. I ended up smashing a rather valuable piece of art in our reception area and marched out the door, cursing the company the entire way." Isaiah stood up, stretching out his back. He walked over to the window and looked out into the fog.

"And then I came here, to Nantucket, to Sconset. Can you believe in all the time we were married that we only ever came back here a handful of times? For the first few years of our marriage, we spent every anniversary here even bringing Jill when she was just a baby. But then Liza was born and the job was getting more demanding. Before I knew it, we had let three years go by without a visit." Isaiah shook his head and turned to Peter. "Three years. What was I thinking? Where were my priorities? So Brenda and I talked and we planned for a big vacation here in the summer of 1998. Three weeks in August. We knew it would be crowded...and expensive. We had a rental all set-up - a cute little cottage over on Evelyn Street - and we were excited to go. Then a week before our ferry reservations, the company made its biggest acquisition yet, a large chain out in California. Being the good company man that I was, I sent Brenda and the girls off on their own while I boarded a flight and headed to LA." Isaiah paused, shaking his head. "I did manage to get back for a couple of weekends, but the vacation was pretty much a bust family-wise. And honestly, I think it was the tipping point in our relationship."

Isaiah left the window and returned back to his chair at the table in front of the fire. He stared first into the fire and then turned to Peter. For the first time since he had started telling his story, his face appeared calm. He seemed at ease.

"So when I lost them I decided to come here. Fortunately, money wasn't a problem. I had done well with the company and despite my outburst at the office I managed to secure a decent package for my termination. Minus ten thousand for the artwork I trashed." Isaiah allowed himself a small smile. "I secured a rental here in Sconset for a couple of months and came to mourn."

CHAPTER TWENTY-SIX

P eter looked at Isaiah intently, unsure of how he was going to respond and asked him tentatively, "So how did you end up here?"

"You mean back in 1828?"

"Yes"

"I was wondering when you were going to ask me about that," said Isaiah. He shifted on his chair. "I had been here only a couple of weeks. It was early October, and I had been walking the beach just about every day just trying to process my feelings. On one unusually warm day - what they used to call an Indian Summer before that became politically incorrect - I decided to go for a swim. And here's the thing, I'm a lousy swimmer. I wasn't going for a swim, I was going to end it all."

"You were going to kill yourself?"

"Yes. I was tired of living with the pain. And the loneliness. Part of me thought that if I were to kill myself, then maybe I'd get to see them again." Isaiah's eyes were once again brimming with tears. "So, I walked down to Low Beach and waded in. The waves were small and the water was still quite warm."

Peter interrupted, "I know that beach - I lost a friend there growing up. The rip there can be really strong."

Isaiah replied, "I'm sorry to hear that. And yes, I knew about the strength of the rip, and honestly, that's what I was hoping for. I had only been swimming for a few minutes when I felt the tug of the rip, almost as if someone had grabbed my ankles and was trying to pull me under. At first, the survival instinct kicked in, and I actually tried to save myself, but no matter what I did or how hard I tried, I couldn't break its grip on me. And of course, there are no lifeguards at that beach. Hell, there wasn't a single person on that beach. All I really needed to do was make my peace, close my eyes, and let my body slip under the water."

Peter nodded his head in agreement and, in some ways, understood. Before his trip to Great Point, he felt like he probably could have survived if something had happened to Charlotte and the kids. He'd be sad, of course, but he could bury himself in his work and get through it. But now? After this experience and what he has learned about himself? He probably would want to die too, just like Isaiah had.

Isaiah continued, "So I did. I stopped trying to fight the rip and just let my body relax. And I tried to think about some of the happiest times with Brenda and the girls and prayed that I'd get to see them. I closed my eyes and let the rip pull me under the water. The next thing I knew, I was lying on the beach just out of the surf, vomiting seawater and covered in sand and seaweed."

"So you didn't drown," asked Peter.

"Unfortunately, no. I didn't. I blacked out when I was pulled under and regained consciousness on the beach. But I have no idea how long I was under. I was alive, if only barely."

"Were you still in 2001?" asked Peter.

"That's the kicker," replied Isaiah. "Of course, I thought I was in 2001. Why would I think otherwise? Time travel is not possible right?" he said with a chortle. "But you and I know better than that now, don't we?" Peter smiled faintly.

He continued, "At first I thought nothing had changed. I mean, I looked up to the bluff, and all the houses looked pretty much the same, at least from a distance. But as I got closer to the cottage, I started to notice little things that didn't make sense. Like there were no power poles, some of the houses were in disrepair or different colors, the paved streets were now dirt tracks, and there was a lot more green space where houses should have been. And a lot of trees seemed to be missing.

"Then I got back to the house, and it looked like this," he said, waving his arms around. "And all of the modern conveniences were gone - no electricity or lights, no kitchen appliances, no television, nothing. All of a sudden it was like camping and I had never been a boy scout.

"But I adjusted and learned and made do. It took me a while to figure it out since I didn't want to ask anyone as they would think me crazy. After a week or so I determined that I was in the early 19th century. And as you've experienced, that's quite a shock to the system. It takes a while to get your head around it," said Isaiah. He stopped and looked at the ceiling and then exhaled, "If my math is correct, that means I have been living this life now for eight years. Wow."

"Forgive me for asking, but what do you do about money? How do you make a living? For me, it wasn't a problem, and I didn't have a choice, I landed on a whaleship. But how do you go about looking for a job in 1820?"

"For the first few days, I pretty much isolated myself here at the cottage. There was food, and I was able to figure things out, like the bathroom. But soon, I was running out of supplies and needed money. I didn't panic about it, but I was certainly very anxious. What was I going to do? Could I find a job? Would I beg on the street? But here's the weird thing, I never had to worry about it."

"What?"

"Some of my money followed me back in time. Heavily discounted, of course, but I was still a pretty wealthy man."

"How did that happen?" asked Peter.

"I have no idea. What I can tell you is that the day I had planned to go to town and start looking for work, I stumbled on an account ledger in an old cupboard. It was from Pacific National Bank, dated 1820, and showed that it belonged to a man named Isaiah Bennet. Me in other words. It also showed the account held a few thousand dollars. So instead of going to town to look for work, I instead went to inquire about this account. I hired a buggy, screwed up the courage, and walked into the bank with that ledger. Funny thing is several people recognized me, I mean, Isaiah, so it was never even a problem. I walked up to the teller window, and that was that. I had money." Isaiah sat back in his chair, his hands clenched in his lap.

"Interesting. So what have you been doing for the last eight years?"

"Hmm. A lot of meditation and thinking. Reading, of course. A lot of walking. And I have been trying to give back. But perhaps most importantly, I try to take care of travelers, like you."

Peter leaned forward, "You said earlier you've seen several dozen travelers."

"Yes."

"Are there any similarities?"

Isaiah thought for a minute and then responded. "Actually there are. It's mostly men and all from roughly the same time, late 20th to early 21st century. All asking the same questions. And all facing a major personal choice."

"A major personal choice? Like what?"

"The common thread seems that each was at a critical juncture in life, a fork in the road so to speak, and needed to make a major decision that would not only impact their lives but those of many others."

"Hmm," Peter grunted. "But what about you? Why were you sent back?"

"I have thought about that a lot, as you can imagine. And in the end, I realized it's about helping others. In my 20th century life, all I did was hurt the people around me; my wife, my daughters, my colleagues, and the hundreds if not thousands of people I fired in the name of efficiency," Isaiah said, his eyes wet with tears. "It was never intended for me to go back. My place was here to help others like you. That's my chance at redemption."

Peter was quiet for a moment letting Isaiah's words sink in. *Redemption.*

Isaiah broke the silence. "Why do you think you were sent here, Peter?

"I think it's to be a better husband and father."

"What else?"

"What do you mean, what else?"

Isaiah smiled. "Everyone can be a better husband and father. If this were all about that, then we would have hundreds if not thousands of travelers popping up every day. There must be more."

Peter thought for a minute. "If I'm frank with myself, I think it was to become a better man. And a more giving man. I hate to admit this, but in 2019 I'm quite the bastard. I'm head of a big plastics company, and I'm rarely home. I don't treat people, or the environment, very well. I have also made a lot of money that my wife wanted us to use to better the lives of other people. And I told her no."

"I think you may have found your answer."

"My answer?"

"On why you were sent here. Do you think you've changed?"

Peter paused and reflected for a minute on his experiences on the Paragon. Of being the greenhand who was lashed for insubordination, of saving Tris on the whaleboat, of being made a whaleman when rounding the horn, and all his work during the hurricane to save the ship and the crew. He looked at Isaiah intently, his blue eyes shining, "I think I do. What I have experienced and lived through has changed me to my core and in the best possible way. I'm no longer the man who arrived here."

Isaiah smiled and held out his hand. Peter took it. "I'm so happy for you. Not everyone has the ability to change, or even the courage to see it within themselves. That's the hardest part, the rest is easy."

For Peter, it was like pieces of the puzzle all coming together. Isaiah had shown him why he had come back, now he wanted to know how to return. He looked at Isaiah expectantly, "So, do you know how I can get back to 2019?"

"Well, as I said, I'm not absolutely certain they go back to their original time. But to answer your question, the dream I mentioned happened just a few days after arriving here. To this day, I can only remember fragments of the images but I fully recall the feelings I experienced."

"And what do those feelings tell you?"

"It's about redemption, a second chance to learn about yourself in new ways to help guide you to make the right choice."

"I understand that," said Peter, a little irritated. "But how do I physically get back to my time?"

"And I'm happy to share those details with you." Isaiah rose and stretched out his back. "But it's getting late, and I think we should call it an evening. Please take the spare bed, and we can continue this conversation in the morning."

"Very well," said Peter, disappointed. He rose and shook Isaiah's hand. "Thank you for sharing your story with me and helping me understand why I'm here."

"You're most welcome," replied Isaiah. "You just need to promise me one thing."

"Of course. What is it?"

"That you will use this experience and what you've learned to become a better man. The man that you know you can be."

Peter nodded solemnly. "I promise."

"Good," replied Isaiah. He squeezed Peter's shoulder, turned, and walked to his bedroom.

Peter sat back down, his mind reeling with Isaiah's words. *You've already completed the hardest part, the rest is easy.* Could this really almost be over? Could he see his family soon? And then a sense of sadness came over him at the thought of leaving Tris. He had become his closest friend, almost a brother, feelings he hadn't experienced since Jack Tate. And the idea of losing another best friend, even if it meant going home, was deeply upsetting.

He rose and walked to the small guest room. In the corner lay a small wooden bunk, not unlike the one he had in the fo'c's'le on the Paragon. He climbed on top and closed his eyes. He fell asleep as a tear slid down his cheek.

CHAPTER TWENTY-SEVEN

Peter woke up to a lovely November morning. The fog had cleared overnight, leaving a vivid blue sky free of any haze or clouds. The air was crisp and cool, and Peter could smell both the salt from the ocean and the unique scent of fallen leaves. He lay in bed, thinking of last night's discussion. Could he really be going home soon? Maybe even today? His heart fluttered at the thought and stirred up butterflies in his stomach. He swung his feet over the side, stood up, straightened his clothes as best he could, and walked out into the hearth.

Isaiah was there, having refreshed the fire and put the coffee on. Already the room was warming and banishing the chill of the fall air. Peter walked to the table and sat in the same chair from the night before.

"Morning," said Isaiah. "Can I interest you in some coffee?"

"Yes, please," replied Peter.

Isaiah swung the arm away from the fire and lifted the kettle. He poured the steaming liquid into a mug and handed it to Peter. "I'm sorry that I don't have any creamer or sweetener as you do in the 21st century," said Isaiah, smiling.

Peter took the mug and a tentative first sip. He smiled and said, "Quite alright. It's delicious just as it is."

"Good," said Isaiah. He grabbed a loaf of bread and a few apples from the pantry and placed them on the table before taking a seat opposite.

They drank their coffee in silence and enjoyed the bread and apples. Peter had just finished a delicious McIntosh when he looked at Isaiah, "Can I ask you a question?"

"Sure," replied Isaiah. "It's the same question I asked you yesterday, which you never really answered. Haven't you ever wanted to go back? Do you miss it at all?"

Isaiah repeated the question, "Do I want to go back?" He paused for a few moments before responding, "Honestly, there is nothing left there for me. Everything that ever mattered to me is gone. And if there is one thing I have learned helping travelers is that you cannot bring people back to life. If they die in your world, regardless of when, they are gone forever."

He sat silently, looking out the window. A cardinal landed on the bush just outside, it's bright red feathers contrasting with the deep blue of the sky. It chirped briefly before taking off.

Isaiah turned back to Peter and continued, "Perhaps if I had come back in time before 9/11, then I could have learned the errors of my ways. But I didn't, and I didn't change. I lost them."

"I understand," said Peter. "But aren't there things that you miss, like electricity or television?"

Isaiah chuckled. "It's funny, Peter. When I left the 21st century, the world was full of people looking for a simpler, easier way of life. Every article I read, every news story I watched, was full of recommendations on how to achieve that. Tell me, has life gotten any simpler in your time? In 2019?"

Peter smiled and shook his head. "No, probably quite the opposite. With the technology we have today, it's more difficult than ever to find peace and solitude. People, like your boss, can reach you twenty-four hours a day, three hundred sixty-five days a year. The workday has become just that, the whole day. No more nine to five with relaxing, hour-long lunches. Now you're expected to be available at all times, regardless of your family commitments or activities outside of work. As a result, stress levels are at all-time highs, and people feel like they are running on a treadmill."

"There, you've answered the question. Why would I want to go back to that? So I can have a refrigerator and some lamps? Or watch crappy television shows about people killing each other?" Isaiah leaned forward in his chair. "Life truly is simple in this time. Sure, there are lots of things I don't have and daily activities can be more challenging. But I'd never want to trade any of that to go back." Isaiah paused to take a sip of coffee. "Besides, I need to be here to help people like you. That's what makes me feel complete."

"And are you happy?" asked Peter.

"I'm as happy as I can be without Brenda and the girls," said Isaiah.

"Good. Because that's the most important thing of all, which I didn't realize until recently."

Isaiah smiled. "I imagine you're anxious to learn how to get back to your time?"

"I am! But also a little nervous."

"Why nervous?"

"Part of it's the unknown. I'm not sure what to expect. But it's also because I do not want to forget this experience, the things I've learned about myself and the friends I have made here."

"Let me ask you this," said Isaiah, "do you remember the day you met your wife?"

"Of course! Like it was yesterday. Meeting Charlotte changed my world."

Isaiah smiled. "Just as this experience has changed your world?"

Peter nodded.

"Trust me, Peter. You will hold this experience close to your heart for the rest of your life. And as you promised me, you will use it to become the man you know you can be; the great husband and father, the generous man who helps others, a selfless man that can truly make a difference."

"I will," said Peter. "I promise."

"Good! So let's talk about getting you home."

The butterflies in Peter's stomach notched up. *Home!*

"We haven't talked about this, but I need to know what was the last thing you were doing before you came to this time," said Isaiah.

Peter replied, "I was on a picnic with my family at Great Point. We had set-up about a half-mile south on the Nantucket Sound side. Charlotte and I got into a nasty argument and I went for a walk, all the way to the tip, where the ocean and the Sound meet. I got knocked into the water by a large wave and pulled into the rip. The next thing I knew, I was on the deck of a whaleship."

Isaiah took a sip of coffee. "You need to return to where you disappeared at Great Point. Reflect on everything you've learned and how you've changed. And if it's to be, then something will happen again."

"What do you mean if it's 'to be'?" Peter asked nervously.

"You were sent back for a reason, Peter. If you've not really changed, that everything you've shared with me is bullshit, then nothing will occur. But if you truly have become a better man, and committing to being a better man in your time, then it will happen."

"Okay. Will it be like last time?"

"It will be similar, yes."

Peter nodded and looked out the window. The blue sky was so vivid it was almost painful. He turned back to Isaiah. "Can you do me a favor?"

"I'd be happy to," said Isaiah.

"I have a close friend from the Paragon, Tristam Coffin. He reminds me so much of a friend I had growing up and we have become quite close. He is about to marry, and I'd like to give him the money I earned on the ship as a wedding present."

"I'd be happy to. How much did you earn?"

"A little over twelve hundred dollars."

"Twelve hundred dollars? That's very impressive!"

"Really? I thought it seemed kind of low to me, but of course, I have no frame of reference."

"Twelve hundred dollars is a lot of money in 1828, and I'm impressed that you were able to earn that much. You must have done quite well for yourself on the Paragon."

Peter felt a sense of pride. He had done well and learned a lot about himself - who he really was, and what he was able to accomplish. From being a flogged greenhand to managing the helm through the hurricane. He blushed.

"Well, I'd like to give that money to my friend, Tris. Tell him it's from me, and it's my downpayment for a whaleship."

"A whaleship? Interesting. I will take care of that for you."

"Thank you," replied Peter. He looked out at the blue sky again and whispered, "Will he know I'm gone?"

"Your friend, Tristam?"

"Yes."

"He will. The people here and the connections you've made are real. But don't forget as much as you've learned from them, they have also learned from you. It works both ways."

Peter was quiet, upset at the sadness that his disappearance would have on Tris.

"Peter?"

"Oh, sorry. Just lost in thought."

"I think you should get going. You have a long walk in front of you and I'm sure you'd love to be home by dinner time," said

Isaiah with a broad smile. He grabbed the remaining bread and the last apple and handed them to Peter. "You'll need this."

Home by dinner time? Oh my God, this might soon be over.

Peter rose from the table and held out his hand. "Thank you for everything."

Isaiah stood, took Peter's hand, and pulled him into a hug. He whispered into his ear, "Keep this experience close to your heart and become the man you are meant to be."

Peter withdrew from the embrace and smiled broadly at Isaiah. "I will. And you promise me to stay safe, healthy, and happy."

"Always."

Peter turned and walked to the door. He gave Isaiah one last look and smiling, opened the door, and stepped outside. He walked through the gate and turned left. He had ten miles to walk and barely seven hours to sunset. Like the Paragon rounding the Horn, Peter was finally, at long last, heading home.

* * *

The cool air and a brisk northerly breeze chilled Peter, and he buttoned up his coat. The wind blew the leaves off the trees sent them skittering across his path, their life's journey nearly done. He wasn't sure what roads existed to Wauwinet and Great Point and didn't have time to spare to explore or get lost. Instead, he decided that the safest and most direct path would be to follow the beach. He walked north along the rutted road that ran in front of The Shanty. As he neared the last cottage in the village, he found the path that would lead him down the bluff and out onto the sand. He and Charlotte had walked it hundreds of times, and he was surprised it was there. He followed the path down to the beach, turned north, put his hands in his pockets, leaned forward against the wind, and started walking.

One thing he noticed hadn't changed much in nearly two centuries was the beach. The sand was still quite fine, making walking very difficult. He made his way closer to the surf and found the damp, more densely packed sand much more comfortable to navigate. And just like 2019, the beach was covered in shells and pebbles, the gulls called out in their raspy voices, and the sandpipers twittered on the edge of the water looking for food. Every so often, he'd see a seal pop its head out of the water just past the breaking waves and eye him curiously. He smiled. *I could be back in my time.*

Then with a shock, he realized what he didn't see; trash. The beach was free of washed-up fishing nets, broken glass, empty beer and soda cans, and all those plastics. He thought of his last time at Great Point and seeing one of his plastic bottles in the sand. *Is that what I'm in business for? Creating trash for the beach? There has to be something I can do about that,* he thought with some dismay.

He progressed up the beach and was soon walking past the high bluff where Sankaty Head Lighthouse would be built a few decades in the future. And not long after, found himself looking out over Quidnet, the brackish pond where he had raced a sailing dinghy as a boy. He smiled at the thought. *I need to teach Sophie and Spencer how to sail.*

By noon, he had reached what he thought was Wauwinet and where he'd enter the beach if he were driving. He made his way up to where the sand and seagrass met to find some shelter from the wind. Sitting down, he pulled the apple and bread out and enjoyed them while watching the waves criss-cross the ocean making unique patterns that only he would ever see. A few gulls approached him hungry for some of his food, which he gladly shared. He could barely eat, his stomach filled with butterflies.

Finishing his food, and nodding to the gulls, he stood up and walked across the heavy sand and down to the water's edge. The other thing missing from the beach were tire tracks. Usually, the sand would be covered in them from all of the vehicles heading to the Point. But today, the sand was smooth, the only blemishes were the little ripples caused by the wind.

It was mid-afternoon when he reached the Galls, that narrow strip of sand that connects the main body of the island with the Point. Over the years, this thin piece of the island had been breached time and again during hurricanes and Nor'easters, often taking months or years for the sand to build back-up and reconnect. Peter wasn't sure what he'd find and was relieved that it was sand as far as he could see. And still narrow. He could make out Nantucket Sound just a few hundred feet to his left.

He continued along, his body tiring and his feet sore. The leather boots he was wearing were blistering his feet, and he began walking with a slight limp to accommodate the pain. It took him just under an hour to cross the Galls and make his way to the lagoon, a small saltwater pond where he and Charlotte would always see the swans. Crossing the edge of the lagoon, he made his way over to the western side of the beach and soon found himself at the same spot where he, Charlotte, and the kids would picnic nearly two centuries in the future. The butterflies ramped up even further, and a wave of anxiety spread through him. *What if this doesn't work? What if whatever force manages all of this doesn't think he has changed? What then?*

Pushing his doubts aside, he tried to think of the fight that he had with Charlotte. She had really only asked two things of him; spend more time with the family and be generous with their wealth. He had refused both. But his time on the Paragon had transformed him from a greedy, self-centered, one-percenter to a more modest, humble, and generous man.

He was ready to go home.

Limping his way up the beach, Peter finally made it to the very tip of Great Point, where just a few months ago, he had been pulled out to sea and sucked back into this time. He stood a few feet from the surf, looked out over the water, and wondered again what Charlotte had done during all these weeks he had been gone. Did she think he was dead? Had she already moved on? Or was she still mourning and praying for his safe return, just like Abigail will be doing with Tris when he's out to sea?

There's only one way to find out.

Peter stepped forward into the surf. The sea was relatively flat, and the small waves broke over the top of his boots. Taking a few more steps, he was up to his knees with the small waves lapping at his thighs. The water was quite warm, almost inviting. His anxiety grew stronger now. The last time he had been here, he thought he was going to drown and had panicked. But now his fear was whether or not he was going to be transported ahead in time. Back to Charlotte, to Sophie and to Spencer.

He closed his eyes and took a few more steps. The waves were now up to his waist, and he could feel the slight tug of the rip on his legs. A hundred yards to the east, the water rose as a wave, larger than the others around it, approached. It traveled quickly, and as it neared the shore, it could no longer maintain its height and started to break. Peter kept his eyes closed, but the sound of the rushing water made him smile.

The wave hit him and swept him off his feet, carrying him a few hundred feet out into the water. The rip here was strong, but Peter didn't fight it. He let his mind and body relax, allowing himself to be gently pulled under. As the water closed over him, he thought of the beautiful family he hoped he was going to see and of the people he was leaving behind. The smiling faces of Charlotte, Spencer, and Sophie were the last thing he remembered as his world went black.

God creates out of nothing. Wonderful you say.
Yes, to be sure, but he does what is still
more wonderful: he makes saints out of sinners.

Soren Kierkegaard

CHAPTER TWENTY-EIGHT

Peter was flat on his back and lying in the sand just out of reach of the light surf at Great Point. He rolled over, opened his eyes, and found himself face-to-face with a large seal splayed out next to him. The seal eyed him quizzically and then let out a tremendous belch, the foul air blowing over Peter's face. Peter responded by vomiting a significant quantity of seawater straight at the seal. Wiping his mouth, he thought, *take that you piece of blubber*. The seal, apparently insulted by nearly being vomited upon, grunted heavily, flopped himself around, and slid into the water.

The rip had once again sucked Peter in and coughed him out. But *when* had it coughed him out? Had he made it back to his time? He propped himself up on his elbow and looked around him for clues as to what time this was. He was looking out over the horizon when he heard the distinctive sound of a twin-engine aircraft, its propellers moving in and out of phase. Looking up, he saw the outline of a Cape Air Cessna passing overhead on its way to the Cape, its familiar seagull logo on the tail. His heart quickened.

He slowly rose to his feet, looked out over the water, and saw the high-speed ferry cruising against the horizon heading toward Nantucket. Just in front of it, one of the slow ferries, the Eagle, was making its way back to Hyannis.

Yes!

Peter jumped for joy, turned, and started running down the beach, the heavy sand quickly tiring him. He slowed to a quick walk and realized he better pace himself as he had ten miles back to Sconset. With luck, maybe he could hitch a ride from someone heading back from the beach. He scanned the sand, and a few hundred feet ahead of him saw a green pick-up truck. A man was standing next to it and waving frantically at him. The man then leaned in the driver's side window and honked the horn several times.

Maybe he can help me?

Peter half walked, half ran directly toward the truck, hoping that perhaps this man could get him back to Sconset.

"Thank you. I hope you can help me," said Peter.

"Sir, I'm afraid that area is off-limits to pedestrians," said the man. He was dressed in olive-colored slacks with a matching button-down shirt. A patch on his breast pocket read Park Ranger.

"Excuse me?"

"You were walking in a protected area. It's not allowed. Did you not see the signs?" The ranger pointed to a small sign that had the outlines of several seals on them along with the image of a person walking covered by a big red X.

"Are you serious?"

"Yes, sir, I am. The tip of Great Point is off-limits. That area is reserved for the seals."

As the park ranger continued to lecture him about why the seals needed protection from dangerous people like Peter, he looked over the man's shoulder and saw the distinctive outline of his Range Rover. He could just make out Charlotte sitting in her beach chair and the heads of Spencer and Sophie playing in the sand, their hair blowing in the breeze. Behind them lay the blue of the water, the sun dancing over the ripples like millions of diamonds.

Peter felt a warm rush through his body.

"Sir?"

He turned to see that the ranger was still talking to him. "What?"

"As I was saying, if I catch you out there again, then I'll be forced to write you a ticket."

"Oh, whatever!" said Peter. He pushed his way past the ranger and started running. He only got twenty feet when he stumbled into a tire track and fell flat on his face. He got up quickly, wiped the sand off, and kept on running. As he approached the car, he saw that Charlotte, Sophie, and Spencer were precisely where he had left them. Charlotte was in her beach chair reading her book, Spencer was building a fort down by the water, and Sophie was making a mosaic from pebbles. His beach chair sat empty next to hers, his beer bottle still in the cupholder.

"Charlotte!"

She turned and was shocked to see Peter running at her so quickly. He came flying across the beach and stopped in a spray of sand a few feet from her. He looked down at her, his eyes wet. "Is it really you?"

"Peter? Are you okay?"

He dropped to his knees next to her chair and hugged her hard, nearly knocking her over. "Oh, Charlotte. Oh my god, it really is you!" Peter was crying, tears rolling down his cheeks.

"Peter? Is everything okay? Peter?"

"It is now. It is now. Sophie, Spencer! Come here!"

The children warily came up to him, and he grabbed them both into a bear hug. He pulled away, his eyes shifting back and forth between them. "I am so, so happy to see you two," said Peter, his eyes shining and cheeks wet with tears.

"We're happy to see you too, daddy," said Sophie, concern in her voice. Spencer just looked at his father, his mouth agape, bewildered.

Peter gave them one last quick squeeze and turned to Charlotte. "Oh my god, you don't know how happy I am to see you."

"What has happened to you?" asked Charlotte warily.

Peter wiped his cheek with the back of his hand and sniffled. "It's a long story. And I want to share all of it with you. But not here and not now. Let me just enjoy this moment, seeing you and the kids."

Confused, Charlotte said, "Okay, hon, whatever you like."

Peter took a long look over the water and then settled down into his chair. He turned to Charlotte, looked deeply into her blue eyes, and smiled. "This is the happiest day of my life."

"Hmmm, okay," said Charlotte. "It's a beautiful day, and I'm glad we're all here to enjoy it together." She returned to her book.

"Me too," said Peter. He paused for a minute and then asked, "How long have I been gone?"

"You mean on your walk?"

"Yes. How long was I gone?" asked Peter.

"I don't have my watch on, but I'd say about an hour, maybe a little more."

"An hour? That's all?" Peter was shocked. Is it possible that all that time in 1828, those months on the Paragon, could be compressed to little more than an hour here?

"Yes, does it seem longer?"

He turned and smiled. "Oh hon, you have no idea."

Peter watched Spencer and Sophie playing and then looked out over the water to see the high-speed ferry making its return trip to Hyannis. He could make out dozens of other boats, some power, some sail, that were enjoying the beautiful weather and calm seas. *A far cry from the hurricane on the Paragon*, he thought.

"Charlotte?"

"Hmm," she said and raised her eyes up from the book and looked at him.

He paused for a minute and then said, "I'm so sorry about that argument we had. You were one hundred percent right, and I was a jerk."

Charlotte was a bit taken aback. It was not like her husband to apologize. "Really?"

"Yes, really." He looked back out over the water and the memories of his time on the Paragon flooded over him. He thought of Tris and of Captain Nelson. He thought of being made a whaleman and rendering oil in the trypots. He thought of the men who died and how he was nearly killed several times from whales and weather. And he thought of Isaiah and all that poor man had lost. "I want to do it all."

"What do you mean?" asked Charlotte hopefully.

"I want to be home with you and the kids, permanently. I want to set-up the foundation and let our money do good things for the island and the people here."

"Really?" said Charlotte, excited.

"Yes, really. It's long overdue. And I have some ideas about the company that I want to get your thoughts on. I think there are some good things we can do there as well."

"Oh my god, that would be so wonderful!" She leaned over awkwardly in her chair, embraced Peter and began to cry. "I know we can do so much good for this island and for others," she said through her tears.

"I didn't mean to make you cry," said Peter with empathy in his voice.

"Oh, hon. These are tears of joy. You've just made me the happiest woman on the face of the earth." She buried her head into Peter's neck.

Tears running down his cheeks, Peter hugged her harder and whispered into her ear, "You're the best thing that has ever happened to me. I'm so sorry for causing you pain, and I promise that I will be the man you want me to be."

Charlotte pulled back from the embrace and looked into his eyes, "What happened to you?"

Peter smiled, his eyes brimming with tears, "Let's just say that I learned a lot about myself on that walk."

"I don't know what has come over you, but I love it!" said Charlotte smiling broadly, her blue eyes sparkling. "Now, why don't you relax and finish your beer. Actually, let me get you a fresh one as I'm sure that one is warm." Charlotte stood and went to the cooler, grabbed him a beer, and handed it to him. He looked at the label on the bottle. It was from an island brewery and featured a large whale fluke about to sink into the water. He smiled and took a long sip.

Peter sat in his chair and looked out over the water. The sky was a hazy blue, the temperature was warm, and a refreshing sea breeze was blowing over him. A few hundred yards out, he saw the distinctive plume of a whale breaching, followed by another. He watched fascinated as the backs of the two whales slid under the water, followed by two broad flukes that appeared and then slipped under the surface. It was the first time he had ever seen a whale on Nantucket.

Thank you, Isaiah. Thank you, Tris.

Charlotte looked at him, quizzically and said, "Have you lost weight?"

* * *

They stayed at Great Point to watch the sunset and were rewarded with a natural show of splendor, the clouds lighting up in deep reds, oranges, and yellows. It reminded Peter of when the Paragon had finally come into Nantucket after their long voyage. He thought wistfully of Tris and the men aboard the ship. He thought with sadness that those men were all dead now, nothing more than memories.

As the day darkened around them, they packed up the car and headed home. What had taken Peter hours to walk earlier in the day took him now just thirty minutes. They made their way back, down the bumpy dirt road and by the big hotel. Peter pulled over a few hundred yards past the hotel to fill the tires back up with air. He grabbed a flashlight and gauge from the center console and jumped out. He was done in minutes - much faster, adding the air back than taking it out - and they were on the road to Sconset.

The drive home was quiet. Spencer had fallen asleep, and Sophie was busy looking out the window, watching for rabbits and deer. Peter was just relishing being in the company of his family and held Charlotte's hand as he drove.

It was well past dark when they got home. Peter parked the Rover by the front door to make it easier to unload, he wasn't going to bother to put it away tonight. He then carried Spencer up to his room and helped him into his pajamas. He tucked Spencer in and gave him a big kiss on the forehead. "I love you," he said.

Spencer whispered back through half-closed eyes, "I love you too, daddy." He turned and was instantly asleep.

Peter crept out and looked across the hall to Sophie's room. She was still up, reading. He slipped into her room and sat on the edge of her bed. She raised her eyes up to his. He brushed her hair from her face. "I'm sorry that I haven't been around much, hon."

"It's okay, daddy," said Sophie.

"No, it's not. I have been away from you far too much in the last few years. That's going to change."

"Really?" said Sophie expectantly.

"Really, hon. I'm going to be around so much you're going to get sick of me."

"Never!" said Sophie, and she jumped up to hug him. "I'd never get sick of you being here."

Peter savored the hug and felt a pang of sadness thinking of Isaiah and his two girls. He owed it to him to enjoy his children as much as he could.

"Thank you, sweetie. And we've had a busy day. I think it's time to turn off the light."

"Okay, daddy."

He took her book, placed it on the nightstand, and turned off her lamp. He leaned down and tucked the covers up under her chin. "Sleep tight, hon" and kissed her forehead. Peter stood and walked to the door. He looked back and could just barely make out Sophie's face in the darkness. She had a smile from ear to ear.

He padded down the stairs and found Charlotte in the kitchen. She was just finishing putting away the remnants of their picnic. Peter walked up from behind and put his arms around her. "Care to join me on the patio for a drink?" he whispered into her ear. He followed the question by kissing her earlobe.

"Hmm, how can I resist when you ask so nicely," she teased. She rotated in his arms, so she was facing him and kissed him long and hard on the mouth. She pulled back, breathing heavily, and said, "I'll take a glass of wine, please."

Peter kissed her again, this time using his tongue to part her lips. "Why don't you go get comfortable on the chaise, and I'll be right there?" he whispered.

"Okay," she replied breathlessly.

Peter got a wine glass from the cupboard and filled it with her favorite sauvignon blanc. He grabbed himself a beer and walked through the French doors and out onto the patio. It was a clear evening, the stars radiating their light down on them. He could clearly make out the Milky Way spread out across the sky. Every fifteen seconds or so, the light from Sankaty Head would swivel by overhead.

"Scootch over," said Peter, and he handed her the glass of wine.

Charlotte looked up at him, smiling. She wriggled over to free up space on the chaise for him. Peter laid down next to her and held up his beer.

"To you."

"No, to us."

"To us," and they clinked.

Peter took a deep swallow of beer and then put the bottle down on the ground.

"Charlotte?"

"Yes, hon."

"How long has it been since we have fooled around outside?"

Charlotte looked at him, her eyes shining, and smiled. "It's been a long time," she said. "Way too long."

"Well then," said Peter. "I think we need to address that right now."

Charlotte looked at him, eyes filled with emotion. "Peter Bois, I don't know what has gotten into you, but I love it."

Peter kissed her and then said. "I love it too, hon. I love it too."

CHAPTER TWENTY-NINE

P eter and Charlotte made love on the chaise and fell
asleep in an embrace, covered only in a couple of beach
towels they had used on their picnic. They woke up a
few hours later. The fog had rolled in, and both were damp from
the mist. Laughing, they made their way quietly up to the bedroom
and made love again. Peter fell almost instantly into a deep sleep.

He opened his eyes to the sun streaming in their bedroom
windows. It looked to be a warm and hazy day outside, the sky
white with light clouds. He turned to give Charlotte a kiss, but her
side of the bed was empty; she had already gone down to the
kitchen for coffee. *She does love her coffee*, thought Peter. He
looked up at the ceiling and felt completely happy and content. His
voyage on the Paragon and his brief time on the island in 1828
seemed a distant memory, almost dreamlike. But he vowed to
himself that he'd never forget that time or those people.

He pulled the covers back, sat up, and swung his feet on to the
floor. Naked, he walked over to the closet and found some shorts
and a polo. He pulled them on and headed downstairs.

He walked into the kitchen to find Sophie and Spencer at the table, eating sandwiches. Charlotte was at the sink washing off some dishes and loading up the dishwasher. He walked up behind her and gave her a big hug then turned his attention to the table where he kissed both his children on the forehead and tousled their hair. "Good morning!" he said.

Charlotte smiled. "Well actually, it's almost afternoon."

"What?" said Peter.

"Yeah," said Charlotte. She came back over to him and gave him a kiss on the cheek. "It's quarter to twelve. You certainly had a good night's sleep," she said and winked.

He put his hands on her hips and pulled her toward him. "I guess I must have needed it," he said with a smile and kissed her firmly on the lips.

"Ugh," said Spencer.

"What?" said Peter looking at him.

"That's gross."

Peter and Charlotte laughed and kissed again.

"What do you think about dinner in town tonight?" asked Peter, releasing Charlotte from the embrace. "I'd like to tell you what I learned about myself on that walk."

"Ooh, that sounds good. Shall we do 56 Union again?"

"No, I'm in the mood for something a little more casual. How about we go to the Brotherhood? I'd kill for one of their burgers."

"Hmm, okay, that sounds great."

"Excellent," said Peter. He gave Charlotte another long kiss.

"Ugh," said Spencer.

Sophie was smiling, pleased to see her parents so happy.

Peter withdrew from the embrace and smiled at his family. "I just need a little coffee."

"Just coffee? Can I make you some breakfast?" asked Charlotte.

Peter, thinking of hardtack, salt horse, and foul water, said, "You know what? That sounds wonderful."

"Bacon and eggs?"

"Perfect," he said. "And maybe some Portegeuse toast?"

Charlotte smiled. "Done. Just give me ten."

"I love you, hon."

"I love you too."

"And, I can't wait to start this next chapter in our lives. I think it's going to be a lot of fun."

Charlotte came up to Peter and embraced him. "It will be more than fun. It will be wonderful."

* * *

Peter eased the Range Rover out of the carriage house and headed down the driveway and proceeded left toward Milestone Road.

"What's the over/under tonight?" asked Peter teasingly, knowing that their last trip to town for dinner had been a bust.

"Hmm." Charlotte paused a minute. "I'm thinking ten."

"I'll take the under. I don't think we will see that many tonight. Too much traffic. Are we playing for the usual prize?" asked Peter.

Charlotte smiled, "I think we both won the prize last night, but I'm up for a replay."

Peter reached over and held Charlotte's hand. Milestone Road was busy with summer traffic, although fortunately, the mopeds were few and far between. They did get behind an older gentleman driving a nicely restored Wagoneer. The car looked brand new, but the driver must have thought the speed limit was 35, not the posted 45. Charlotte tensed, worried that being stuck behind this driver was going to set Peter off. But he rolled the window down, put his elbow out, and seemed to just enjoy being in the car with her. She relaxed.

They made it into town and started the challenge of finding an available parking spot in August. Eventually, they crept behind a couple who looked like they were walking to their car. "You're such a vulture," said Charlotte, chuckling.

Peter laughed. "It's the only way to get a spot. This is crazy!"

His bet paid off, and the couple proceeded to get in their car and start the engine. A few seconds later, they were backing out, and Peter was able to swing the Rover in. They jumped out and walked the few blocks to the restaurant. When they got there, they saw that the line for a table was out the door.

"It looks jam-packed," said Charlotte nervously, knowing Peter's lack of patience and penchant for taking his frustrations out on the hostess. "Shall we go somewhere else?"

Peter took her hand and said, "Nope. This is good. We're not in any rush, are we?"

"No, we really aren't. Are you sure you don't mind waiting?" asked Charlotte.

"I don't mind at all. It just gives me more time to be with you and stare into those lovely eyes," said Peter. He leaned over and kissed Charlotte hard on the lips.

"Wow," said Charlotte. "I'm really looking forward to hearing about your walk."

They waited nearly an hour before the hostess showed them to a table in the corner. They were just below grade and could look out through the windows and see the feet of people walking by. It was dark, the candles at each table providing just enough light to make out the exposed brick walls and low, wooden beamed ceilings. For some reason, the place reminded Peter of the belowdecks on the Paragon. He found it comforting and, in some ways, a perfect venue to share his story with Charlotte.

The waiter arrived and took their drink orders. As usual, Charlotte had a glass of sauvignon blanc while Peter settled for a local draft beer.

"No Manhattan?" asked Charlotte.

"No, just want to keep things simple." He took a swig and placed his glass down on the table. He reached both hands over to Charlotte. She took them.

"Have I told you today how lucky I'm to have you?" said Peter.

Charlotte smiled. "Actually, I think you've said that maybe once or twice. Or a dozen," she giggled. "And I love hearing it."

Slowly, her smile was replaced with a pensive look. "What did happen to you on that walk?"

Peter was quiet. He squeezed her hands and looked into her eyes. "I learned about who I could be as a man," he said.

"All that from an hour-long walk?"

"It was actually longer than that, quite a bit longer."

"What?" asked Charlotte, confused.

"I really don't think you're going to believe me, but I need to share with you what happened."

"Oh, okay. But you have me worried now."

"Don't be worried, it's all good." He squeezed her hands again. He took a deep breath and started. "Remember that terrible argument we had? About you wanting me to be home more and starting the foundation?"

Charlotte nodded and smiled, "It was just yesterday, I think I'd remember it."

"Oh, right. Sorry, it's just that it's been a little longer for me. Anyway, I was so angry and really not sure what I wanted to do. I ended up walking straight to the tip of Great Point and decided I was going to go back to Connecticut. Alone. Thought maybe a few weeks without me would teach you a lesson," he said sadly.

"Teach me a lesson?" asked Charlotte, her good mood starting to evaporate.

Peter gripped her hands. "I was so wrong, hon. So wrong. I'm ashamed of myself for even having a thought like that." His grip on her hands relaxed, and he continued, "Anyway, I was at the

Point trying to call the jet to take me back to Connecticut when a wave hit me and knocked me off my feet. It pulled me out into the rip and then sucked me under."

Charlotte's eyes went wide. "Did you almost drown?"

Peter looked at her nervously. "Well, yes, but I landed on a whaleship."

"A whaleship? I didn't know there were any around. Usually, when an old ship visits they'll have something in the paper about them."

"There aren't any around, at least in 2019."

"In 2019? What do you mean?"

"I did indeed land on a whaleship. It was called the Paragon. But the year was 1828."

"1828?" Charlotte looked at him, confused.

"I know it sounds crazy. But I promise you it happened. It was captained by a man named Nelson, and one of the mates was a young man named Tristam. Do you remember me telling you about my friend Jack who drowned swimming with me?"

"I do. I know how much it devastated you."

"Tris looked exactly like Jack. It was almost as if they were related. And as I got to know him, I realized his personality and nature were very similar as well."

"Really?"

"Yes. And he helped me to settle in on the Paragon, and showed me how to do things."

"What do you mean 'settle in'? Hadn't they just rescued you from the water?"

The waiter interrupted them, "What can I get you folks tonight? Any questions about the menu?"

Peter looked at Charlotte, "Do you know what you want?"

"Yes," and she looked up at the waiter. "I'll start with the small Caesar, and then I'll have a bowl of the French onion soup for my entree."

"Very well," said the waiter. "And you, sir?"

"I'll start with a bowl of the chowder. And then I'll have the Brotherhood burger, please. Medium with the Boursin cheese."

The waiter finished writing down the order. "Can I refresh your drinks?"

"Yes, please," said Peter.

He turned his attention back to Charlotte and reached for her hands. "Honey, I know this is going to sound crazy, but I was on the Paragon for nearly four months."

Charlotte looked shocked. "Four months? How is that possible? You were only gone an hour. Peter, you're worrying me now."

"I know what it sounds like, hon. But trust me, every bit of this is true. Time is strange, and time travel is stranger still."

"Time travel?" said Charlotte, her voice barely a whisper. She was getting more concerned.

"Hon, trust me, please. Hold off on any judgments until you hear the whole story."

315

"Okay, babe, I'll try. But this isn't easy for me to hear."

"I can imagine," replied Peter. "But, I need to share everything with you and how it has impacted me."

She held his hands firmly and stared into his eyes. "Okay. I'm all yours."

He paused for a minute and then started, "As you can imagine, I was very confused when I landed on the Paragon. We were off the coast of Chile and looking for whales...."

Peter talked for several hours, stopping only to enjoy their food as well as order additional rounds of drinks. Charlotte was patient and listened intently, asking just a few questions along the way.

"...and then Isaiah told me how to get back to you and back to this time," said Peter tapping on the table with his finger. "He said I needed to go back to Great Point, stand in the rip, and reflect on who I wanted to be as a man. And then I was hit by another wave and pulled under. I woke up on the beach, right next to a big seal. That was yesterday. I was home."

Charlotte sat back and stared at Peter. "This really happened? All of it?" she said.

Peter leaned forward and took her hands. "It did, hon. All of it. And it was exactly what needed to happen to me. I needed to learn what was most important and why I'm here." A tear trickled down Peter's cheek.

"What is it, babe?"

Peter smiled sadly. "I am just so lucky to have you. I keep thinking of Isaiah and what that poor man lost. I never, ever, want to take you and the kids for granted again."

Charlotte clutched Peter's hands and smiled. "I love you, Peter Bois. And while your story sounds fantastical, I love what it has meant for you."

"Thank you, hon. And thank you for listening, as crazy as it sounds." Peter leaned back into his chair and said, "so let's talk about the future."

Charlotte relaxed, happy for a change of topic, and excited to hear Peter's thoughts. "Okay," she said, "tell me what you're thinking."

"I don't want to sell the company," said Peter. "Instead, I think we can use it to do good things."

"Like what?" asked Charlotte, a little wary about where this was going.

"Plastics are a significant problem in the world's oceans right now. In fact, plastic trash is killing whales, dolphins, and other sea life."

Charlotte nodded in understanding.

"If you remember our discussion a few weeks ago, I told you about that new resin technology we developed that breaks down in saltwater. So, for example, a water bottle made with this resin will quite literally degrade in just a few days. It essentially melts away, leaving nothing behind but some harmless residue that can be eaten by plankton. So instead of trash, it's more like producing food."

"But didn't you tell me that it was too expensive and would cost millions in lost margins?"

"Yes, but I was a jerk and an idiot," said Peter. "There are things that are more important than profits."

Charlotte smiled knowingly. "So, what do you want to do now?"

"I think we should spin off all our production capability, all of the factories, and set-up a separate company to focus on licensing this technology to plastic companies everywhere. All the profits generated would be donated to those organizations that are dedicated to cleaning up the world's oceans, like Clean Seas Forever."

Charlotte was shocked, even more so than in hearing Peter's story. "Would you still be the CEO?"

"More of an honorary chairman. We would hire a full-time CEO."

"Oh. Peter. That would be wonderful. The thought of having you home with us. And think of the positive impact you can have."

Peter smiled, "Yes. Which would leave me with the time to manage our new foundation."

"Really?"

"Really. But only if you will manage it with me. Be my partner?"

"Oh my god, yes!" She reached out and grabbed his hands. "Of course! I would love that!"

"You had originally asked for half of our money to start the foundation. But I think we can do better than that. We don't need much to pay the bills, and I'm done with that CEO lifestyle, the private jets, limos, you know. We can put a few million in some conservative investments, which would generate all the income we need to maintain our current lifestyle. And provide a nice inheritance for Spencer and Sophie."

"Oh, Peter. That would be amazing. Just amazing."

The waiter arrived. Peter and Charlotte were the last people in the restaurant, and the waiter looked like he was ready to head home and go to sleep. Or more likely, head out to party. "Can I get you anything else?" he asked, hesitant of the answer.

"No, just the check, please."

The waiter, relieved, produced the bill from his apron and laid it on the table. Peter quickly whipped out his wallet and threw his card down. The waiter retreated to process the payment.

Peter looked over at Charlotte. "Oh, and one more thing."

"What's that?" said Charlotte a little nervously.

"I want us to get a dog."

Charlotte laughed out loud. "That sounds perfect. I know that will make Spencer and Sophie very happy. They've wanted one for a while now."

"And I'd like to name him Tris."

"Tris it is," said Charlotte, smiling. She paused. "Peter, I cannot tell you how happy you've made me over the past twenty-four hours."

He reached over to take her hand, rubbing her knuckles with the tips of his fingers. "When I was on the Paragon, all I could think of was you, Sophie and Spencer. It kept me alive." His eyes filled with tears. "All I wanted was to get home to you and the kids. For me, this is a dream come true."

"It's a dream come true for me as well. I love you," said Charlotte. "With all of my heart."

"I love you too," said Peter. He wiped a tear from his cheek and said, "What do you think about joining me on the patio for a drink when we get home?"

"Absolutely," said Charlotte.

Peter signed the check, added a very generous tip, and then walked Charlotte back to the car, holding hands the entire way.

Heading home, they saw ten deer but didn't bother counting. They knew they had both won.

CHAPTER THIRTY

T he next day broke cooler, with light overcast and dense fog. Nantucket was living up to her reputation as the Gray Lady.

Peter was in the kitchen at the table with Charlotte and the kids. They were working on a puzzle and had nearly completed the border. He had just put a corner piece in when he looked up and said, "You know, it's such a crappy day that I think I'm going to go into town and do a little research."

"Research?" asked Charlotte.

"Yes. I'd like to understand a bit more about the Paragon and what happened to her and her crew. And I'm hoping I can learn more about what happened with Tris and Abigail."

"Okay, hon. Do you want to meet for lunch?"

"That sounds good, although town will probably be bustling. Not a very good beach day."

"Maybe a late lunch, then? How about we meet at the pharmacy at 2:00?"

"Perfect. I'll leave you the car, then."

Charlotte looked at him. "How are you going to get to town? Uber?"

"I'll take the bus."

"The bus?" said Charlotte, shocked.

Peter smiled. "Yes, honey. The bus. You know, public transportation."

"Wow, okay. That just doesn't sound like the Peter Bois I know."

"The Peter Bois you knew is gone. This is the new and improved version," said Peter smiling, tapping his chest. "And he doesn't mind taking the bus." *After three months in the fo'c's'le on the Paragon, public transportation is luxury by comparison.*

He got up and grabbed his wallet. Charlotte looked at him, "Don't forget your phone, in case I need to text you."

"Um, I don't have a phone anymore."

"What? What happened to it?"

"I, um, lost it on my walk," said Peter and winked. They had agreed not to share any of Peter's story with the kids.

"Oh, okay then," said Charlotte. "Then just plan on meeting us at two, and if we don't show, I guess just take the bus home."

"Sounds like a plan," said Peter. He kissed Charlotte and then the kids. "I'll see you all in a few hours." He walked out the front door and headed toward the Sconset rotary and the bus stop. He had to wait a few minutes but he enjoyed watching the tourists coming into the village on their bikes having made the seven-mile trek from town. They were taking out their maps to check their progress and figuring out how to get to the beach. The bus appeared a little after ten and Peter got on. After a few stops and nearly thirty minutes, the bus deposited him on Washington Street in downtown Nantucket. He got off and walked casually down Washington Street to South Water and the eight short blocks to the Nantucket Whaling Museum.

Entering the front door, he proceeded over to the information kiosk where an older woman, probably in her seventies, was standing. She looked up with a broad smile as Peter approached. "Good morning. Can I help you?"

"Hi, yes. My name is Peter Bois, and I'd like to do a little research on whaling."

"Of course. Anything specific?"

"Yes, I'd like to know more about a whaleship, she was called the Paragon and sailed out of Nantucket in the 1820s."

"Hmm," said the volunteer. "I'd suggest you start with a visit to our research library. It's just a short walk over to Fair Street, and the staff there can assist you in researching the details around that ship and maybe even her crew."

"Terrific," said Peter. "Thank you."

"You're welcome. Enjoy your day."

Peter turned, headed out the door, and walked the ten blocks to the research library. He opened the door into a sunlit reading room with bookcases and cabinets lining the walls.

"Can I help you?" said a young lady. She was wearing a green polo shirt with Nantucket Historical Association embroidered on the right breast. Just above that was a small name tag. Judy.

"Yes, My name is Peter, and I'm looking to research a whaling ship from the 1820s. It's a ship called the Paragon."

"Of course. What would you like to know about her?"

"I know she set out on a voyage in early 1829. I'd like to know how that voyage went and how long it lasted."

"I think we should be able to track that information down through our ship and voyage database. Anything else?"

"Yes, I'd like to research a young mate on that ship. His name was Tristam Coffin."

"Coffin? There were a lot of Coffins on Nantucket back then," she chuckled. "But let's see what we can do. Give me just a minute." She turned and walked through a door marked *employees only*. She returned ten minutes later with a large, black, leather-bound book.

"Okay. You said the ship was the Paragon?"

"Yes. I believe she departed Nantucket on a whaling voyage in early 1829, maybe March?"

She flipped through the pages and then stopped. "Here she is. The Paragon under Captain Nelson. Is that the one?"

"Yes," said Peter excitedly. "That's the one."

"Hmm, okay. It looks like she was lost in a storm off Cape Horn, around June or July 1829."

"What?" said Peter, shocked. He felt a stab of anxiety through his body.

"Yes. This shows she was lost at sea, most likely in a storm. Her last known position was just east of Cape Horn."

"Did anyone survive?" asked Peter.

She scanned the ledger. "No. It shows all hands lost." She looked up at him and smiled, not realizing the impact her words were having on him. "Anything else?"

"Is that all the information you have?"

"Well, yes," she said, laughing. "You're talking nearly two hundred years ago, and many of the records have been lost or destroyed. It's not like we had the technology back then like we do today."

Peter nodded solemnly.

"Are you okay, sir?"

"Yes, I was just hoping for a different answer." *Oh my god, the Paragon was lost with all hands?*

"I'm sorry that wasn't the information you were looking for. Can I help you with anything else?"

He took a deep breath. "Yes. Can you please look up Tristam Coffin? He was a mate on that ship."

"Oh right, sorry forgot about that. Give me just a minute." She departed again and returned a few minutes later with another large ledger.

"You know, sir, you can do some of this online."

"Really?"

"Yes, especially a lot of the genealogy. We have a very powerful database that allows you to trace thousands of Nantucketers, from the 1700s all the way through the late 18th century. You might want to give that a try."

"I will when I get home. But while I'm here…," he said hopefully.

"Sure," she said and flashed him a wide smile. "Yes, let me see." She flipped through a number of pages and landed on one. "Any idea on when he was born?"

Peter did some quick math. "I would guess between 1800 and 1805."

She used her finger to trace down the paper. "There he is." She swung the ledger around to show Peter and pointed at the information. "Looks like he was born 1802 and shows he was married in 1828 to an Abigail Folger." She continued reading, although slowly as the text was upside down to her. "And look, it appears he died in 1885, at the ripe old age of eighty-three." She looked up at Peter, smiling.

"Tris," said Peter in a whisper.

She looked down at the ledger. "Oh, wait, that symbol means we have a picture of him in our collections. "Let me see if I can find that." She took note of the item number and disappeared again into the back.

Tris lived! thought Peter, his mind reeling. *He didn't go back out on the Paragon. What happened to change his mind?*

The librarian returned with a photocopied picture. "Here he is," she said and handed it to him.

Peter took the picture and stared into the eyes of his old friend. Tris was older, probably in his early sixties and dressed in his Sunday best, his hair gray and sporting a neatly trimmed beard of the same color. He was sharing a sofa with Abigail, who was also dressed in her finest and looked lovely. Both bore a slight smile and were looking to the left of the camera lens. Behind them stood four men and three women, probably their children with their spouses. Spread out in front of them were ten young boys and girls, all looked to be under the age of six. Only two of them were looking toward the camera, the rest were playing with a handful of toys scattered on the carpet. Tris and Abigail looked happy, prosperous, and content.

What a brood! thought Peter. "This is terrific, thank you. Can you tell me any more about him?"

The librarian turned the ledger back to face her so she could read it more easily. "Hmm," she said. "Let me check one more thing." She disappeared again.

After a few minutes, she returned. "I thought there was something familiar about his name. I was just updating one of our databases last week and remember him." She had an iPad this time and pulled some information up on the screen. "I'm looking at our whaleship database, and it says he was the owner of a whaleship called the *Greenhand*. It shows that it had many successful voyages between 1830 and 1862 under three different captains." Reading some more, she said, "It looked like the ship was retired in 1865."

"Really?" said Peter excitedly.

"Yes. It's all here. If you want to access it in the future, I'd suggest you go online to our digital databases."

"I will. And this is terrific. Thank you for all your help."

"You're welcome, sir."

"Oh, and can I keep this?" asked Peter, holding up the picture of Tris and Abigail.

"Of course, that's your copy."

"Thank you," said Peter, "I really, really appreciate all of your help." Clutching the picture, he turned and walked out the door. As he walked down Fair Street, he reflected on Tris and Abigail, the thought of them living a long and happy life pleased him immensely. But those happy thoughts were heavily weighed down by the news of the Paragon. He had just spent four months with the crew, had literally been with them just days ago, and now they were all gone. Memories of the hurricane flooded back, and he could imagine Captain Nelson at the helm steering the ship through the storm amid rising waves and turbulent seas. *Could I maybe have saved them? Did my leaving the ship in any way impact their destiny?* His mind was as confused as an ocean in a storm, bouncing back and forth between feelings of sadness for the Paragon and happiness for Tris.

He glanced at his watch and saw it was just past one. He had a little time to kill before meeting Charlotte and the kids. At Main Street, he turned left and decided to take a stroll by many of the beautiful homes built by the captains from Nantucket's heydey as the whaling capital of the world. He was not well versed in their history but could appreciate their exquisite architecture and magnificent construction. *Could one of these homes have been Nelson's?* A stab of sadness shot through him at the thought of Nelson's widow learning the news and having to take full responsibility for their home and family. A whaler's wife was used to that burden, but knowing now she'd be alone forever must have been incredibly difficult for her.

He made his way down to the pharmacy, his mind still turning from what he had learned. He swung open the screen door and saw that Charlotte, Sophie, and Spencer had already arrived and had claimed three of the handful of turn stools at the lunch counter. Peter smiled at them and came up behind Charlotte. He leaned around and gave her a kiss on the cheek.

"Hey, how did your research go?" she asked.

Peter smiled sadly. "I learned a lot, but it was not the news I was hoping for."

"Oh, I'm sorry. Did you want to talk about it?"

"Maybe on the way home. Let's just think about lunch now and enjoy this time."

"Sounds good," said Charlotte. "Split a chocolate frappe with me?"

"Only if it has malt," said Peter and smiled.

"Deal. Egg salad?"

"Yes, please."

* * *

They finished lunch quickly and headed to the car. It was still cool and damp out, but the fog had lifted, and there were patches of blue sky visible in the overcast. Charlotte had found a parking spot on Main Street. Peter looked at her smiling, "Prime parking spot. I'm impressed, it must be all that clean living."

Charlotte smiled back, "Did you want to drive?"

"No, thanks. I'd prefer to just ride and watch the world go by," he said and climbed into the front passenger seat. Spencer and Sophie jumped into the back, Sophie helping Spencer with his seatbelt. Charlotte slipped her sunglasses on, put the car in reverse, and backed out. She moved the shifter to drive and headed up the street, the car bouncing wildly from side to side on the cobblestones. After a hundred feet, she made the left on Orange Street, and the ride smoothed instantly as the surface transitioned to pavement. She looked at Peter, "Do you want to tell me what you found out?"

Peter shared his findings of the Paragon with her. Charlotte could see how sad he was and how hard the news was hitting him.

"The ship was lost? With her entire crew?"

"Yes," said Peter, his voice trembling.

"I'm so sorry."

"But, there is actually some good news."

Charlotte looked at him expectantly, "What's that?"

"Tris didn't sail on her. It looks like he stayed on Nantucket and bought a whaleship of his own, just like he and I talked about."

"Really?"

"Yes. And he named it the Greenhand."

Charlotte smiled warmly. "That's wonderful. I think it shows the impact you must have had on him."

"Yes," said Peter, laughing. "I was quite a challenge for him when I first landed on the ship. I was essentially helpless and he

330

steered me through those very difficult few days." He was smiling but with tears in his eyes. "And do you know what's really cool?"

"What's that?"

"The research library had a picture of him with Abigail and what looks like their whole family, including at least ten grandchildren."

"Ten grandchildren?"

"Yes," said Peter laughing, "Ten. I think Tris must have died a very happy man."

"All because of you."

"No, not because of me."

She took one hand off the wheel and reached over to Peter. "You gave him your earnings and showed him the importance of staying home with the woman he loved. If he had gone on that voyage on the Paragon, he would have died."

Peter thought for a minute. "Maybe, I did."

They were nearing the big rotary when Peter spoke, "Would you guys mind if we made one more stop?"

"Sure, we're in no rush. Where do you want to go?"

"To the Inquirer and Mirror offices. Right there," he said pointing at a small shingled covered building. "I want to look up and see if I can find any information on Isaiah."

"Sure, hon." Charlotte wheeled the Rover through the heavy traffic around the rotary and pulled into the parking lot. Peter jumped out and then leaned back in, one hand on the door, "Why don't you guys go grab an ice cream? I'll need a few minutes."

"They just had milkshakes for lunch. I think their sugar intake is maxed out for the day. We'll just wait here."

"Okay. I'll be right back." Peter slammed the door and entered the building. He walked in and found a young man at the counter looking down at a laptop and typing furiously away. "Excuse me," said Peter.

The man slowly and reluctantly lifted his head from the screen and looked at Peter. "Can I help you?"

"Yes, hi. I'm looking to do some research."

"Oh sure, but that's all online now."

"It is?"

The young man talked as if explaining it to a toddler. "Yes. Just visit our website and go to the bottom left and click on the digital archives link. We have issues dating all the way back to 1821."

"That's great. Thank you."

"No problem," and resumed his typing.

Peter walked out and hopped in the car. Charlotte looked at him, "Did you get what you needed?"

"Yes. It's actually all online now. I guess I should have tried that first."

"Hmm, okay." Charlotte backed out of the parking spot, navigated her way around the rotary, and proceeded down Milestone road to Sconset.

When they got home, Peter headed into the house and went straight to his office. He cracked his laptop, signed-in, and launched his browser. At the Inquirer and Mirror homepage, on the bottom left of the screen and just as described was the link to the digital archives. Clicking on that opened up a description screen along with a search box. Peter paused for a minute and then typed in "Joseph Chamberlain" and hit enter. The browser wheel spun for a minute or so and popped up with a short note from the October 8th, 2001 edition.

New York Man Feared Drowned Off South Shore

Joseph Chamberlain of New York City is believed to have drowned while swimming off the South Shore this week. Chamberlain, 44, was renting a cottage in Siasconset for the month and had not been seen or heard from in several days, according to a neighbor. Tragically, Chamberlain had just lost his wife and two daughters in the attacks on the World Trade Center buildings last month.

Peter sat back in his chair. *Isaiah.*

He thought for a minute and then hit the back button of the browser to return to the search screen. In the search field, he typed 'Isaiah Bennet' and then added a date range from 1828 through 1890. He hit enter, and the wheel on his screen spun for several minutes before popping up with several results. Scrolling through, he clicked on a highlighted section in the October 18th, 1862 edition of The Inquirer and Mirror. The screen filled with a scanned edition of the paper, it's three pages filled with news, notices, and advertisements.

He zoomed in on a column section that was simply marked *Died* and found a handful of words on the death of Isaiah.

In this town, 15th inst., Isaiah Bennet, aged 86.

"Eighty-six years old," said Peter out loud. "Good for him. I wonder how many travelers he helped. How many men and women got back to their own times with his guidance."

Peter looked out his office window, across the manicured green expanse of his lawn and out across the moors, and whispered, "I hope you're with Brenda now. And with your girls."

CHAPTER THIRTY-ONE

I t was a late October evening, and Peter and Charlotte were in the large family room at Fernweh, a fire blazing away in the hearth, throwing out warmth and flickers of light. The sun had just set, and the horizon held a remaining smudge of purple, showing that the day was not yet entirely done. Facing the fire, Peter sat on one side of their large sofa with his computer in his lap and his feet stretched out over the cocktail table. Charlotte was on the other end, her feet folded under her with Tris, their yellow lab puppy, sound asleep and snoring slightly with his head in her lap. She was slowly rubbing his fur, focusing on the soft ears and the area between his eyes. On the television, over the hearth, the Patriots were at home and losing to the Chiefs.

Peter looked up from his laptop and over at her. "It's nice to spend Sunday night with you."

Charlotte smiled. "Me too. I used to really dread Sunday evenings. It usually meant saying goodbye and knowing I'd be spending a lot of my week alone. Even when we were together in Connecticut, it still felt the same."

Peter smiled knowingly. "But now we don't need to feel bad. We will be together so much you'll be sick of me."

"Never," she said, laughing.

Peter turned back to his laptop and typed a few keys.

"Wow," he said out loud.

"What is it?"

"Oh, I've been playing on one of those genealogy websites, you know the ones that claim you can track your family back for centuries.""Yeah. Did you find something out about you?""No, actually, I've been researching Jack Tate and his family. Remember I told you how much Tris looked and acted like him?"

"I do."

"Well, if this website is to be believed, then Jack Tate was indeed related to Tristam Coffin."

"Really?" said Charlotte leaning forward. The movement woke the dog, but he stretched, yawned, and laid his head back down. The light snoring resumed almost immediately.

"Yes. There are some gaps in the records, but it looks like Tris was Jack's great-great-great-great-great-grandfather." Peter was counting it out on his fingers.

"Oh my god. Then..."

"I know," said Peter, finishing her sentence. "That means that by keeping Tris off the Paragon and saving his life meant that Jack could be born. And be my friend."

"Oh honey, that's too much for me to get my head around." Charlotte thought for a minute and then said, "Peter?"

"Yeah?"

"Do you think Jack could have gone back in time as well? Like you did?"

"I'd love to think that, Charlotte. But I know that's not the case. Unfortunately, Jack just died. They found his body a few days later."

"Oh," said Charlotte, disappointed. "I'm sorry."

"It's okay, hon. I'm just happy that I had my friendship with Tris, which connects me even stronger to Jack."

"I'm so glad," said Charlotte, turning back to the game. She watched a few plays and then looked back at Peter. "Have you done any investigating on your side of the family?"

"Me? What do you mean?"

"Well, you told me that your name on the ship was Peter Starbuck, not Bois. Why don't you look up your family tree and see if there is any truth to that?"

"You think I should?"

"I mean, what do you have to lose?"

"Why not?" Peter turned his attention back to his laptop and hit a few keys. A few minutes later, he looked up from his screen. "Well, that's interesting."

"What is it?"

"I put my name in and followed the little leaf hints they give you. Within four generations, it shows our family name was indeed Starbuck." Peter looked at the laptop and was nodding his head. "Let's see that would be my great-great-grandfather. According to this, his name was Samuel Starbuck, and he had a daughter, Grace. She married an Antoine Bois who apparently emigrated to Nantucket from France just before World War One."

"That's amazing. So you really are a Starbuck?"

Peter smiled. "It looks like it! And you know what is even better?"

"What's that?"

"I can kind of consider myself a native Nantucketer!"

Charlotte smiled, "That is so great. I know that has bothered you in the past."

Peter closed the laptop, feeling content, and looked at Charlotte. Her eyes were back on the television, the Pats were trying to pull out another fourth-quarter comeback.

"Charlotte?"

"Hmm?" She was still watching the game.

"Are you happy we moved here full time?"

She turned to Peter and thought for a minute. "I am. It has been a bit of an adjustment, but Sophie and Spencer seem to love their new school and have made a bunch of new friends." She paused. "And don't forget what you promised."

"What's that?"

"That we'll have a long vacation off-island every winter. Somewhere warm."

Peter smiled. "Of course."

338

The game ended, and Charlotte raised the remote and turned off the television. She looked at Peter and said, "Are you nervous at all about tomorrow?"

"Well, maybe a little. It's been a while since I've had a new job."

"I know it's going to go great, and you're going to love it. It will keep you challenged and, most importantly, will keep you home with us," said Charlotte, her blue eyes sparkling.

Peter smiled warmly at her. "I could not be doing it without you." He stood up, "Now, why don't we retire to the patio?"

"But it's so chilly out!"

"It's okay, we have this," said Peter and grabbed the woolen blanket that Charlotte kept folded on the back of the sofa.

Charlotte smiled and said softly, "Okay, I'm in."

She stood slowly, unwrapped her legs, and gently lowered Tris's head down to the sofa. The puppy continued snoring lightly. She walked over to Peter and put her arms around his neck.

"I love you, Peter Bois," she said huskily. "Or should I call you Peter Starbuck?"

Peter leaned down and kissed her neck. He paused between kisses and whispered in her ear, "Call me Starbuck."

Charlotte giggled. Peter grabbed her hand and led her slowly through the kitchen, through the French doors, and out onto the patio. They reclined on the chaise together and covered themselves with the blanket. Above them, a brilliantly black sky was ablaze in stars.

* * *

Peter's alarm sounded at little after five. He hit the off button and slipped out of the bed, careful not to wake Charlotte. Tris, laying by her side, raised his head and looked at him. "Come on, Tris," whispered Peter. "Let's go for a walk."

The dog stood up on the bed and shook his head, waking Charlotte. She mumbled, "Peter, what are you doing?"

"Ssshhh, it's okay. Tris and I are going to go for a walk, that's all. I want to see the sunrise."

"Hmm, okay. But please be careful."

"Always," said Peter. He threw on his jeans with a turtleneck and a heavy cable knit sweater and made his way down to the kitchen. He fed Tris a little kibble while he made himself some strong coffee. Peter walked over to the pantry and grabbed an insulated mug. He filled it with the fresh coffee, grabbed Tris's leash, and headed toward the front door. He paused a minute to put on his heavy woolen coat and slip the leash onto Tris.

"Let's go, Tris," said Peter and stepped out into the cool morning air. There was a light fog that shrouded the streetlights and clung tightly to the ground. He and Tris walked down the driveway and headed toward the beach. They made their way down Main, past the rotary, and headed toward the bluff. The streets were quiet as the few remaining residents of the village were still asleep.

They made their way the few blocks to *The Shanty* and stopped outside the gate. Tris sat on his haunches while Peter stared at the door, lost in reflection. Thoughts of Isaiah, of Tris and of the

Paragon and the men who sailed her clouded his mind. Today he started work in their honor, to repay the debt of their kindness, their sincerity, and their guidance to make him a better man. The puppy stood and tugged on the leash as if to say *enough already*. Peter looked down and rubbed his head. "Okay, Tris, let's go down to the beach."

The dog sprang forward and led Peter through the path between the houses and then down to the beach. They walked out onto the sand and found an area by the seagrass where Peter sat down, putting his mug next to him. He pulled on the leash gently and encouraged Tris to sit next to him.

Looking due east over the water, he could just make out the faintest of light on the horizon. Much of the fog had lifted, but there were still wisps of it in the moors farther down the beach. Sitting with his arm around Tris, Peter thought of how much he had changed since he had been sucked into the rip just a few months ago. That man, that arrogant, self-centered, greedy CEO, had landed on a whaleship and had been broken and humbled. From that, he had learned much about himself and about life. True to his promise to Isaiah, he had kept that experience close to his heart.

The last few weeks had been busy with lawyers, banks, and paperwork. Peter had sold his outstanding shares in Shimmo Plastics and used some of the proceeds to acquire the natural resin technology and all worldwide patents from his old firm. He then formed a new company, Greenhand Plastics, to manage licensing of the new technology as broadly as possible. He had also called his old prep school friend, Chuck Thompson, and made amends with him. It had been an awkward conversation at first, but Peter apologized profusely for his behavior and had convinced him that he wanted to make things right. Chuck would be starting next week as the CEO of Greenhand. If all went well, the new firm would generate several hundred million dollars a year for the foundation.

Peter took a sip of coffee and looked out over the water. The few clouds lit up with color as the sun neared that perfect line between the ocean and the sky. A seal popped it's head up out of the water and looked at Peter. Tris barked, and the seal splashed and dove underwater. "Good boy," said Peter, rubbing the dog's head.

At a little after seven, the sun broke the surface of the horizon, it's light brightening the day. Peter sat a bit longer until the sun was well above the water and then stood, wiped the sand off his jeans, and started walking home. They followed Gully road under the old bike bridge, past the rotary, and then up Main to the house. At the entrance to the driveway, he slipped the leash off Tris, who proceeded to run down the path chasing rabbits and barking with joy. Peter smiled.

He walked in the door with Tris following him, panting, and took off his coat, still damp from the fog, and hung it in the closet. Walking into the kitchen, he found Spencer and Sophie at the table having breakfast. Charlotte was pouring milk into their cereal.

"Hey. How was your walk?" she asked.

"Wonderful," said Peter. "Such a beautiful sunrise this morning." He came up and gave her a hug. "Next time, I want you to join me."

"Hmm, okay. I guess," she said, laughing lightly.

"I'm going to run upstairs and get ready," he said and turned to Sophie and Spencer. "You guys be ready in twenty?"

"Yes, dad," said Sophie. Spencer just nodded, a spoonful of cereal in his mouth.

"Great," said Peter and headed upstairs.

He returned fifteen minutes later after a quick shower and shave. He was dressed in pressed khakis, a blue gingham button-down, a light yellow sweater, and freshly shined loafers. "How do I look?" he asked Charlotte.

"You look great," she said and gave him a kiss. He returned it and was tempted to walk her back out to the patio.

Smiling at the thought, he turned to Sophie and Spencer. "Ready?"

The kids pushed back from the table and grabbed their backpacks. Charlotte handed each of them a small brown bag and kissed them on the forehead. "You guys have fun at school today. And remember, I love you."

"Love you too, mom," said Sophie. Spencer was quiet but ran over and gave his mom a hug.

She turned her attention to Peter. "Good luck today, hon."

"Thanks, babe," he said and hugged her. "See you around five."

* * *

Peter dropped Spencer and Sophie off at school and then made his way down Atlantic Avenue toward Main street. He and

Charlotte had found the perfect spot for the new offices, a second-floor space over a popular clothing store with the luxurious benefit of private, off-street parking. He pulled the Rover into the parking spot, shut off the engine, and reached over to the passenger seat for his backpack.

He walked around the corner and made his way down the brick sidewalk to their building. Passing several retail stores and a small restaurant, he came to a simple white door with a brass knob. It had raised panels on the bottom half and glass panes on top through which Peter could make out the wooden stairs leading to the second floor. A handwritten note taped to the inside of the glass gave a phone number and directions for deliveries.

Peter took a breath and opened the door. He walked up the narrow staircase, the well-worn treads creaking and groaning with each step. At the top of the stairs was a small foyer with a glass-paneled door to the left. On the wall to the right of the door was a small, shiny brass plaque that read *The Jack Tate & Tristam Coffin Foundation.*

He smiled at the plaque and touched it lightly with his right hand. *Here we go.* He turned the knob and door entered into a bright, airy room. The walls were of exposed brick with large windows that looked out over the cobblestones. Four desks were spaced across the wooden floor. Three of the desks were empty, but behind the first sat a woman with short brown hair and green eyes. She was dressed comfortably in jeans and a white turtleneck sweater. A simple gold chain with a pendant shaped like Nantucket hung around her neck. She stood as Peter entered and walked over to greet him.

"Good morning, Peter," she said. "Welcome to our official first day!"

"Good morning, Jen. And thank you." He walked over to the desk closest to the window and put his backpack down. On the desk were three framed pictures. The first was one of Charlotte and the kids they had taken the prior year professionally at Sconset beach. The second was of him and Jack, from the summer they worked together and just a few weeks before his death. It was taken at a job site, and both were sweaty from hard work. But they were happy and smiling and looking like they didn't have a care in the world. The third was that of Tris, Abigail, and their family that he had received from the research library a couple of months before.

He touched the frame with Tris's picture and then walked to the window. He looked out over Main, the trees lining the street were nearly bare of leaves. A gusty north wind was working on the remaining stragglers. Peter turned to her, "I'm so happy you decided to join us."

She smiled. "My brother thought the world of you. It was tragic that we lost him so young. But the work you will be doing in his name? How could I not be part of that."

Peter smiled warmly. He could see a little of Jack and some of Tris in her face. "It just means so much to me to have you here as part of this. You have no idea."

She smiled again and clasped her hands. "So, what's the first order of business?"

"Would you mind finding a phone number for me?" asked Peter.

"Sure. Who do you need?"

"I need the number for Jasper Norrington. He is the CEO of an organization called Clean Seas Forever."

"Just give me a minute." Jen walked over to her desk and tapped some keys on the keyboard. She jotted down the number on a yellow sticky note and walked back over to Peter.

"Here you go."

"Thanks, Jen."

Peter sat down at his desk and picked up the telephone. He read the note and dialed the number. It rang several times before it was picked up. "Yes, good morning. It's Peter Bois for Jasper Norrington." He paused. "Yes, I'll hold."

A minute later, a voice came on the line. "Jasper? This is Peter Bois. Please don't hang-up. We have a lot to talk about."

Author's Notes

I must first thank you for reading Starbuck, Nantucket Redemption. I really hope you enjoyed reading it as much as I enjoyed writing it and appreciate you taking the chance on a new and unknown author. Thank you. But before you go, I have two requests. The first is to please leave a review and let others know how much you (hopefully) enjoyed the book. The second is to join my mailing list at www.garthjeffries.com so we can stay in touch on future projects.

The story of Peter Bois and the Paragon draws heavily on historical records to reflect as accurately as possible what the fictional ship and her crew must have experienced in the early 19th century in their pursuit of whales. And with that I must recognize the outstanding resources available through the Nantucket Historical Association's Whaling Museum as well as the New Bedford Whaling Museum. I thank them both for their outstanding work and dedication to preserving this important era of American history.

The characters represented are works of fiction but draw on the well documented families of 19th century Nantucket including the Starbuck's, Coffin's, and Folger's among others. For those curious, the Nantucket Historical Association's Barney Genealogical Record is an amazing peek into the family trees of white Nantucketers during the 17th, 18th and 19th centuries.

I must also thank those organizations that work diligently to protect the unique landscape and personality of Nantucket. This includes the Nantucket Land Bank, The Nantucket Conservation Foundation, the Sconset Trust, and the The Trustees of Reservations.

And no acknowledgement would be complete without a word of thanks to our men and women in the military, our first responders, and all our healthcare providers. Thank you for all you do in keeping us safe, healthy and free.

Garth Jeffries
Kansas City
May, 2020

Made in the USA
Monee, IL
30 June 2020

35058100R00215